“As a storyteller myself, I found Bill Siems’ latest novel intriguing and gripping, inventive and entertaining, hard to put down because of my desire to see this sacred life and events through Bill’s powerful tale.

Hane and the Centurion recounts the key events of Jesus Christ’s mortal life in a combination of some of my favorite themes—the incomparable life and teachings of His life interwoven with themes reminiscent of high fantasy like Tolkien and C.S. Lewis. If you are a believer you will enjoy the interplay of light vanquishing darkness, memorable characters with whom you will form emotional bonds, and a heightened desire to follow the Savior yourself.

I highly recommend this story!”

Barry Rellaford
co-author of A Slice of Trust: The Leadership Secret with the Hot and Fruity Filling

“With his elegant, yet lighthearted style, William Siems has crafted an engaging tale with deep, distinctly human characters that you will come to know and love. Hane and the Centurion tells the story of Jesus Christ in a new and intriguing way, intermingling history and fiction to create a story unlike anything you have ever read. Pick up this story and read it today; you will not regret it.”

Tyler Appleby
author of The Triqan Trilogy and The Ten Kingdoms Trilogy

Hane and the Centurion

Chyeem Chronicles Book Two

By William Siems

a Gospel Fantasy sequel to "The Magi and a Lady"

Hane and the Centurion

First printing - Fall 2019

Scripture quotations from the SUV (Siems Unauthorized Version) of the Bible

Contact the author at chayeem10@gmail.com

Cover by Jacob Bridgman from artwork by Gil Henry

Interior design by Alane Pearce of Professional Writing Services apearcewriting@gmail.com.

Dedication

I thought I would write a novel. It took forty-five years. Its sequel came much faster. Initially, I had no intention of writing a sequel to my third novel, *The Magi and a Lady*, but while in the middle of it I realized that I had left a door open for one. So, here it is. Again, without the faithful support of so many it still would have remained simply a doorway. Thanks again to my wife, Nancy, who was my constant inspiration and encouragement; my good friend Keith Timmer, who listened to each new chapter and was still excited when it ended; the editing of my daughter Angela who edited with, "What color would you like to see the corrections in this time?"; and of course the center of the whole thing, the Promised One, Jeshua.

For seven of the fifteen years I taught full-time at Boeing Airplane Company, Gil Henry was my partner. Those were incredible years. I have never had a teaching partner his equal. In the late 1990's he drew me a bookmark which has been adapted to the cover of this book and one of his other drawings I have used to depict a young Chayeem. He has taken the "ultimate upgrade" (Heaven), but I'm pretty sure he is pleased, both with this book and that his art is included.

Preface

Although just a work of fantasy-fiction, its inspiration has come from two major sources. The star and its promised return comes from a second century manuscript called "The Revelation of the Magi" by Brent Landau, published by HarperOne. Much of the rest of the story is inspired by the New Testament Gospels. Research into the Gospels was aided by Stevens and Burton's "A Harmony of the Gospels," published by Charles Scribner's Sons. The rest of the story comes from my own fertile imagination and is purely supposition or speculation. You will notice that I continue to use my own names for many of the characters as it fits better into my Siems Fantasy Universe. I hope this is not too confusing. I have included a list of Scripture references as they apply to some chapters just after the Table of Contents, as well as a glossary of names at the back of the book. As with all my fiction, this is written for your enjoyment, challenge, and with the hope that you may be encouraged on your life's journey.

This second edition of the book now contains a twenty-seven week daily devotional. I would suggest you read the entire book first and then go back and use the devotional to read it more deeply a second time. I believe you will find that second reading even more enriching.

Blessings,

Bill Siems
Winter 2020

Table of Contents

Chapter Scriptural References

Chapter 4 - Uriel's Purpose	Matt. 2:19-23
Chapter 8 - The Journey Begins	Luke 10:30-36
Chapter 9 - Adventures on the Road	Matt. 5:38-39
Chapter 10 - Mekah's Companion	Luke 8:2
Chapter 11 - Passover in Jerusalem	Luke 2:41-45
Chapter 13 - At Simeon's for Lunch	Luke 2:25-34
Chapter 17 - In the Temple with the Teachers	Luke 2:46-52
Chapter 20 - There was a Man Named John	Luke 3:2-16
Chapter 22 - The Jordan River	Matt.3:13-17
Chapter 24 - The Tempter	Matt. 4:1-11
Chapter 25 - Political Intrigue	John 1:19-51
Chapter 26 - It's Just a Wedding	John 2:1-11
Chapter 27 - Their First Passover	John 2:13-22
Chapter 28 - Nicodemus at Night	John 3:1-15
Chapter 29 - His Teaching's Disrupted Again	John 8:2-11
Chapter 30 - Tax Collectors and Sinners	Luke 5:27-39, 19:1-10
Chapter 31 - Just Getting a Drink of Water	John 4:1-42
Chapter 32 - The Boldness of John	Mark 6:17-20
Chapter 33 - Synagogues	Luke 4:16-30, Mark 6:1-5, Luke 13:10-17
Chapter 34 - Who is Blind Here?	John 9:1-41
Chapter 35 - Four Good Friends	Mark 2:1-12

Young Chayeem

Prologue (Recap)

They had called him the "Promised One" since virtually the dawn of time, the one who would set all things right, the one who would make all things new. The promise included that his birth would be proceeded by an angel, or perhaps a star, something which had formerly covered the ancient garden of Delight, where Chayeem, the Tree of Life grew. The angel would lead some special travelers to discover the new king of the Jews.

Now, all of the promises had come to pass. The three Masters from the East, Seph, Chok, and Raz, had traveled to Jerusalem led by the angel Uriel, who appeared most often as an old man. There, while talking to Herod, the current king of the Jews, they learned of the prophecy that a great leader would be born in Bethlehem. The Masters were accompanied by Mishimar, a soldier who possessed a mysterious singing sword named Hane, which means Favor, and by Hannah who acted as their cook and their horse whisperer but was much, much, more. While the five of them journeyed to Bethlehem with Uriel, Herod sent his chief wizard Nebo, Nebo's son Nesher, and their spies to find out where the new king slept.

When the Masters found the boy Jeshua with his mother Mary and his stepfather Joseph, they knelt, worshipped the boy, and gave him gifts. That night the angel warned the Masters that Herod sought to destroy the boy and that they should return to the East by a different route.

Meanwhile, the fallen archangel Halel had called himself the god Marduk, and sent Nebo to intercept the travelers. Nebo's son Nesher ambushed the travelers while Nebo returned to tell Herod the location of the child. Marduk had given Nesher the singing sword called Balak, meaning The Void, and with it Nesher challenged Mishimar. The battle of the two singing swords caused the very atmosphere to reverberate as chord matched discord, light clashed against darkness, and the two fought each other to a stand still. When a small animal bolted in front of Mishimar, startling him and breaking his concentration, Nesher knocked him to the ground, senseless. Nesher stood over his fallen form and demanded Mishimar's singing sword, which had landed a few feet away. While appearing to comply, Hannah picked it up and launched her own attack on Nesher. Suddenly the god Marduk materialized, but before he could assist Nesher, the angel Uriel also appeared, and the battle of the four singing swords began. Rarely had the world ever seen such a cataclysmic engagement. Untamable, beautiful light confronted darkness, the full fury of each released against the other. Hannah fought Nesher with such ferocity that he barely had time to breathe, let alone utter any of the incantations which his father had taught him. Breathless and exhausted, he faltered. Hannah took advantage of the slip, and slew him. Marduk tried unsuccessfully to claim both Nesher's sword, Balak, and Mishimar's sword, Hane. But Uriel frustrated him in the attempt and he backed through the reappearing portal and disappeared, spewing oaths of later vengeance.

Mishimar had slowly returned to consciousness as Hannah, cradling him in her arms, kissed him. After a moment's surprise, and to assure himself that he had really returned to reality, he had kissed her back. She had helped him to his feet, handed him his sword, and retrieved the fallen sword Balak from Nesher's corpse.

The three of them, Hannah, Mishimar, and Uriel, had turned to face the Masters, who had dismounted to watch the conclusion of the battle. Their mouths still hung wide open in utter amazement.

Seph had muttered, barely above a whisper, "What have we just witnessed?"

Uriel had replied calmly, "The child and his family have fled Bethlehem in a direction of which the enemy is unaware. Mardok wanted to eliminate us before continuing on to eliminate the child, but I have warned Jeshua's parents."

Seph had continued, "Warned them of what?"

"That they needed to flee to Egypt, for Herod seeks to destroy the threat to his throne."

Chok had finally found his voice, "And what now?"

"It will be safe for you to return home. You are no longer in immediate danger," Uriel had said.

Chok had spoken again, "And what about the three of you?"

Uriel had looked at Mishimar and Hannah, "I can't speak for them, but I will join myself to the child and his family. Every one of the Lord's little ones needs a guardian angel." And he had disappeared.

Raz had also looked at the couple, "And you two?"

Maishimar had looked at Hannah and she had nodded in agreement. "I think we will follow Uriel a while longer."

Seph had raised his hand skyward, "Then the peace of Chayeem, the One Tree, be upon us all, as we travel our separate ways." The two groups had come together and embraced one another, last of all Seph and Hannah.

As they had broken their embrace, she had reached out, touched his cheek, and said "Goodbye, 'Other Father,' may the time between us be short."

With either a twinkle or a tear in his eye he had pointed to Mishimar, and responded, "Take good care of her, you have my blessing." Mishimar and Hannah had raised their singing swords to them in salute, turned, and rode off in the other direction, hoping to intercept the holy family as they fled to Egypt.

The Masters had mounted up, turned their horses towards the East, and began their journey home.

The dark sword, Balak, was later restored to its original glory by Jeshua when Hannah and Mishimar pledged their swords to his service. It became once again Oz, one of the seven singing swords forged for the archangels before time began.

PART ONE

In Egypt

Chapter 1
Three Years Later

On a clear starlit night, they relaxed around the fire in the back of the yard. Simon and Elizabeth were both nearly three years old and they sat each on one of Mishimar knees as he pointed out the stars and constellations. Mishimar had not imagined a life this happy, but since he and Hannah had accompanied Mary, Joseph, and Jeshua to Egypt everything had been peaceful, calm, and nothing short of wonderful. He and Hannah had married in a small village along the way and soon conceived Simon. Elizabeth had been born to Mary and Joseph shortly after Simon's birth. It had been a blessing for the two women to be pregnant together, although sometimes a curse for the rest of them. Yet often young Jeshua would walk to the two of them as they sat, grumbling after supper, and climb up onto a cushion between them. He would then place a hand on each of their abdomens, begin humming a song, and all the tension would leave them and the room.

Tonight, Mary had gone inside. Joseph had gone to the shop to put the finishing touches on a bed frame he was making for the leader of one hundred chariots. While Mary prepared things for bed, Jeshua studied a copy of the Torah, the first five books of the ancient Hebrew scriptures. Joseph had taken it in trade for some of his woodwork.

Simon reached over and touched his father's sword. "Sword story, Papa," he asked firmly. Elizabeth smiled and nodded.

"Simon," Mishimar smiled, "you've heard that story over a hundred times."

"Please, Papa, please?" he pleaded as Elizabeth nodded along with him.

"Okay, okay," and he began, almost regally. "Seven singing swords, forged before the world began, were given to the archangels when the stars sang and the sons of God shouted for joy. But during the rebellion of Halel, he who had once covered the sacred garden Delight, one sword fell with him and two swords fell with the Nephilim who joined him. A final sword vanished when R'gel was slain during the conflict."

"What then, Misha?" Elizabeth had called him "Misha" since she began to talk.

"*They could probably both recite it themselves,*" he thought, but Mishimar continued, "Twice Nephilim lay with Moabite women who bore children from those unions. These boys were half human and half divine. One of these two became the giant Goliath, the champion of the Philistine armies. He stood over six cubits tall and carried a javelin with a shaft as large as a weaver's beam. Before he reached the day of his "being welcomed into the ranks of manhood," he killed an Ariel with his bare hands. The Ariel were lion-like beings worshiped by the Moabites. You understand what an Ariel is, Simon?"

"Yes, Papa."

He looked at Elizabeth, "and you?" who nodded. While Simon talked a lot, Elizabeth just usually nodded in agreement.

"Well, to commemorate his reaching manhood and his slaying of the Ariel, the fallen archangel Halel visited him and gave him the singing sword that had belonged to his father. Its name was Hane, which meant Favor. When Goliath fought against the Hebrew shepherd boy David, he wore that sword. However, he did not consider David a worthy enough opponent to unsheathe

the sword, but he simply planned to pin him to the ground with his javelin. However, David felled Goliath with a stone from his sling, ran up to him, drew the sword, and cut off Goliath's head. The sword became David's possession, a trophy of his victory. David later dedicated it to the Lord and had it enshrined in the tabernacle. Then, one day, when David fled from King Saul who sought to kill him, David stopped at the tabernacle for some food and while there, retrieved the sword. Years later he still had the sword when he fought against the other offspring of the Nephilim, the giant Ishbibenob. David almost saw defeat in that battle because Ishbibenob also had a singing sword, Balak, that his father had given him. Fortunately, one of David's men, Abashai, snuck up behind Ishbibenob while focused too intently on his battle with David to notice, and slew him. David's singing sword passed on to his son Solomon, but later Solomon dedicated it to the false god Chemosh when his foreign wives led his heart away. Before the sack of Jerusalem, Jeremiah had the task of hiding the ark and the tabernacle. Along the way he also decided to retrieve the sword, Hane, from the false god's temple and took it along with him. He hid them all in a cave. The sword lay hidden for many years until one day my grandfather, your great-grandfather, stumbled upon it while sheltering in the same cave during a rainstorm. He passed it on to my father, who finally passed it along to me." Mishimar left out his intention of one day passing the sword to Simon. He was too young to appreciate that.

"Other sword, Balak?" Simon asked.

Mishimar continued, "Because Abashai slew Ishbibenob, David gave him that giant's sword. But after that it fell into obscurity until the battle of the four singing swords. That story will have to wait for another night, it's time for bed."

"Please, Papa, please?" Simon pleaded again as Elizabeth looked up with hope in her deep brown eyes.

"No," Mishimar said softly but firmly, "another night, children."

Simon looked crestfallen until he saw Jeshua coming from the house.

"Sleep Jeshua?" more pleading.

"*We might have to work on that, the pleading*," Mishimar thought as he smiled, shaking his head. "Yes, I'll ask Joseph if you can sleep with Jeshua."

Off Simon ran, up to Jeshua, who held out his hand, and the two of them nearly danced back into the house. Elizabeth remained and looked longingly up into Mishimar's eyes. He smiled again, "It is all right, Elizabeth, you'll probably all get to sleep together." She climbed off his lap and dashed towards the house. Mishimar's smile deepened as he relished a night alone with Hannah, his wife.

Chapter 2
Earlier in Jerusalem

After the attempt to find and destroy the child who threatened his throne turned into a debacle, Herod became even more paranoid. He had been betrayed so many times that he saw enemies around every corner. His chief wizard's son had been slain in the attempted attack on the Masters. When Nesher's body had been returned to his father, Nebo had laid him on his sacred black altar in his secret demonic temple and lit him afire. He had then stepped into the fire himself and perished. They only found the fire, much too late, when smoke started appearing from places they did not even know existed. Herod's trusted centurion, Anthony, had cleaned up the mess and returned that part of the palace to some semblance of decency only to have it become the residence of Herod's latest lust, the sorceress Batel. Through her own dark arts, she restored the hidden temple and reconsecrated its black altar. She dedicated it to the god Chemosh, the conqueror, and gained an even deeper hold on the king. Soon, he did not even remember Nebo. Batel brought along her daughter Meshel and a young girl, Mekashephah. Mekah, as she liked to be called, was rumored to have been the offspring of Chemosh and a virgin, and was dedicated to sorcery from the womb. Mekah's first words were those of occult power and she cast spells before she could walk. The invisible dead kept her company and her familiar, a scrawny black cat called Qadar followed her everywhere.

Herod's second wife, Malthace, came from Samaritan heritage. That had not particularly pleased the Jews, but he was already having trouble with them. She bore him a son, Archelaus, who eventually became Herod's favorite over Archelaus' brother Antipas and half-brother Herod II. Herod attempted to regain favor with the Pharisees by even murdering some of their foes, but the relationship was still tenuous. Shortly before he died, Herod revised his will to give the throne to his son Archelaus, and had a golden eagle affixed over the temple. Two teachers of the Law and some forty students chopped the defiling eagle down, even though they were captured and burnt alive in the square. Herod then fled to Jericho where he died. Archelaus' brother Antipas tried to contest Herod the Great's will, but Caesar sided with Archelaus who had come to Rome for the ratification of his father's will. Herod Archelaus became the ruler of Samaria, Judea, and Idumea and the army proclaimed him king. Herod the Great, king of the Jews who had sought to destroy the Promised One, was dead.

Where Batel had been Herod the Great's consort, Mekah stole Archelaus' heart while she, still a child, became a formidable force in his kingdom. One day, while playing with her invisible companions she discovered Nebo's ancient spell book. Even though he had concealed it with a spell of visual misdirection, her ancient, invisible friends had shown it to her. They gave her the simple words of power to both nullify its concealment and reveal its presence.

She brought it to Batel, who she called Gram. "Gram, look what I found." She held out the book, opened to a particular page.

"Mekah, dear," Batel murmured astonished, "where did you find this?"

"Judas showed me." she said. Judas was one of her invisible playmates, supposedly a former military general who had died under mysterious circumstances and although incorporeal, remained tied to the material world. "He gave me a word to speak and it…appeared."

Batel reached to take the book from her when Mekah jerked it back.

"Mine!" she nearly screamed.

Batel reached out again, speaking soothingly, "No, Mekah. This is not a book for a child."

Mekah looked down at the open page and spoke a word in a language that Batel had no idea the child even knew. Suddenly Batel could not breathe. She tried to say something to counteract the word, but she had taken her final breath, and only exhaled a gurgling from deep within her throat. She dropped to the floor, turned blue, and lay still. Mekah, smiled, closed the book, and went to her room.

Only when one of the king's guards came to call them for supper did he see Batel lying cold and lifeless on the floor of her living quarters. He called both a physician and a wizard, but she had obviously been dead for quite some time with no visible marks to identify the cause of death. The wizard seemed to discern some inarticulate, indistinct aroma of witchcraft, but what exactly had occurred lay beyond his art to reveal. They presumed that Batel had finally over-extended herself and had paid the ultimate price with her life.

They found Mekah in her bedroom happily humming some ancient military march. When informed of her Gram's untimely death, she did an adequate job of crying and pretending grief, but inwardly she felt free to now pursue her sorcery unrestricted. Her mother's death did not particularly upset Meshel either. Batel had always been a hard taskmaster. She had shown little praise or love, except on herself. The attention Batel had lavished on the former king could not be called love at all.

Archelaus allowed Meshel to stay in Batel's living quarters because of the fondness he had for Mekah. He gave Mekah unlimited access all over the palace, with the exclusion of his private chambers, and she soon discovered Nebo's hidden temple of sorcery which Batel had restored and dedicated to the god Chemosh. Her own incantation opened the door. She had the presence of mind to enter it with a sacrifice, a mouse her cat had caught. Although she could barely reach the top of the black altar and the sacred bowl, she found an ornate bronze box that had probably once contained scrolls and parchments to stand on. The sacrificial knife lay next to the bowl and with it she disemboweled the mouse and laid it in the bowl. She muttered some unintelligible word and it burst into flame, producing pungent smoke. She inhaled the intoxicating smoke deeply and continued to mumble incantations until the smoke nearly filled the room. With a burst of light and the concussion of an implosion, a being of indescribable beauty stood before her.

"Chemosh?" she exclaimed.

The Being responded, "That will do."

She bowed until her forehead touched the altar. "What may I do for you?"

The being smiled wickedly. "Much my little one. We have much to plan and prepare for."

Chapter 3
Still in Egypt

Joseph and Mishimar arrived home after dropping off the new bed frame that Joseph had completed. Pleased, the Egyptian chariot officer had taken them into his home and served them refreshments while they discussed plans for a new table. He also mentioned that he would be proud to recommend Joseph's work to his men and fellow officers. Soon Joseph would have much more business than he could possibly handle. Work in Egypt had initially been difficult with the lack of wood, but the wealthy and influential had their wood imported. They lived off the gifts the Masters had given Jeshua until word spread that a new master woodworker had arrived in town. Mary and Hannah both made friends quite easily and their daily time at the well and in the marketplace soon proved fruitful. Now, Joseph felt very glad he had been teaching Mishimar to work as his apprentice. Mishimar enjoyed working with him as well as learning the trade. For a lad of six Jeshua also showed signs of becoming a talented apprentice in his own right. He had great instincts, read wood well, and above all worked meticulously and patiently.

Jeshua and Hannah greeted them as they returned to the yard and helped them by unhitching the horses while they put away the wagon. Jeshua's way with horses rivaled that of Hannah's and yet he showed a willingness to learn from her and loved to work alongside of her. They seemed kindred spirits in many ways. Although Mishimar and Hannah were both fierce warriors, she also had a strong compassionate side to her character that powerfully drew everyone to her, people and animals alike. Jeshua exhibited that same wonder, a compassion so deep it mesmerized. Where Hannah displayed it in a distinctly feminine fashion, Jeshua's compassion was decidedly masculine.

Although only three years old, Simon and Elizabeth were turning into scrappy little warriors themselves. Mishimar had made them their own little practice swords, complete with leather-wrapped blades. They had both mastered many of the basic sword movements and although comical, their careful sparring showed a certain beauty. They would work hard for ten to fifteen minutes and then one of them would do something incorrectly or even silly and they would end up falling over themselves in laughter. Hannah also taught them rudimentary hand to hand combat skills. While they might seem quite young for such training, their precocious minds soaked up knowledge and skill like sponges.

When Mary called them in for supper, they all stopped at the well to clean up first before they entered her house. They knew from experience not to cross her threshold unless they had done so. They ate simply, but well. Joseph said often that Mary could make as much as he did if she started a small bakery, but she enjoyed working at home and raising the children.

As they all gathered around the table for the blessing, Jeshua turned towards the door and announced, "Uriel."

An old, but vigorous man stepped through the doorway. "It is obvious that the blessing of Chayeem rests on this house, but I acknowledge it, in all of its fullness."

Jeshua had slipped away and returned with a towel and basin of water. He knelt at the angel's feet as he lifted first his right foot, removed the sandal, washed it, dried it, kissed it and said, "Jeshua blesses you." Then he did the same to the left foot, saying, "Welcome home," as he looked up into the angel's face.

There may have been a tear, at least a twinkle in Uriel's eye as he said, "It is very good to be here, Jeshua."

Mary had also slipped away unseen and now returned with a bowl, a plate, and a cup which she set down. They motioned for him to join them at the table.

He did and looked around at them all as he said, "It is always a pleasure to share a meal with you."

Simon and Elizabeth could no longer contain themselves and said almost in chorus, "Did you bring us anything, Uncle Uriel?"

Into the ensuing laughter Jeshua returned, having discarded the bowl and towel, and asked, "May I pray?" Joseph nodded and he began, looking towards the cushion at the end of the table, the place they always left open. "Papa, You give us each day what we need. It all comes from Your hand and for that we are very grateful. Thank You especially that Uriel gets to join us tonight." They all said, "Amen."

Uriel then reached around behind him to the bag that still hung over his shoulder, opened it and removed two objects. He held them, one in each hand, and then reached his hands out to the children. They placed their hands beneath his, palms up, and he dropped a small, smooth stone into each of their hands. The children gasped as the stones touched their palms. They were agates, Simon's a smoky grey one and Elizabeth's a cloudy amber.

"I took those two stones from the river that runs from Delight," he explained. Delight was the garden where the Tree Chayeem grew and that made both the river and the stones special. In glee, both the children showed the stones to everyone. However, Uriel had not finished.

He asked, "Jeshua, would you come here?" Jeshua did, kneeling next to him. Uriel took Jeshua's head in his hands as he whispered, "Jeshua, I am very proud of you." Those words meant much more than a pebble from any river. Uriel then held his hand out to Jeshua. Jeshua placed his palm below Uriel's. The angel opened his hand and then closed Jeshua's hand around an object. He placed his mouth next to Jeshua's ear and whispered even softer, "That is a seed from Chayeem. He gave it to me Himself."

Jeshua's eyes widened, he embraced Uriel, and his eyes filled with tears, "Thank you, Uncle, thank you sooo… much," and he reverently placed it in the pocket of his tunic.

Although no one could hear what Uriel had whispered to Jeshua, they could see its effect. Mary brought things back down to earth, saying, "Please put the gifts in your tunics and let's eat my supper before it gets cold."

And they did. As always, the bread practically melted in their mouths and the rest of the meal, the lentil soup, raw vegetables, wine and water, seemed even more savory because they ate together. Conversation forgotten, they devoured the meal. As soon as the children finished, they asked to be excused and went into the other room where Jeshua had set up a game of "towers" on the floor, building towers from the wooden blocks left over from Joseph and Mishimar's woodworking. The rest of them resumed their small talk, updating Uriel on their current events, although as an angel he probably knew most of them already. Finally conversation lagged and they looked to Uriel.

Joseph posed the question that disquieted all of their hearts. "And why have you come to visit us?" Uriel smiled his disarming smile as Joseph continued, "You know we consider you part of the family, but…." His voice trailed off into silence.

Chapter 4
Uriel's Purpose

With all eyes on Uriel, he sat up a bit straighter, "I do have some good news. I was going to share it with you in a dream, but decided to come right out and say it here at supper." He paused for just a moment. "Those who sought the life of Jeshua are dead: Herod, Nebo…." He let the words hang there for a bit and then continued. "You can return to Israel. Mishimar and Hannah probably need some time to discuss whether this ends the period of their commitment, but of course I will continue to go with you, whether you can see me or not." They all looked at Mishimar and Hannah.

Mishimar looked at Hannah, she nodded, and he spoke for them both. "We pledged our lives and our swords to you for as long as you need us. As far as we are concerned that means for life. Besides," and he smiled his usual, although sometimes mischievous smile, "I was thinking my use as an apprentice might have now proved to be indispensable," and he chuckled. They all joined in.

Joseph spoke up, "Is there any sense of urgency at our return or do we have enough time to make a smooth transition?"

Uriel's response brought relief to them all. "There is no sense of urgency. You can take all the time you need." Their relief deepened. "I do have one small request, if I may? Actually, I'd like to fulfill a promise, or maybe it was just a wish?" He looked at Mishimar. "We once talked of a chance to spar together. I think this might be it, if you have a few minutes?"

Mishimar's eyes widened, and a smile graced his face as he responded with nearly childlike glee. "Really? That would be incredible. I would love that!"

"Well," Uriel's smile matched Mishimar's, "go get your sword and meet me in the back yard."

Mishimar's eyebrows furrowed, "Will I be sparring with you as a man or an angel?"

Uriel laughed, "You should probably try me in this form first. I'm not sure you're ready for the other."

Mishimar practically leapt to his feet, excused himself, and headed for his and Hannah's room. Hannah and Mary started picking up the dishes. The rest of them got up and headed for the back yard, all except Jeshua, who lingered and then followed the women into the kitchen.

"Hannah, you should go join them." His words soothed like a warm ointment. She often had difficulty believing he was only six. He continued, "I would love to dry the dishes while Momma washes." His ability to touch the human heart even this young consistently amazed her. It rivaled his ability to calm a stallion, and nearly brought tears to her eyes.

"Thank you, Jeshua, I would like that." She let her hand rest a moment on his shoulder as she passed him. He certainly did inspire devotion. He looked up and winked at her as if a secret passed between them before she left.

When she entered the back yard, they had lit the torches and a blazing fire in the fire pit. While cool and crisp for this time of year, it felt friendly. This was, after all, their home, or at least had been for the past few years. The house sat far enough outside of town that their land bordered the desert.

Uriel and Mishimar faced each other, smiling in anticipation. Mishimar had never actually seen Uriel in action. He had been unconscious on the ground during the battle of the four singing swords when Hannah had fought Nesher with Mishimar's sword and Uriel fought the god Marduk. Now, Uriel drew his blade and Mishimar drew Hane in harmony with it, and the concert began.

The sacredness of the moment brought tears to all the observers' eyes, and only sheer force of will kept them from their knees. Simon and Elizabeth proved the exception. They gleefully fell to their knees. What they all saw and heard defied description as the beauty of Uriel and Mishimar's dance together transfixed them. This was not light against dark as the battle of the four swords had been. This was light enhancing light, and the swords' song rivaled those sung only in heaven. The clash of blade meeting blade resounded like cymbals, adding to the symphony's crescendo which built and built until Mishimar abruptly disengaged and stepped back, panting deeply and sweating heavily.

Stepping unexpectedly from the shadows, Hannah drew her own blade, Oz, the sword once wielded by a fallen archangel, then by his son Isbibenob, and finally by Nesher, before she took it from him at his death. Jeshua had redeemed it and returned it to its original purity. Now, as she drew Oz from its sheath, the symphony entered its second movement. When their blades touched, Uriel smiled as though his fondest hopes had materialized. This second movement played out even more powerfully than the first, not outshining it, but embellishing it. Just as the creation of Dawn and her presentation to Clay had brought about the "Very Good" in the beginning, Hannah's entrance into the dance with her sword made this symphony very good too. Now tears ran recklessly down all of their faces, and all those assembled had fallen to their knees, wishing that this could go on forever. But heaven touches earth only as a foretaste of things to come. When Hannah too finally disengaged, exhausted, and sheathed her sword, the music stopped, leaving a palpable void. It took a few minutes for everyone to slowly regain their senses. Only Uriel seemed unfazed, being used to the things of heaven. His eyes slowly swept them all, coupled with the smile they all knew.

"I will see you all in Israel." The children scrambled to their feet, rushed him and embraced him. As they stepped back, he looked over them all to where Jeshua stood. They followed Uriel's gaze as he nodded his head, and disappeared.

If his departure could make the void any deeper, it would have, but Jeshua stood there and his spreading smile refilled their emptiness. With adult-like wisdom and gentleness he addressed them all, "We should probably go to bed. We have much to prepare for, beginning tomorrow."

Chapter 5
Preparations While in Egypt

Homes and land sold easily in Egypt, especially ones with room for a shop, and coupled with the favor of God they quickly found someone to purchase their home. Jeshua had placed at the top of his class at Sabbath school, having already memorized much of the Pentateuch. With pleasure his Rabbi wrote a letter of introduction to his next rabbi, preparing for wherever they settled. Joseph completed the table that he had promised the Egyptian officer and fully realized how indispensable Mishimar had become to their carpentry business. When they delivered the table, the officer expressed amazement, first at how quickly it had been finished and then at how incredible it had turned out. He wanted to have Joseph make him some other furniture, but they informed him that they had begun preparations to return to Israel. Joseph did, however, give him the names of two of his competitors who also did exemplary work. That impressed the officer even more.

He responded, "If you ever return to Egypt, please come and stay with us. It would be my pleasure to have you." Besides giving Joseph a generous bonus for his excellent work, he took them in to meet his wife and family. One of the officer's sons, Cymon, looked about Jeshua's age. Maybe someday they may meet.

Meanwhile, Mary and Hannah began to clean the entire house. Hannah did not even have to ask why. She knew it expressed their gratitude to Chayeem for providing them a sanctuary, as well as serving as a gift to the purchaser of their home.

They gathered around the table for their last supper in Egypt. In the morning they would start towards Jerusalem. It would be a long journey, but this time they felt no fear. With a wagon and the kids as a distraction, it would seem more like a holiday. They reminisced about the many good times they had these last few years in Egypt, especially with the favor of God. It reminded them of the first few years in Bethlehem. Jeshua then entertained them with stories about Egypt from the Pentateuch. He had turned into quite a story-teller. The women tucked the children in for the night and then met the men in the back yard around the fire.

The full moon and the stars shown brightly in a crystal clear sky.

Mishimar asked the first question. "So, where are we heading, Bethlehem?"

Joseph responded, "I'm not sure, but we all know that we can trust Chayeem to guide us. Uriel wasn't very clear about where we should go, only that we could go since Herod and his wizard are dead."

Mary added, "And if Jeshua is to save Israel then it would seem necessary for us to be back in Israel someplace."

"And what exactly has been said about him?" Hannah questioned.

"The angel told us to name him Jeshua, for he would save his people from their sins. I'm not sure what that really means," Joseph replied.

"The angel also said that God would give him the throne of his father David and that there would be no end to his kingdom. Further more, Simeon, at his dedication, said he would be the cause of the rise and fall of many. Really, there was so much said that it's hard to make sense of it all." Mary intentionally left out parts of the story. Some she feared, some she could barely begin to believe.

"Isn't it going to look a little strange to have two soldiers riding with you?" Mishimar looked at Hannah.

"It would only look strange if you were riding with us…." Joseph paused, "…as soldiers. If you are just my apprentice, Hannah is your wife, and the swords are hidden, we should be okay. You should be used to traveling in disguise by now," he laughed. "In the morning, we will pack up our final things and be on our way home. Well, to our new home."

They got up to head for bed, but Hannah and Mishimar lingered behind. "So, I suppose this is goodbye to peace, quiet, and a normal life?" he whispered as he drew her into his arms.

"And when has life with you ever been normal?" She kissed him passionately.

Chapter 6
Dreams and Nightmares

In Jerusalem, Anthony, the Roman centurion, awoke with a start, his wife, Julian, shaking his shoulder, "Anthony, Anthony, you were dreaming." His eyes flared wide with pain and he sweated profusely. "Was it the same one?" she asked. He fought to catch his breath.

He could see it clearly as if he still stood there. The husband attempted to block the way, but the soldier had him unconscious on the ground before the man could blink, revealing a mother, who clung to a young boy. They huddled in the corner of the small house, her four-year-old daughter trembling next to them. The boy looked less than two. If only he had been significantly older. The soldier turned to Anthony for orders.

"Take the child from her, but do it," they both knew what "it" meant, "outside. We're not savages." Anthony spoke commandingly over his own emotional pain, finding this mission harder than he had ever imagined. Years of fierce battles had given him vivid fodder for his imagination, but this was a slaughter. His soldier struck the woman, grabbed the baby boy, and yanked him from her stunned arms. As he retreated with the screaming child, Anthony stepped between the mother and his departing soldier. She crashed into him and fought to get around him. He held her tight and put out a hand to also restrain the girl from following the soldier outside. The child's screams stopped. He placed the woman, now limp in his arms, on the cushions on the floor. He sweated heavily, amidst his own turmoil. The mother roused and whimpered. He looked at her quivering form and then to the little girl. "I'm sorry, I have my orders." It did not excuse his behavior, probably did not even help, but he had to release his own pain somehow. The nightmare mercifully receded.

He nodded, trying to catch his breath in deep gulps. He felt like he had been drowning. "Yes, it was the same one." The agony slowly dissipated. He counted the nightmares as his penance, but it did not comfort him when compared with how much innocent blood had been spilled that night. He threw the sheets aside and struggled to sit up on the side of their bed. He still did not have his full faculties, and for a man of his discipline, that frightened him. He focused his breathing and quieted his heart, as Julian moved over and wrapped her arms around him.

"It's okay, it's okay." Her voice meant to reassure him, but he had already retreated to the private garden of his mind.

He turned slowly and deliberately kissed her. "Thank you, I'm all right now." He disengaged from their embrace and got to his feet. "What time is it?"

"Still hours before sunrise," she replied sleepily, "come back to bed."

"In a minute." He walked to the door of their bedroom. "I'll be right back." In the wash room he splashed some cold water on his face, dried off quickly on the towel, and silently padded barefoot to their son's room. Markus lay sleeping peacefully. He was older than the children slain that night so many years ago, but still looked just as vulnerable. He had kicked his covers askew. Anthony straightened them, pulling them up to his chin, and lightly tousled his hair. He loved this boy more than life itself. Every time the nightmares came he felt like he had lost his own son.

After the slaughter of the children in Bethlehem that night, it had taken months to calm the resultant uprisings. Herod's low popularity turned into open hostility and hatred with that debacle. The uprisings had been a blessing in disguise, because those next few months kept Anthony too busy to think about the slaughter. All his energy went into keeping the peace. If he had any consolation, he felt pretty sure they had not slain the new king. By the time they arrived, the home had been long abandoned. They searched the town and the farms in all directions for many miles, but found no sign of the carpenter and his family. It seemed they had simply vanished. When soldiers asked the neighbors and the townspeople about them, everyone had very good things to say. They all uniformly praised the carpenter's work and said the family seemed kind, peaceful, and had kept mostly to themselves. When the uprisings finally died down, the nightmares began. They increased in occurrence, intensity, and duration, until they occurred almost every other night. He had to do something. He considered drinking, but valued his role as a husband and father too much for that. Still, he had to do something.

Days later, after taking care of an exhausting domestic dispute, early one evening he settled down in the baths and accepted a slave girl's request to rub his shoulders. He knew this young woman, but his tiredness prevented him from recalling her name. She knew him too, and well enough to know she would be safe with him. Not all of the officers treated the slave girls well. She worked his shoulders quietly, efficiently, and he began to relax.

Then she asked, "Would you like to follow me to one of the massage rooms?" and reached out a hand. He looked around, noticing they were alone. Reluctantly he held out his hand, which she took and helped him to his feet. His feet felt a little unsteady, and he began to wonder if he had been in the water longer than he thought. She lifted his arm around her shoulders, walked him to one of the rooms, and helped him onto the low table, face down, his head on his hands.

Saying, "Excuse me while I change into a dry tunic," she left him for a moment.

Rebecca. Her name came to him suddenly. She was one of the few slaves who had earned everyone's respect because she differed from the others. Although a slave, she actually seemed to enjoy her work. His thoughts, jumbled from the exhaustion and warm water, caused him to doze off. The next thing he knew she softly touched his shoulder.

"Centurion?" she whispered, as he startled wide awake and up on his elbows. Some strong emotion lay behind her words, fear maybe?

He lay back down, "It's okay Rebecca, I won't harm you."

"I know." That emotion still echoed under her words. She knelt down next to the table and began kneading his lower back. She had strong hands and powerful thumbs for one so small and young. She had learned her art well. "Centurion, you appear to not have been sleeping well. Is there something I can do to help?"

He smiled as he said, "No, I will be all right, thank you."

But she continued, "Please forgive me for seeming impertinent, but I think you are being troubled by nightmares."

"*What? How could she know that?*" He froze, stunned, and replied so low she could barely hear him, "Only my wife knows that. Who told you this?"

She went on, "And I think it has something to do with what happened in Bethlehem a few years ago."

"Get away from me!" he commanded, actually afraid.

"I'm sorry. Maybe I shouldn't have said anything." She moved back from him. "I didn't mean to make you angry, but I can help."

He sat up, livid. He began to scramble to his feet and do something he would later regret, when he caught the look in her eyes. He flinched, cold-cocked. Large tears rolled down her cheeks and he looked into a gentle face like he had never seen before. She no longer looked like Rebecca the slave girl, she seemed somehow otherworldly. He nearly said, "How could you help me?" when he realized he almost believed she could. The anger drained away leaving him weak again, as he mumbled, "How.....how could you possibly help me?"

"Which god do you serve?" That emotion echoed behind her words again.

"I suppose Mars, if any," he responded. "Why?"

"From what I know about Mars, he is not particularly forgiving."

As he gazed into her eyes, he thought, "*Compassion, that's what it is. This is what compassion looks like.*" It had been so long since he had seen it in anyone besides his wife towards their son. "Forgiveness?" he ventured.

"What if I could introduce you to a God who could forgive you, so that you could forgive yourself?" Compassion dripped like honey from her words.

"Is that even possible?" He could hardly get the words out.

"Yes it is, because He is here," she said with certainty.

"Here?" He looked about the massage room. Maybe she was joking. He looked her in the eyes again, "*No, she's not joking.*"

"You can't see Him, but He's here. You can't see the wind, only its effects, but you know it is here." She smiled. "You can simply ask Him to forgive you and He will."

"Who is this god?" His faith in what she said wavered and he tried a diversionary tactic.

She answered, undeterred, "His name to us is sacred, but in the beginning of creation he was called Chayeem, the Tree of Life."

"You worship a tree?" He moved towards sarcasm.

"He manifests Himself in many forms, that was just one of the earliest." She definitely believed in Him. "But what if He could take away the pain in your heart, let you forgive yourself, and cause the nightmares to cease? Didn't you say that 'you had to do something'?"

"*Wait, he hadn't said that aloud, had he? Surely he had only thought that this morning*?" What he did say was, "Okay what must I do?"

"Simply tell Him what you did, why you need forgiveness, and ask Him to forgive you. Talk to him like He's right here, because He is." She made it sound so simple.

"Why should He forgive me?" He sounded unconvinced, but then he really did not need to be absolutely certain. Just the slimmest chance of forgiveness would be enough.

"Because He loves you and wants you to know that." *How could she be so confident?* "Would you like me to introduce you to Him?" He tentatively nodded and she began, "Chayeem, You have known Anthony," she used his given name, totally out of character for a slave, "all of his life. He has something to say to You," and she gestured to him.

He felt really stupid, talking to the air, or an invisible tree, or whatever, but still he ventured, "Chayeem," and before he could say another word the room seemed filled with something, Someone, so wonderful he could not breathe. He paused, "I am a soldier, I have had to do many terrible things, but in Bethlehem..." he gasped, overcome with emotions, as tears welled up in his eyes, "I'm sorry, I'm sorry, I'm so, so sorry," and he let himself go as the grief overwhelmed him. When he came to himself, he found himself wrapped in Rebecca's arms, and she wept also.

"Keep going," she coaxed, as she released him.

"Please forgive me," and that was all he got out before a powerful compassion knocked him over. He lay on his side on the massage table, curled in a ball, as Rebecca sat at his head, one hand on his shoulder, the other caressing his hair, like a child's.

"And, Chayeem, help him to forgive himself," she whispered softly.

Chapter 7
Anthony's Explanation

That evening when Anthony returned home he said nothing about his experience with Chayeem. He feared to find it all a product of his imagination, and worried that the feeling of deep seated peace and companionship might dissipate, but it did not. If anything, it grew stronger. When he spent time alone, especially in the early morning or late at night, he would talk to Chayeem and listen. He heard nothing audible, but definite pictures and impressions formed in his mind as he listened. Finally after nearly an entire week without the nightmares he decided to tell his wife.

However, she broached the subject first. "You haven't had a nightmare all week. What has happened?"

He wondered, "*Where do I start*?" He began when he encountered Rebecca in the bath. Initially his wife feared he was about to confess to infidelity. That would have almost made more sense to her than the truth.

"You've met a god and are striking up a friendship with him?" She wore her incredulity on her sleeve.

"I don't know that I'd call it a friendship," but as he thought about it, maybe he would, "and it's not a god. Rebecca would say He is the only God. The rest are just pretenders."

"How much time have you spent with this slave girl? I think she has brainwashed you." Her tone might have been spiced with a little jealousy. He had, after all, kept this from her for most of the week.

"Not much, just a little while she's giving me my rub downs." Hmmm, that did not come out quite right.

"She's a bath slave?" He could see her working up a head of steam.

"Chayeem," he whispered, "help me." Suddenly the fury of her anger evaporated like a burst soap bubble and she wept. He put his arm around her, pulled her close, and continued to pray under his breath until she stopped. "Julian, you know me. I have always and will only ever love you. God just used Rebecca as a tool in His hands to bring me to Himself. I want you to meet her and see for yourself."

"Really, you want me to meet her?" She had moved back to incredulity.

"Yes," he whispered endearingly. "I think you will see her as the daughter you have never had." He continued, "May I invite her to dinner?"

She looked at him hard for a moment and then her gaze softened. "Yes," was all she said.

Anthony did invite Rebecca to dinner and she came that next day. She was much more than Julian could have imagined. She had not expected this small, slim bath slave with an undefinable aura of peace, confidence, and compassion rare in someone so young. Markus fell in love with her immediately and followed her around like a puppy dog. She seemed genuinely taken with him too. Markus did not see her as a girl, just as a fun playmate. Imagine their surprise when he asked her to play his favorite game, "soldiers" and handed her a wooden sword, only to see her adeptly wielding it. Yet she played with him in a way that never made him feel inferior.

Anthony broached the topic at supper. "Rebecca, where did you learn the sword? You are quite good."

She smiled rather shyly, "Oh, I didn't know you were watching. I hope I wasn't offensive. I know women are not supposed to be good at swordplay." She seemed ashamed, like she had been caught doing something wrong.

"No, no," he quickly interjected, "It was rather wonderful." He reiterated his question, "Who taught you how to use a sword?"

"My father started me when I was quite young. We had lost my mother at my birth and since I was his only child, he trained me himself once he found out that I took to it like a duck to water. He was killed when the Romans attacked our city, so as a slave I have had to practice in secret." All this she shared with gentle confidence.

Anthony looked at his wife, who seemed to read his mind. He asked tentatively, "What would you think of coming to live with us, initially to help us raise Markus?"

She looked truly and utterly surprised at his question, tears welling up in her eyes. "Is that even possible?" she questioned, daring to hope and nodding her assent.

"I'll see what I can do," he said as Julian smiled broadly.

Chapter 8
The Journey Begins

The adults ate breakfast early, then packed the wagon and hitched the horses while the children had their breakfast, washed the dishes, and packed up their few final items. They arranged the boxes in such a way as to leave a small play area in the front of the wagon for the children, complete with cushions and a few of their toys. They left most of their home's furnishings as part of the sale of their home and land. As a carpenter, Joseph had proved himself exceptionally inventive at building their furniture from the scraps left from the items he had sold. That significantly sweetened the sale. Besides, it would have taken a number of wagons to carry it all to Israel and would have slowed them down. Joseph could always make more, especially suited to their new home, wherever that might be. Mishimar rode ahead, in his normal scouting position, with Hannah to the rear as protection from that direction. Joseph drove the wagon with Mary at his side, their former pack horses now pulling the wagon and their riding horses tethered to the back. It seemed rather minimalistic, but they wanted to travel light.

The journey back to Israel passed more leisurely than the one to Egypt. They rode at an easier pace with the wagon than they would have with a caravan of horses. They also made frequent stops for the children. All of this allowed the horses to remain rested and strong for the entire trip. Most evenings they camped in a location Mishimar remembered from the trip to Egypt. They found enough towns and villages to provide both a chance to replenish supplies and a diversion from their long hours on the road. The children did not seem to mind at all. Throughout this grand adventure they improvised numerous ways to make their travel more exciting. Jeshua would read them stories from the Pentateuch. He read the same stories often enough that they began to learn many of them by heart.

One evening, after they had set up camp and had begun to get ready to sit down to supper, a man burst out of the trees, grabbed Jeshua, and with a knife to his throat demanded, "Your money or I will kill the boy."

Joseph slowly stood, as did Mishimar and Hannah, their hands on the hilts of their swords. Joseph spoke, "No, you won't kill him. That would give away your advantage." Mishimar and Hannah drew their swords together and the harmony they caused made the thief begin to tremble where he stood. He looked in danger of cutting Jeshua accidently. Joseph continued, "Put away your knife, share supper with us, and perhaps we can help you."

The robber removed the blade from Jeshua's throat, put his knife back in his belt, and looked at them all in astonishment. "Who are you people?"

"Just travelers," continued Joseph. "Come, eat with us." His words were disarming all by themselves. Mishimar and Hannah resheathed their swords, but even so the music took a few moments to dissipate. Released from the thief's grip Jeshua took a step away from the man, turned around, and offered him a hand. Mesmerized, the robber took Jeshua's hand, followed his lead to the fire, and sat. As they ate in nearly palpable peace, the man began to share his story.

"My name is Thaddeus. The Roman invasion destroyed my family. A number of years ago, while traveling, I fell among robbers. They beat me, stripped and robbed me, and left me for dead. I lay barely conscious when a priest came by, but when he saw me he crossed over to the other side of the road and just left me there. Later, a Levite also came by, but he did the same. Then a Samaritan came upon the scene of my calamity, took pity on me, bound up my wounds, gave me something to drink, placed me on his donkey, and brought me to the next town and to an inn. He left me there and paid for my care. I stayed there a few days until I regained my strength. The innkeeper said the man would come back and settle the account with him, but before he did, I left. I had nothing, only the clothes he had dressed me in, some of his own."

He stopped for a moment, took a drink of water, and continued. "I was ashamed of my circumstances. I felt everything, everyone, had turned against me and looked down on me. Surely the priest and the Levite, even the innkeeper had. Only the Samaritan had shown me compassion, but he left. So, I suppose it began that moment, when I left the inn in shame after sneaking into the kitchen to steal a knife. My life of robbery waited just around the next corner." He hung his head and stopped.

"What if all that could change in an instant?" Hannah knelt at his side. Jeshua, sitting next to him, reached out and placed his hand on Thaddeus' shoulder. "We have all been engulfed in pain, betrayal, fear, and shame, but what if someone could take all of that away?" she continued.

His head still hung low, muffling his words, "Is that even possible?"

"What if I could introduce you to the God who is here?" She now reached out her hand and touched his other shoulder. He looked her in the eyes and there, around the quiet of the campfire, they introduced Thaddeus to Chayeem. He had bowed his head again, in shame, as he had spoken with Chayeem, but when he looked up once more they saw joy and peace in his eyes.

Joseph invited, "We are headed towards Israel. Would you like to, join us on our adventure?"

Thaddeus replied, "It would be my privilege."

Chapter 9
Adventures on the Road

As they settled into their new routine, the entire family soon wondered how they had gotten along before Thaddeus joined them. He worked tirelessly, ready to help whenever and wherever needed. He usually rode one of their extra horses, but sometimes he just walked alongside the wagon and captivated the children with his stories. He had traveled extensively as a wine merchant, mostly a purchaser of fine wines around the country for inns and establishments, but sometimes even for kings and courts. He had an extensive network of contacts and because he was such a likable fellow, always made new ones. Soon everyone forgot that because he had lost everything for a time he had become a robber.

One afternoon, the children played in the back courtyard of the inn where they were staying while the men took the wagon and animals to the stables and the women went to the market to replenish some of their supplies. The children had been left with Thaddeus, who had gone back inside for a moment to get them some cups of water. That very moment three rough-looking teenagers stepped out of the bushes.

"Ah, what have we here?" the oldest and apparent leader took another step towards them. "What a pretty little girl. What should we do with her, fellows?"

Jeshua stepped between Simon, Elizabeth, and the boys, "No!" he said commandingly.

"Look, it's a little hero," the leader leered and then threatened menacingly, "Step aside, squirt!"

"You are making a terrible mistake." Jeshua stated firmly.

"You think so?" and he knocked him to the ground with a hard right to the face.

Jeshua slowly stood up and replied, "Yes, I do."

He knocked him to the ground again, this time with a left to the head.

Jeshua's head bled slightly from the second hit. He got up again.

Thaddeus walked out of the back door and quickly sized up what was going on, "Heh, what are you doing?" He set the platter of cups aside.

The bully hit Jeshua square in the face, turned, and ran, his compatriots with him.

Thaddeus made as if to go after them, but Jeshua had regained his feet and stood in his way. Thaddeus stepped forward, took Jeshua's bloody face in his hands, "Are you okay?"

Jeshua took a cloth from his pocket, began to wipe the blood from his face. "Yes, I AM."

At his words the ground shivered. Thaddeus looked around quickly. "*Was that an earthquake?*" he thought, but nothing else happened. He held out his hand for Jeshua's cloth which he gave him. He poured some water on it and gave it back to him, and Jeshua washed the rest of the blood from his face.

He looked up at Thaddeus, "Thank you for not going after them."

Thaddeus responded, "I probably wouldn't have been able to catch them."

Jeshua tried to smile, but it hurt too much.

❖

That evening after the two younger children climbed in bed, Mary and Joseph took Jeshua aside. "What happened today?" Joseph asked.

Jeshua frowned. "Who told you something happened?"

"Jeshua," Mary whispered tenderly, "you have a black eye."

"Ah," he replied, "I guess that gave it away," and he relayed the story of what happened.

"You didn't fight them?" Joseph did not know whether to be concerned. "You just stood up to them?"

"And kept getting up and standing up to him each time he knocked me down." He smiled a bit, although it still hurt.

"You didn't fight back?" Mary asked.

"There are different ways to fight," he replied simply.

"I'm glad Thaddeus showed up before they could hurt you any more," she said.

"It's okay, Mother. There are things much worse than getting knocked to the ground." Jeshua spoke quite seriously.

"Yes, there are," Mary murmured as a tear formed and she remembered, "*and a sword will pierce your own soul.*"

"Off to bed?" Joseph questioned.

"In a few minutes," Jeshua got up, walked out the back door, and sat on the porch steps. An old man walked out after him and sat beside him.

Uriel looked down into his eyes, "I was very proud of you today."

"You were there," more a statement than a question.

"I am always here." Uriel lightly tussled his hair, put his arm around him, and drew him to his chest. Interesting how he said "I am always here" rather than "I was there." As Jeshua drank deep of Uriel's protection, he also realized that he might not avoid the pain, but he would always have Uriel's presence to count on, seen or unseen.

Before they went to sleep that night, Mary shared with Joseph what she heard in the market. Archelaus now reigned in Herod's place. The son behaved no better than the father. The next morning dawned clear and bright, perhaps the harbinger of things to come. At breakfast Joseph recounted a dream from the previous evening.

Uriel had appeared to him and warned him of the dangers in and around Jerusalem.

"I am of the opinion that, with this recent information, we shouldn't go back to Bethlehem," Joseph added. Seeing a general nodding of heads, he continued, "I'm proposing that we bypass Jerusalem and head up north to Galilee."

Mishimar looked to Hannah and then said, "That would be fine with us." Thaddeus nodded his agreement too.

Joseph looked to Mary, "What would you think if we tried Nazareth again? Do you suppose enough time has passed that they might accept us now?"

Mary took a deep breath and sighed, "Sure, let's give it a try."

The men went to get the wagon and horses, while the women and children cleaned and packed up. They left the inn and began the journey to Nazareth.

Arriving in Nazareth they did find acceptance as a family. The years had covered the ugliness of the past, everyone needed an expert carpenter, and Joseph's work spoke for itself. The quality of it, coupled with his fair prices, soon had him more than enough work. With the money from the sale of their property in Egypt they purchased a house large enough for them all with room to grow and an excellent out-building for a shop.

Early one morning, Jeshua took a shovel, a wineskin of water, and the seed that Uriel had given him up into the nearby hills. He found a place where a grove of oak trees had been recently harvested. There he prepared and planted the seed of Chayeem. From then on, he stopped and watered it whenever he could.

PART TWO

Six Years Later

Chapter 10
Mekah's Companion

Herod Archelaus had procured a companion for Mekah. The king thought it might tame her down a little, but it merely provided her a disciple. Her name was Marie and her parents had lost everything in a fire. In hopes of gaining some of their investment back, they sold their oldest daughter. Marie had grown up in the small northern fishing town called Magdala on the western shore of lake Galilee. She was a quiet young woman with a dark complexion, but a few years older than Mekah. Being in awe of the fifteen-year-old Mekah, laced with a healthy dose of fear, probably contributed to Marie's getting along with her. Wherever Mekah went she acted like she owned the place, not in a particularly condescending manner, but as though she thought she truly did. Her aura of power had its roots in darkness and sorcery. No one knew of the secret temple that Mekah frequented. She had faithfully kept it hidden and only visited it in such a manner that it remained concealed. She had covered the door to it with a tapestry woven with elaborate and arcanely occult symbols.

Like sisters who shared a room together, the girls slept in beds side by side. This morning as Marie opened her eyes, Mekah sat on the edge of her bed smiling at her.

"Mistress," Marie whispered. "What is it?"

"Bathe and dress quickly, I have something important to show you," she replied briefly. While Marie did so, Mekah sat and watched approvingly. When she finished, Mekah stood and approached her.

"You are right-handed?" she asked. Marie nodded. "Hold out your right hand, palm up." As she complied, Mekah so quickly produced a knife and slightly sliced Marie's palm that she hardly felt any pain. "Make a fist!" she commanded. As she did, Mekah took a small bowl from her tunic pocket, placed it under Marie's fist, and had her squeeze some of her blood into the bowl. She then turned, opened a drawer to the nearby nightstand, took out an embroidered cloth and handed it to her. "You may wrap your hand in that." Marie took the cloth in her left hand and first brought it to her nose, noting its wonderful fragrance. She doused her hand in her bath water, quickly dried it before it could bleed more, then wrapped it in the cloth. Mekah extended the small bowl of blood towards Marie's left hand and she took it. Mekah then tenderly took Marie's right hand in her left, and hand in hand they walked out of the bedroom, through her quarters, until they stood before the tapestry.

Mekah let go of Marie's right hand, dipped her own right thumb into the blood in the bowl and made a mark on Marie's forehead. "I am swearing you to secrecy." Her gaze intensified. "No one must ever know this door exists. Do you agree?"

Marie timidly nodded, "Yes."

Mekah lifted the right corner of the tapestry away from the wall to reveal the door, said a word, and the door opened. "You may go in," she whispered and they entered the temple. Mekah dropped the corner of the tapestry and closed the door behind them.

The room disoriented Marie, as though they had entered another realm entirely. A number of well-trimmed oil lamps reflected across the hard sheen of a dark obsidian altar in the middle of the room. Mekah took the bowl from Marie, stepped up to the altar, set the bowl of blood on it, and muttered something unintelligible that set it ablaze. Startled, Marie stepped back and crashed against the closed door. With the sound of a muffled implosion, there stood before them a Being of indescribable beauty.

Mekah simply said, "Chemosh" and bowed. Marie stood paralyzed with fear, not knowing what to do. The Being drew his sword, producing a sound of such discordant beauty that Marie found herself writhing on the stone floor. Chemosh lay his sword on the altar. A portal opened to his right and seven lesser beings stepped through. Marie finally struggled to her knees. She looked up hesitantly at the beings.

Chemosh spoke and it took the breath from her lungs. "My soldiers: Passion, Desire, Allure, Stealth, Pleasure, Disguise, and their captain Deception." Then to the Beings, "Welcome to your new home."

With that, Chemosh disappeared. Mekah reached behind her and opened the door. Keeping the beings in sight the entire time, she stepped backwards out of the room, leaving Marie alone with the seven of them.

Their captain spoke hissingly, "Come join us, my little one."

She arose and walked trance-like into the midst of their demoniacal glee. She awoke much later on the floor, alone, sore all over, very much afraid, her clothes in tatters. She burst into tears, then a near maniacal euphoria exhausted her.

Chapter 11
Passover in Jerusalem

This would be Jeshua's first experience of the Passover Festival in Jerusalem, the greatest of their holy festivals. While they had celebrated each of the feasts at home every year, he could barely contain the wonder of celebrating Passover in Jerusalem. Surely, this would be one of the highlights of his short twelve years of life. Many special things had happened, but everything falling into place now seemed to imply that this celebration would eclipse them all. Jeshua knew the Pentateuch, the first five books of Moses, by heart and could easily quote almost all of it from memory. He knew the story of the original passover well: how God had brought His people out of Egypt, the land of bondage, through the plagues that He had rained down on the Egyptians, culminating in the death of every firstborn of man and beast. That night all those who had followed God's instructions and had slain a perfect lamb, put its blood on their door posts and the lintel of their home, and remained inside until morning, had heard the Devourer pass over their home. The celebration of God's deliverance was a perpetual statute, and God's people celebrated it each year by this festival, an act of remembrance.

He found it difficult to sleep that night because of the anticipation. Soon they would celebrate one of the holiest of their days in the City of God's own habitation. On their journey the next day they sang the Songs of Ascent, those special psalms penned so many years ago, and dedicated to the pilgrimage and pilgrims on their journey to the Temple. They approached the temple itself, that place on which God chose to let His name rest and the place where He manifested His presence, even if most people could not see Him. An awe inspiring building, designed to elicit a sense of worship, it did not disappoint Jeshua. Since they had crested the hill outside the city and first viewed it, it had taken his breath away. Even as they came closer, it became more difficult for him to wait. Here sat God's house, His dwelling place. He could hardly wait to get inside.

An incredible multitude filled the Temple. Some had brought their sacrifice with them, the most special thing to do. The personal cost of sacrificing your own lamb to which you felt a deep attachment made the sacrifice that much more meaningful. Sin, sickness, and decay had infected every part of society, even within God's own people. All the sacrifices in the world would not change that, but each family could in some small way atone for it personally. Although not shepherds, they had raised their lamb themselves, as part of the family. To have him slain for their sins brought a deeper meaning to the ceremony. This personal, terrible loss, starkly illuminated that a restored relationship with God came at a high price. That, plus the memory of this personal cost, provided an additional motivation to keep from sinning again. Love remained the greatest deterrent to wrong doing. Why would one want to hurt someone who loved them so much, whom the scriptures said should be loved with all our heart, soul, mind, and strength? Amidst all the suffering, pain, and death, they also celebrated. Their sins gone, their atonement complete, they were free to love fully.

No longer a child holding his mother's hand, Jeshua found himself free to discover all that went on around him. Joseph had reminded him, "We leave when the Sabbath is over, so don't forget, we will meet you back with our friends for the journey home."

Joseph received a simple, "Yes," in reply from the young man with stars in his eyes, completely drinking in the fullness of this experience. And so they parted ways. Mary found it more difficult, but as her son entered manhood, he needed the space to grow.

Jeshua drifted towards the teaching, listening to the rabbis and teachers. Fortunately still young and lithe, he wiggled his way through the crowd until he reached near the front. He found a place next to an older man, sat, and listened. Occasionally the rabbis would ask if any had questions and someone from the crowd would pose one. A brave soul did just that, presenting what he considered a difficulty with the scriptures: "Why does God command us 'Do not kill,' and then condone the murder of men, women, children, and flocks as His people conquered the promised land?" Most of these questions the learned men had heard before., although they seemed new to this particular crowd.

One of the rabbi spoke up, "God does not condone murder, but killing during war time differs. When a surgeon removes the diseased part of the flesh, he often must also remove some of the apparently healthy flesh around it to make sure that the disease does not return. When God's people entered the land of promise, they found much of it diseased and it needed to be surgically cleansed. Does someone have another question?" A number of hands raised, including Jeshua's. The rabbi pointed to him, "You have a question, young man?"

Jeshua asked them, "In the beginning, He who created them male and female said, 'Therefore, a man shall leave his father and mother and cleave to his wife, and the two shall become one flesh.' Why then did Moses give a man a certificate of divorce that he might send his wife away?"

The rabbis and the teachers of the Law began to argue among themselves, one saying this and another saying that. Finally one of them stood up, "It is time for the noon meal. We will come together after that and hear more of your questions." They all got up and began to leave, still arguing among themselves.

The old man who sat next to Jeshua leaned over to him and chuckled, "They didn't answer your question, young man." He continued, "I would be privileged if you would share the noon meal with me." Jeshua smiled, helped the old man to his feet, and left with him.

Chapter 12
After Encountering the Seven

Mekah waited what she deemed an appropriate amount of time through horrific noises, grunts, groans, pounding, scraping, and screaming, until the sounds on the other side of the door ceased altogether. Yet still she waited. She prayed to Chemosh, again, and again, and again. Then finally, when all had been quiet for some time, she spoke the word, and the door opened. Marie lay on the cold stone floor, her clothes in tatters, her beautiful body a mass of abrasions and contusions, spittle dripping from the corner of her mouth. Mekah experienced more compassion than she had felt in a long time as she lifted the limp, seemingly lifeless body and took her to their chamber.

Marie slept, if it could be called that, all the rest of that day and through that night. Nightmares troubled her and repeatedly had her thrashing the covers from the bed as she mumbled in terror at unseen demons. Fortunately for Mekah, she was nearly impervious to fear or she definitely would have been afraid. She did, however, worry. Had Marie been driven insane by her experience with the Seven, or would she awake in some semblance of her former mind? While it seemed somewhat beneath her, Mekah nursed Marie back to health. Chemosh had made it quite clear to her that Marie was extremely special and her care could be trusted to no one else.

Finally Marie regained consciousness. She had no recollection of the hidden temple room, its altar, nor her encounter with the Seven, as though it had never happened. Yet Mekah soon began to notice subtle changes in Marie's behavior. She began to dress more provocatively. Not blatant, more latently, subconsciously. However, any man in the room seemed inextricably drawn to her, partly because of how she dressed. Chemosh had seen enormous possibilities in all of this, so he had introduced her to the Seven. Mekah just needed to groom her.

Sorcery did not interest Marie at all, but she easily learned the fine arts of seduction. For that Mekah drew on the Sanskrit she had learned to translate a nearly complete copy of the Kama Sutra, the Indian tome on the "Art of Love." Far more than a text of eroticism as some supposed, it guided the reader into a life of desire, pleasure, and satisfaction. Together they studied it extensively, page by page, although Mekah saw it as primarily an academic exercise. For the practical application of this information, Mekah decided to turn Marie over to a young, but highly experienced courtesan, Ahlam.

Even at her young age, Ahlam had become famous in the courts of the king. Her exceptional skill at giving pleasure and her high prices made her doubly desirable. Only the wealthiest of patrons could experience her charms. So, late one beautiful morning, out on a sunlit terrace, Mekah introduced the two. Ahlam stood at the terrace's railing with the mid-morning sun surrounding her like a halo. Poised with her back towards them, dressed in the lightest of gossamer blue gowns, she turned slowly and gracefully when Mekah called her name.

"Ahlam, I have someone I want you to meet." Mekah's voice dropped to just above a whisper. "This is Marie and she has served me well, but your master has purchased her contract."

Everything about Ahlam thrilled the senses, even her voice. "Then she will be joining me in my quarters?" she whispered seductively in return.

"Yes. With your approval, I will have my servants take care of that immediately," Mekah replied.

Her devastating smile fired her eyes, "Let me have her for an hour and then I will send you word."

Mekah nodded, turned, and left Marie behind on the terrace. Marie thought herself confident, but Alham's presence unbalanced her in a way she did not understand. While similar in age, their life experiences differed greatly. Ahlam gestured towards a table on the terrace replete with fruits and beverages.

"Marie, I am very pleased to meet you." Suddenly Marie felt completely at ease. "And what is your favorite beverage?"

She felt so comfortable that she sat down and then wondered if she had committed a breach of etiquette. "Thank you," she paused, at a loss as to how to address Ahlam.

That slow smile spread again, "You may simply call me Ahlam. I think we are going to be friends."

Marie looked at the array of beverages, "Actually, I prefer water."

Ahlam poured her some water, in the clearest of crystal goblets, then some for herself, and sat beside her. Her gown flowed gracefully like a gentle breeze as she sat and crossed her legs chastely. Her perfume seemed almost absent, yet it somehow captured Marie's senses. Ahlam watched Marie intently without making her feel self conscious, taking in every nuance, and gesture. What she saw impressed her. Marie exhibited a rare comfortableness in her own skin.

"So, did you realize that you now belong to my master?" she asked gently.

Marie shook her head "*No*" almost ashamedly.

"Are you comfortable with that?" she continued.

Meekly Marie responded, "I don't know your master. Are you comfortable with him?"

"Most definitely," and she added, "and as far as he is concerned, you will work for me."

"Then that will be fine with me, too." Marie met Ahlam's eyes and matching smiles graced both their faces.

Chapter 13
At Simeon's for Lunch

While the old man may not have been extremely wealthy, he did seem to be a man of means. He resided within walking distance of the temple and in one of the better parts of town. When they entered, a servant greeted them, removed their sandals, washed their feet, and anointed them. According to custom, the servant cared for the old man's feet first and then Jeshua's. Afterwards, the old man turned, embraced Jeshua, kissed him, and welcomed him into his home. As a carpenter's son, Jeshua could tell quality furnishings when he saw them. The old man reclined at the table and indicated that Jeshua should join him, which he did.

"Excuse me, son," the old man lightly pleaded, "for my lapse in manners. I should have introduced myself as we journeyed to my home, but I'm afraid that sometimes it takes all my concentration just to successfully put one foot in front of the other." He handed Jeshua a cup of sparklingly cold water, obviously from a very deep well. "I am Simeon, and in my later years I wish I had studied to become a rabbi in my youth. It is interesting what becomes important as you get older and what no longer matters very much though you thought it did in your youth."

"I am very pleased to formally meet you, Simeon. My name is Jeshua," he responded.

With actual interest Simeon asked, "Tell me about yourself, Jeshua. The question you asked in the temple showed an unusual grasp of the scriptures."

Jeshua recounted, "I was born in Bethlehem and after my dedication and circumcision in Jerusalem, moved back there for a few years. We traveled to Egypt right before the massacre of the children, and stayed there for about four years. We moved back to Nazareth in Galilee about six years ago and this is my first time to observe the Passover in Jerusalem. Regarding the scriptures, I have always been fortunate that everywhere we have gone I have been taught by an excellent rabbi. That, and I get so excited every time I study them. It's like He's speaking to me directly."

A sudden gleam sparkled in Simeon's eye, "Excuse me, how many years ago were you dedicated in the temple?"

"It would have been twelve years ago, right after the Feast of Tabernacles," Jeshua elaborated.

As though someone had punched Simeon in the stomach, he seemed to struggle for breath.

With obvious concern Jeshua asked, "Simeon, are you alright?" and he began to rise from his place.

However, Simeon held up his hand, restraining him, until he had his breath back again, then asked, "What are the names of your parents?"

"My mother is Mary, and my…." he hesitated, "stepfather is Joseph."

Simeon's awe deepened, "I met you as a baby, at your dedication."

Now came Jeshua's turn to be awed, "You're that Simeon?"

He nodded. "Your mother told you about me?" Jeshua nodded.

With a far away look in his eye, Simeon spoke, "It had been revealed to me by the Holy Spirit that I would not die until I had beheld the Lord's anointed. That day they brought you to the temple, I took you up in my arms, and declared, 'Lord, Your servant may now depart in peace, according to what You have told me. For I have seen with my own eyes the salvation You have prepared for all people, a light of revelation to the Gentiles and glory to Your own people, Israel.' I said some other things too, but I don't recall them clearly."

Both of their eyes held tears as Jeshua leaned towards Simeon, who drew him to his breast. They savored the sacred moment, then Simeon spoke again, "I was surprised to awake alive the next day, and the next, and the next, for all these years. Never in my wildest dreams did I imagine I would be privileged to see you again."

"And I share that privilege," said Jeshua. "So, you believe that it is my destiny to bring salvation to all people? What does that even mean?"

Simeon pondered his response, "I'm not sure. It may mean any number of things and many people will try to tell you what it means, but you must listen to Him," and he pointed upward.

"He is also here." Jeshua pointed to his heart, "closer than my next breath."

Simeon's servant had brought their lunch, silently and discretely. They finally both realized that it sat in front of them. Simeon asked Jeshua, "Would you bless our food?" Jeshua nodded, looked towards the end of the table, and began to speak. It seemed like heaven suddenly joined them and when he stopped, Simeon added his own "Amen" with difficulty.

They spoke mostly of the scriptures over their lunch. The breadth and depth of Jeshua's understanding astonished Simeon. As they finished, he asked Jeshua, "Are you going back to the temple and the teachers?"

"Yes," he said simply. "I have a number of other questions for them."

"*I hope they're ready for you, but I doubt that they are,*" Simeon thought, but all he said was, "I think I will take a short nap. I will join you at the temple later." Simeon walked Jeshua to the door and kissed him before he left. "*Whose soul was going to be pierced?*" he thought as he watched him leave. Then he went to his bedroom and his bed, but it took him a long time to fall asleep. Jeshua walked pensively back to the temple, his mind swirling with questions.

Chapter 14
Anthony's New Orders

Julius, one of the king's personal guards, opened the door to Herod Archelaus' private council room and ushered Anthony into it. Anthony wondered why he had been summoned. It had only been days since he had met Chayeem. He did not think anyone else even knew, but he still struggled to understand how their new relationship would affect his allegiance to the king. He had no particular problem enforcing the laws of the land, but he had no idea how he would respond if commanded to slaughter children again. While he felt forgiven for that incident, and cleansed from the stain it had left on his soul, the memory of it still popped up on occasion to remind him of the potentially immoral demands of his position. He did not have a problem with using deadly force when it was required, but he could not imagine ever slaughtering innocent children again.

Although he needed no introduction, Julius announced, "Anthony, my lord," and backed out of the room the way he had come in.

"Anthony, Anthony, it's good to see you. How have you been?" intoned the king through a mouth full of food. "Would you like something to eat?" as he gestured to the banquet spread before him.

"Thank you, my lord. No, I am fine." He patted his stomach as though full. "I have been very good. Thank you for asking. What can I do for you?" Anthony had served Archelaus' father faithfully for years, had equally served Archelaus, although his personal contact with the king had been less than with the king's father.

"You are familiar with my Master of Arms, Claudius?" and the king took a long pull from a golden goblet.

"Yes, my lord, he trained many of us, especially as we advanced in the ranks of your service." He wondered where this conversation led.

"And he spoke very highly of you, as did my father," the king smiled as he took another drink.

Anthony thought it interesting that the king spoke of both Claudius and his father in the past tense. "Has Claudius retired, my lord?"

"In a manner of speaking," the king alluded to something quite different than retirement. The door to his personal chambers opened and out stepped the sorceress Mekah, tying a light robe around herself. Mekah had quickly replaced Batel in the king's heart. Perhaps she stole his soul also. Her presence in the room brought the slaughter back to Anthony like a punch in his gut. He whispered Chayeem's name beneath his breath. As though she heard it, Mekah shuddered where she stood. She regained her composure, walked over to the king, and kissed him lightly on the cheek. He seemed not to notice, but as she sat in the chair next to him, his hand unconsciously fondled her.

"As I was saying," continued the king, "I am in need of a new Master of Arms and I would like that to be you." Mekah seemed to blanch a little at that proclamation and whispered in his ear. He turned to her and uncharacteristically said sharply, "No! I am sure he is the man for the job. My father put his life in Anthony's hands. I will put the future of my officers there too!" Mekah looked startled and turned away, like a petulant child.

It took a moment for Anthony to regain his own composure before he replied, “It would be my honor to so serve you, my king.”

Mekah had now regained her composure also. “I'm not sure Chemosh would agree, but the decision is rightfully yours, my liege.”

Archelaus looked sternly at her again, “Yes! It is! Julius will show you to your new quarters. Julius!” he said rather loudly and Julius opened the door and re-entered.

“Yes, my lord?”

Archelaus said commandingly, “Anthony is our new Master of Arms. Please accompany him to his new quarters.” Then to Anthony, “You will also inherit his residence, slaves, and all other property. Julius is at your disposal to see to the transition of your belongings,” and he nodded a curt dismissal.

“Yes, my lord,” Anthony managed to get out of his mouth before he turned and walked out the door, followed by Julius.

Archelaus sighed as though a large weight had just been removed from his shoulders and did not see the scowl on Mekah's face. He reached down, squeezed her hand, and turned to face her. She now smiled in false approval.

As a soldier and an officer, Anthony had superb control of his emotions. That saved him from making a fool of himself in the king's presence, but once Julius had closed the door behind him, the incredulity of the last few minutes engulfed him. He shook his head, trying to make sense of it all, then Julius slapped him on the shoulder and said, “Congratulations, I can think of no one more deserving.”

Anthony smiled, retorted, “I hope it comes with a pay increase,” and chuckled lightly.

To which Julius added, “Most certainly! You'll need it to keep up with all the expenses of your new home. Wait ‘till you see this place,” and they marched off together.

Claudius' home was nearly a palace in itself. It featured a beautiful garden and an open air pavilion over a close cut lawn that could be used for a multitude of purposes. The pavilion had sliding doors that could virtually enclose it in inclement weather, but be left wide open in the usually nicer seasons. Tables and chairs could be set up on the lawn to entertain. He knew his wife would fall in love with this place. After the grand tour by Julius, he made that his next task, going home to tell his wife the good news.

When he did reach home, he began with, "The king called me into his presence this morning," and paused for dramatic effect.

It worked. She came over and lovingly pushed him, "And...."

He feigned injury and then smiled, "I have been promoted to Master at Arms. Do you realize all that means?"

She played along, "No, tell me. What all does that mean?"

He started slowly, wanting to build up momentum, "No more long campaigns away from home." She smiled coyly and winked. "More regular hours each day." She still smiled. "And we inherit Claudius' home, servants, pay, and property."

She allowed a petulant look to cross her face, "But I have grown so fond of this little place." She emphasized "little."

He concluded, "and you will fall madly in love with this new one."

She perked up, "When do we move?"

His smile deepened as he pulled her into his arms and kissed her. "We begin today."

Chapter 15
Returning Home from Passover

Mary and Joseph spent an amazing week celebrating the Passover in the Holy City. They had not seen much of Jeshua, but when they had seen him he practically vibrated with excitement. Joseph had told him their plans to leave that morning, and since he had always obeyed them, he must be with some of their friends. So, they and hundreds of pilgrims left Jerusalem to make their way back to their respective homes. The journey back to Nazareth would take about six or more days. They did not hurry. The rest of the children had been left with Thaddeus and Hannah, while Mishimar had traveled with them, adding an extra measure of safety with his singing sword. Not that he had ever recently been required to use it, but it still brought them comfort.

That evening as they made their camp, they expected Jeshua to find them for supper. When he did not, Mary began to worry. After supper, she had Joseph and Mishimar look for him among their friends and acquaintances, but they found him nowhere. Now her concern turned to fear for his safety.

"He must still be in Jerusalem and probably panicking," she fretted.

"We better go find him," Joseph said calmly, although his own mind raced with possible scenarios.

They quickly packed up their belongings and turned back towards Jerusalem that night. Although already late in the evening, someone usually stood guard at each encampment they passed. They would stop, ask them if they had seen a frightened twelve-year-old boy, and, receiving a negative response, move on. Unfortunately, nothing about Jeshua particularly stood out, other than that he was only twelve and rather polite. After describing him for the umpteenth time, they asked if they could join that encampment and bedded down for a few short hours of sleep though none of them slept much.

They awoke, had a cold breakfast, repacked, and arrived back in Jerusalem early the next morning.

Before they began looking, Joseph took Mary's hand, looked at Mishimar, and said, "We should pray." Mishimar nodded his assent. Joseph spoke quietly, "Chayeem, it seems that Jeshua did not follow us home and we don't know where he is. Jerusalem is a huge city, still filled with hundreds of thousands of people, please help us find him. He's only twelve and probably scared. Thank you." He dropped Mary's hand. "Do we have a plan?"

They conferred, decided to split up to cover more territory, and did just that. Mary headed towards the public wells and markets where most of the women would be with their gossip, hopefully about a lost twelve-year-old. Joseph headed for the marketplace. He knew that Jeshua had been looking for a new cover to his rare copy of the Pentateuch, and being an excellent shopper and negotiator, would be focused on getting the most for his meager funds. As Joseph's apprentice, he had received a small percentage of each sale he had helped with, and he had carefully saved it for this special purchase. Mishimar headed for the local militia. As a soldier, he hoped their extensive network might find the boy more quickly. They were all disappointed when they met at an inn they had frequented during their time at Passover, hoping he might return there, only to find they had each been unsuccessful in their search, nor had he gone back to the inn. They had a small meal and spent the night in their rooms praying. They tried again the next day and the next, all to no avail. Only prayer kept Mary from hysteria.

Their frustration continued to mount and they were running out of options, when late the third night there came a polite knock on the door. Mishimar opened it to reveal the centurion, Anthony, whom he had met so many years ago when the Masters searched for the new king. Mishimar froze, uncharacteristically flabbergasted.

Anthony spoke first. He looked down to Mishimar's hip, "I see you still have the sword."

Mishimar's hand went to its hilt as he finally found his voice, "Anthony!" he exclaimed as he embraced him and then turned to introduce him. "Mary and Joseph, this is Anthony, the centurion we met when Hannah and I traveled with the Masters in search of your son."

Now came Anthony's turn to be astonished. "This twelve-year-old you are seeking, he is the king who was born in Bethlehem?"

Mary and Joseph turned to each other, not sure how to respond. Mishimar looked deeply into Anthony's eyes, knew he could trust him, and prompted by Chayeem replied, "Yes."

Anthony smiled, "Well then, I have some good news and some bad news. I don't know where he is right now, that's the bad news, but I know where he will be tomorrow, that's the good news. These last few days there has been a young lad, about twelve years old, amazing the people and the teachers in the temple with his questions and his answers. They are awed at his understanding of the scriptures. I am told that he speaks as no rabbi the people have ever heard, with such familiarity that it's like he knows God personally."

Mary sounded nearly frantic, "We can't find him right now, tonight?" Joseph placed a hand on her shoulder.

"No," soothed Anthony, "But I'm sure he is safe. You just need to wait until morning and you will find him in the temple, sitting among the teachers."

She seemed to relax. Joseph drew her into his arms. "Thank you, Anthony. We'll withdraw to bed then and see if we can get some sleep. We didn't have much last night."

Mishimar and Anthony remained behind, alone. "I have been promoted to Master at Arms," Anthony said as almost a confession. "So I teach the sword, rather than actually have to use it in battle." Then, he asked almost sheepishly, "I would be in your debt, if I could hold your sword once again."

Mishimar still remembered fondly the one time they had switched swords and sparred together in the palace courtyard, late that night when they found out they would be searching in Bethlehem for the new king. He smiled, drew Hane, who softly sang a note of pure beauty. "Remember, I told you that the two of you might meet again, and here we are." He handed the sword to Anthony, who took it almost reverently

"May I?"

Mishimar stepped back, "Be my guest."

In a continued atmosphere of near worship, Anthony swung Hane over his head and practiced a few thrusts and parries. The smile on his face glowed with light, and then it darkened. "You know," he forced the words out with difficulty. "It was I who led the slaughter of Bethlehem that attempted to slay their son?" He pointed in the direction Mary and Joseph had left.

"No, I didn't. I'm sorry." The joy at watching Anthony with his sword had softened into real concern.

"Chayeem has forgiven me," Anthony's voice faded to a whisper.

Mishimar's eyes opened in astonishment, "You have met Chayeem?"

"Yes, only recently, and He is with me constantly," Anthony continued, as he offered the sword back to Mishimar, hilt first.

Hane's soft melody ceased as Mishimar sheathed him and stepped forward to draw Anthony into an embrace. They held each other for a moment, and as they released each other, looked to find their eyes glistening.

"Do you want me to assign some guards to take you to the temple tomorrow?" Anthony asked politely.

"Thank you, but that won't be necessary. It would cause too much attention," Mishimar grinned.

"I think you will find," Anthony nodded towards Mary and Joseph's bedroom, "that their son is creating quite a bit of attention all by himself."

As Anthony turned to leave, Mishimar asked "Anthony, before you go, would you like me to quickly tell you the story of my sword, Hane?"

He stopped dead in his tracks and slowly turned back around. "I would like nothing more. Should we sit down?"

"Sure, but it won't take very long. I've told the story so many times to the children that I could do it in my sleep. Hmmm, I probably do." Mishimar smiled.

They sat and Mishimar began, "Seven singing swords, forged before the world began, were given to the archangels when the stars sang and the sons of God shouted for joy. ….." Anthony sat on the edge of his seat in such rapt attention that he reminded Mishimar of the children. A few minutes later Mishimar concluded with, "…and then my father gave the sword to me and as they say, 'The rest is history.'"

Anthony took a deep breath, unaware of how long he had been holding it, and stood up. "Thank you. Now, I must leave you to your rest." He reached out a hand and they grasped forearms Roman style. "And may His favor," Anthony pointed upward, "continue to rest on you all." Then he pointed to the hip on which Hane rested, "Thank you for the story and a chance to wield him once again."

"You are entirely welcome. He still sings for you. Perhaps you will meet even again."

"I would like that. I would like to see you all again," Anthony turned, opened the door, and walked out into the night.

"*Hmm, Anthony, Chayeem, and Hane, will wonders never cease?*" Mishimar thought to himself.

Chapter 16
Meeting Ahlam's Master

As Ahlam began to introduce her to the life of pleasure, Marie realized that she seemed specifically designed for this. Her instruction involved her entire being, mentally, emotionally, physically, and spiritually, and enhanced her natural gifts and talents in all of these areas. They had begun that very next morning, out in the garden, with breathing exercises and relaxation. This had transcended into deep meditation. She sat cross-legged on the short cropped grass of a small meadow, surrounded by trees and flowers, basking in the morning sun.

"Close your eyes, empty yourself, let everything go, and become a part of all that is around you," Ahlam softly coached her. "Inhale through your nose, slowly exhale through your mouth. Savor the fragrances around you, the sounds, the gentle breeze. Now wait, wait, wait."

Her eyes snapped open. "What am I waiting for?"

"The eagerness to go away for one thing," Ahlam replied, a little frustrated. "*This was after all, their first morning,*" she reminded herself. "He will come to you when you are ready," she explained.

Marie's eyes snapped open again, "Who will come?"

"Close your eyes," she soothed, and Marie did. "Your Guide. He will approach you, you cannot go to him."

Suddenly Marie inhaled deeply, not startled or shocked, but in amazement, awe, and wonder.

"Is that him?" Ahlam questioned. Marie shook her head, no. "Then what?"

The wonder deepened, "It is she," Marie whispered.

Ahlam startled. "*There are no female guides.*" she said to herself. "Ask him his name."

"Her name is Dawn. She is the first woman, the embodiment of beauty, grace, and all that is desirable to make one wise," Marie continued softly, almost mesmerizingly.

Ahlam's jaw dropped. Was that even possible, the spirit of the first woman? She had never heard anything like it, but then with Chemosh anything was possible. "What is she saying to you?"

Marie responded, "You will be my coach, but she will be my guide. She is always with me, wherever I go, even when I am asleep."

This astonished Ahlam. Her guides came and went. No one stayed with her, at least not that she knew. "Ask her if we may move on into the physical routine?"

"She says, 'Yes, flexibility and grace are very important for what she has in store for me,'" Marie replied.

They moved on into the stretching, the bending, building strength, ability, and agility. They worked single muscles, muscle groups, and then put it all together in the dances. The dances themselves were not erotic, nor was the way she would dress or behave. As Ahlam taught her, her purity and seeming naiveté would be her greatest power. Ahlam also taught her much about men, their dreams, desires, wishes, and fantasies. She taught her of their apparent strengths and their many weaknesses. She would become a master of men. They practiced. Each day they practiced, and practiced. Finally came time for her to perform. Ahlam took her to the Master, Janus. She first had dinner with him, then danced for him. Ahlam left them alone together and waited outside his chamber. He came out much later.

"You have done very well by her," Janus said huskily. "For one so young, she is almost as accomplished as you. I think she was born for this," he continued. "Whatever you need for her, you have but to ask."

Ahlam smiled. Janus was after all only a man, a powerful man, but still just a man. She went in to find Marie asleep. She remembered nothing, another part of her gift. Ahlam took her to the baths and then they had another lesson in massage, practicing on some of the King's officers. She had very strong and now accomplished hands. Ahlam had also taught her some self defense, the beginning of the martial arts, including many of the body's pressure points. She could incapacitate most men fairly easily. She would have more difficulty with an accomplished soldier, but they were more apt to appreciate her and less apt to try and take advantage of her. After supper they read and studied. Sharpening her mind was also of strategic importance.

Ahlam woke her early the next morning. They broke their fast, and quickly completed their spiritual and physical routines. Today they planned a special day of observation. They paid particular attention to dressing in a way that would bring them no undue attention. While they worked hard to disguise their beauty, Ahlam explained that disguise had more to do with deportment and mannerisms than physical dress. When they finished, they walked the dusty roads like peasants to the temple.

There they began their observations of men. Ahlam pointed out this and that about each man that they watched, explaining signs and nuances that gave away all kinds of information, from occupation and marital status, to their general emotional state or level of happiness and contentment. Marie took constant mental notes of all that Ahlam pointed out. "Pay particular attention to this. Above all, stay away from men like that one. See how he…." and she went on and on. After skirting the crowd for some time, they actually joined them and found them moving in a specific direction. The rabbis had assembled and were teaching the crowds, but attention seemed to be singularly focused on one young man in their midst. He had just finished answering a difficult question and many of them nodded in agreement. Ahlam and Marie stopped to listen.

Chapter 17
In the Temple with the Teachers

Jeshua had spent the last few evenings with Simeon, sparsely partaking of his fine food, but especially enjoying his good company. Like iron sharpens iron, Simeon too enjoyed their discussions that lingered long into the evening.

"*This boy truly is a wonder*," Simeon thought to himself as he lay on his bed, with the early morning light streaming through his window. Although he enjoyed the festival of the Passover greatly, Simeon had enjoyed these few days afterwards even more. He wondered how long he could keep the lad under his roof. When he finally coaxed his tired old bones out of the bed, cleansed himself, dressed, and presented himself to break his evening fast, Jeshua had already left. Simeon felt a little sad, not for the seeming lack of respect in Jeshua's going to the temple without him. He knew Jeshua meant no disrespect. His excitement to be there with the teachers, deep in the scriptures simply consumed him. Simeon shared that feeling too, but he was old and slow. "*I will miss him terribly when he is gone, but thank You so much for these last few days.*" Although the words remained unspoken, they hung in his heart, regardless. One of his servants walked with him to the temple.

❖

Following Anthony's instruction, Mary and Joseph had entered the temple and followed the crowd to where the rabbis taught and there they stopped cold.

Jeshua sat among the teachers, not just a face in the crowd, but almost as one of them. When they asked him a question, his answer had them all nodding in agreement with this remarkable lad. The crowd murmured the same to one another in astonishment.

"I have a question for you," Jeshua said. "The scriptures record concerning Job, that he was blameless, upright, feared God, and turned away from evil. Why then did such calamity befall him? He lost everything, his children, possessions, even his health!"

They conferred among themselves and then one of them stood up and addressed Jeshua and the crowd. "It was a test. The Lord God was testing him."

"Really?" Jeshua seemed unsatisfied. "God had proclaimed that there was 'none like him on the earth.' Why would God need to test him?"

They looked at one another. The one rabbi still standing shrugged his shoulders, "What would you say?" he asked.

Jeshua smiled, "The Accuser said, 'Does he fear You for no reason? You have put a hedge around him and all that he has, but touch all of that and he will curse You to Your face.' It seems more likely that the Accuser was put to the test. Satan destroyed all that he had, even touched his health, and in all of this Job remained in the integrity of his heart. In the end Job says, 'I had heard of You, but now I have seen You and repent in dust and ashes.' And when Job prayed for his friends, God showed His mercy and compassion by restoring him double all he had lost. It was the Accuser who made a fool of himself."

The rabbis and teachers looked dumbfounded and had nothing to say in return. They just stared at one another, as did the crowd, amazed at the wisdom of this young lad's answer.

Mary finally broke the silence. "My son, we have been searching everywhere for you. Why have you treated us like this?"

A gasp arose among the crowd.

Jeshua stood up and almost seemed confused by her question, "Why were you looking for me? Did you not know that I must be here, in my Father's house?" and he gestured all around him. He walked to their side.

Mary whispered, "Come, we will go home," and held out a hand.

Rather than taking her offered hand, he stepped closer, placed a hand on her shoulder and whispered in return, "I AM home." She involuntarily shuddered.

Marie and Ahlam both stood transfixed in the crowd. Marie turned to Ahlam and barely spoke the words, "Who is that young man?"

She shook her head from side to side, "I have no idea, I have never seen anyone like him."

Joseph placed his hand on Jeshua's shoulder and the three of them walked through a crowd that almost magically parted to let them through. When he passed Simeon, Jeshua raised a hand towards him, waved, and smiled.

Later, as they passed one of the pillars, Mishimar seemed to appear out of nowhere and join them. Initially he startled them, but Mishimar smiled reassuringly, "It's okay, everything is fine," and pointed back to where Anthony stood. They nodded to each other.

Once away from most of the crowd, Jeshua began telling them everything. He told about the excitement of listening to the teachers, about the questions people asked, and the answers given. He told them about his first question and how they were unable to answer it, but adjourned for lunch instead. Then he told them how he met Simeon. That pretty much brought their little trek through Jerusalem to a standstill, as they tried to decide if they had time to go back and meet with Simeon. In the end, they did not have the time, so Jeshua continued with his story. He had spent the last few days with Simeon during the evenings and at the temple during the days. Today had been the most wonder-filled of them all, as he had been asked to sit amidst the teachers and take a more active role in the questions and answers. As he described many of them, including his own, Mary and Joseph kept glancing at each other, raising their eyebrows. Through all of this, Mishimar kept so silent that they almost forgot he walked with them. Mostly he just seemed their silent protector, listening, looking, glancing this way and that, his hand never straying far from the hilt of his sword.

On the evening of the second day after supper, before they had settled around their small fire, at another great campsite Mishimar had somehow found, Mishimar whispered to Joseph, "I'm pretty sure that we are being followed."

That got Joseph's attention, "Pretty sure?" he asked. "Have you seen them?"

"No, they are quite good," Mishimar went on. "One of them must be quite an experienced tracker to keep on our trail, but far enough away that I haven't been able to actually see them."

"What should we do?" concern laced Joseph's voice.

"Nothing, yet. I just thought you should know." He was a soldier after all. "I don't think they mean us any harm, or they would have done something by now, but it's good to be aware." He left it at that and they all went to bed. The rest of the trip to Nazareth passed uneventfully and once there Jeshua submitted himself to them in all things. He continued to grow in wisdom, and in stature, finding favor with God and with men.

Chapter 18
A Soldier's Home

After five years Anthony and Julian released Rebecca from her service to them on the single condition that she stay with them as their daughter and Markus' older sister. She tearfully accepted and everyone benefitted. Markus loved having a big sister who could trounce all the older boys in the neighborhood, not that she ever needed to, he just knew that she could. She prepared him to do the same.

Julian found her nearly indispensable. Because of complications with Markus' birth, she could have no more children, so gaining Rebecca as a daughter proved a b

essing beyond measure. Rebecca helped with everything, including housework and cooking, but shone brightest in her relationship to Markus. They became best friends and although he was nearly twelve he still did not see her as a young woman, perhaps because she did not act like one. She could ride, she could fight, and she could best most men with a sword. She fought skillfully with the left hand and with the right, and even more fiercely with a two-handed sword.

As Master at Arms, Anthony had a special training pavilion at his disposal, dedicated to all the arts and forms of combat. After completing her chores, while Markus attended school, she hid in a secret place of observation at the pavilion. Anthony knew all about her secret, but he never let on that he did. With her prodigious mind and nearly total recall, she needed only to see a move once and she could duplicate it. Her secret place had enough space that she could even practice the move a few times, and she usually had her wooden practice sword with her to do so. Later that evening after supper, she would teach the moves to Markus. Anthony's pride in both of them grew as Markus turned into quite a swordsman himself.

Julian's latest challenge lay in how to coax Rebecca out of being a tomboy the rest of her life. She finally lit on the ruse of teaching her the fine arts of womanhood as a disguise. Surprise is a tremendously powerful strategic weapon and if everyone saw her as just a simple young woman, Rebecca could have that weapon at her disposal. It worked, and because Rebecca excelled at everything she put her heart and mind to, she excelled here too. She soon cloaked her warrior heart with a soft demeanor. She knew that she must discipline her entire being, body, soul, and spirit, so she strove to work heartily in each aspect of her person every day. Each day, for her mind, she had Markus summarize his day's instruction. He helped her learn to read Greek. She had learned Hebrew from a fellow slave who had introduced her to Chayeem many years ago. Manuscripts of both Greek and Hebrew proved hard to come by, but Anthony kept his eyes and ears open. While fighting one battle as a centurion, he had saved the life of a young rabbi named Gamaliel. Seeking a way to repay him for his kindness, the rabbi had clandestinely found out about Anthony's love of Hebrew, and had painstakingly made a copy of the Psalms for him.

The rabbi had arranged a meeting with Anthony in secret. "It was very difficult for me to discover this little known fact as I believe it is one of your best kept secrets," he whispered to Anthony as they sat late one evening in an inn. "And I am probably more conspicuous talking to you than you are to me, but I had long wondered how to repay you for saving my life." Anthony did not know how to respond, so the rabbi continued, "I know, what is the worth of one young rabbi?" Gamaliel smiled. "I have made you a gift. Please don't open it until you arrive home, and thank you once again."

Anthony finally found some words. "I suppose, 'You're welcome,' is not enough, but the gift was unnecessary. Thank you for it, whatever it is," and he smiled at him. They shook hands, and the rabbi got up and left the inn. Anthony watched Gamaliel as he departed, thinking, "*There is something special about that one. My heart tells me so.*"

When he got home and began to unwrap it, he recognized the language as Hebrew. He quickly wrapped the manuscript back up. Rebecca's birthday would arrive soon. As a slave they really did not know when she had been born, but they had picked a date during the Hebrew Feast of First Fruits and made it her day. She had blossomed early into a young woman and Julian's work on her disguise continued to astound Anthony. The evening they celebrated her birth after supper, they reclined around the table. Rebecca had still not grown accustomed to gift giving and found the fuss they made unusually embarrassing. Julian had fixed her favorite meal, complete with a fig torte. Markus, for all his budding manliness, had become quite an artist. Where he had found time to do her portrait in charcoal no one could guess, but finally, Anthony had her sit next to him as he produced the gift, a simply wrapped box.

"You must guess what it is." They normally played this game with gifts, so she knew he had probably disguised the package.

"New leather fighting breeches," she ventured. He shook his head. She only had three chances and she could not squeeze the package. "It's too short for a sword, I'll guess a dagger." He shook his head again.

He thought he would try a bit of misdirection. "Mother's been working on your disguise. Maybe it has to do with that." He smiled at Julian.

She wrinkled her nose, "A dress?" she asked in mock disgust.

"Nope! I win, maybe you shouldn't get to open it after all," he teased.

"Papa...," she pleaded. He folded. She rarely called him Papa.

"Okay, you can open it," he said with a tear in the corner of his eye. He had no idea of its value until she unwrapped and opened the box. Her eyes widened, she paged through the first few pages, turned to the end, and then her eyes filled with tears. She stammered, "It's the entire book of the Psalms." She reverentially placed it on the table, put her head in Anthony's lap, and wept openly. Now Anthony was beside himself. As a tear trickled down his own cheek, he caressed her back, looked over at the tears also filling the eyes of his wife, and shrugged his shoulders. "*I guess Chayeem helped me with that one,*" he thought. Markus made his way over and looked at it himself. They had only recently started studying Hebrew, but he recognized the characters for the Psalms. He winked at his dad, "*Good job, Dad,*" and nodded.

Rebecca finally composed herself, hugged and kissed both Anthony and Julian affectionately and retired to her room. She stayed gone for the better part of the rest of the evening. Markus helped his mom with the dishes. He usually assisted Rebecca, which he enjoyed, but they excused her for chores on her special day. Anthony started a fire in the back courtyard's fire pit and sat near the fire until Markus joined him. They chatted about both of their days, both expressing genuine interest in what the other had experienced. Finally, Rebecca joined them and both the children snuggled close to their dad.

"I think I have told you about the singing sword I ran across years ago before the slaughter of the children at Bethlehem." Strange, how he could now mention that day without pangs of guilt. Chayeem was so good to him. "The three Masters were looking for the new king and were accompanied by a woman who took care of them and their horses," he looked down at Rebecca, "and by a soldier with an incredible singing sword."

"Yes, father, you have told us that story," responded Markus, Rebecca nodding, "and how you asked him if you could handle it and you traded swords and sparred there, late at night, in the king's courtyard, and the sword sang for you."

"The soldier's name was Mishimar and I ran across him again during Passover. It seems he now works with the Jewish family into which this new king was born," Anthony continued.

As if coming into possession of the book of Psalms was not astonishing enough, Rebecca nearly jumped out of his lap. "You've met the new king?"

Anthony shushed her, "I tell you this in the strictest confidence. This must remain our secret and our secret alone."

Markus had to ask, "Does Mother know?"

"Yes, yes, of course she does." How could they have thought otherwise?

"Tell us about him, Papa," Markus nearly pleaded and Rebecca joined her voice to his.

"Well, I wanted to tell you about the singing sword, but I guess that will have to wait. He's twelve now and a most amazing young man. He was in the temple, asking questions of the teachers and astonishing them with his own answers to their questions. I must admit, I've never heard anything quite like it and from such a young man. The crowds were amazed."

"Can we meet him?" they asked excitedly.

"No. He doesn't live around here, and I think it best if his whereabouts remain a secret. Herod tried to kill him once and I'd rather not get mixed up in that again. Now, back to the singing sword." He took a deep breath.

The children reluctantly realized they would have to settle for second best, the story of the sword, as Anthony began, "Before the world began, seven singing swords were forged for the archangels...." and late as it was, they stayed wide awake for the entire story.

Chapter 19
A Delivery in Jericho

Elizabeth no longer needed a stool to reach the sink as she and Jeshua finished the morning dishes and Mary came back into the kitchen. The other children played underfoot and Mary carried the youngest, Abigail, named after her wealthy friend in Bethlehem, on her hip. "Jeshua, your father and Mishimar have to deliver some furniture in Jericho this morning. They would appreciate your help loading and unloading it."

"Certainly, Mother," he said as he hung up the towel, grabbed his cloak on the way out, and headed to the shop.

"See if your brother, James, can go with you. That would help me a lot," she called after him. James heard his name, jumped up from his play, and followed Jeshua out the door.

The men had already hooked the team up to the wagon. Jeshua arrived just in time to help them load a lavish bedroom set for a wealthy customer. Joseph had made it to exact instructions and as with all his work, the intricacy of the details and the smoothness of the finishes would surely exceed their expectations.

Joseph turned to Jeshua, "Good," he exclaimed, "I'm glad you are coming with us!" Then he saw James. "She wants us to take him too?"

"Yes, Father," he said as he nodded.

Joseph sighed. "Maybe he can help you load the bedside tables?"

James followed Jeshua around like a puppy dog. He practically worshipped his older brother, and his willingness to work made him quite strong for a young lad. Together they lifted the tables up to Mishimar's waiting hands, and he carried them all the way forward in the wagon. It took all three and a half of them to lift the bed itself. The massive oak edifice fit the grandeur of the magistrate who commissioned it.

They lashed them all tight, separated by blankets, so they would not scratch one another during the jostling of the trip. Joseph, Jeshua, and James climbed on the wagon, the older ones on the seat and James in the back on top of the blankets, between the tables. Mishimar rode alongside on his newest black stallion, lovingly named Midnight after his predecessor. The crisp, sunlight morning in Nazareth made for a perfect trip to Jericho. James considered this a grand adventure and kept on the lookout for bandits at every turn. At his age most everything seemed like an adventure. Jeshua enjoyed the journey for other reasons. He enjoyed the beauty of the morning, he could discuss his latest readings with Joseph, he got to leave the shop and travel the road. He loved carpentry, but there was more to life than sawing and sanding. He could think, pray, even sing, in the shop, but the noise level prevented good conversation.

He also had time just to think. Jeshua loved Joseph, but also really looked up to Mishimar. He would have described Mishimar as the consummate soldier, father, husband, and gentleman. Mishimar and Hannah's decision to befriended Jeshua's family in Bethlehem so many years ago, follow them to Egypt, and to stay with them ever since had greatly influenced Jeshua's life. He also really liked their son Simon, and he felt pretty sure that his sister, Elizabeth, liked Simon even more.

In the last few months, Jeshua had internalized almost the entire book of Isaiah that his rabbi had lent him. He currently pondered the verses:

"The Spirit of the Lord is upon me, because He has anointed me to bring good news to those with nothing; to bind up those whose hearts are shattered, to bring freedom to those enchained, opening their prison doors; and to proclaim that the Lord's favor has finally come."

He recited them to Joseph and asked him, "Who do you think Isaiah wrote those verses about? Surely not about himself?"

Joseph thought for a moment. "I don't know. Maybe he's not talking about one person. That's quite a mouthful to be completely fulfilled in just one man."

Jeshua might have just thought the words, or did he say them out loud, "Maybe he was speaking of the Messiah, the Lord's Christ?" In any event, he left them hanging in the air for the remainder of the trip.

The Magistrate was so exceptionally pleased with the bedroom set that he broke normal protocol and insisted that as a bonus they all stay for lunch with him, which they did. Jeshua ate with the men. James sulked off to be with the children, but they soon heard him romping joyfully with them out in the courtyard. The servant even offered Jeshua some wine, since he looked and acted older than his years, but he graciously declined, as did Mishimar.

After lunch they started on the road back, traveling through some desolate country. James had built the semblance of another encampment with just the blankets, and suddenly called out, "Bandits!"

Thinking it just part of his game again, Jeshua casually turned around to find three armed riders hurtling down upon them. "Mishimar!" he turned back, yelling ahead of him as he grabbed Joseph by the arm. Within a few heartbeats, Mishimar flashed past them to engage the three. He hit them like a hurricane. Hane came ringing out of his scabbard, clanged against the first robber's sword, shattered it, and practically sliced him in two. Before he could execute a back stroke towards the second robber, he realized Hane was stuck fast. Their horses crashed together and unhorsed them both. The dead robber, Hane still protruding through his chest, landed fully on top of Mishimar as his back hit the ground, knocking the wind out of him. The robbers must have been former cavalry officers as, unfazed by their fallen comrade, they split up and continued the attack. One turned towards the fallen Mishimar, only to find himself facing Midnight instead. Amidst the flailing, deadly hooves, the robber managed to draw and throw a dagger, catching the struggling Mishimar in the throat. The robber retreated a few steps and looked to his partner. Midnight now stood over Mishimar who was bleeding out, one hand to his throat. His other hand grasped Midnight's leg and with Herculean effort, he pulled himself to his feet, removed the knife out of his throat, threw it at the robber, and collapsed again to the ground.

The robber blocked the thrown dagger, but momentarily suspended both his attack and his retreat. His companion had reached the horses harnessed to the wagon and attempted to grab the reigns, startling them. They reared and overturned the wagon, throwing Joseph and Jeshua clear. James's head hit the side of the wagon and he landed unconscious on the ground. Joseph struggled to his feet, but the robber swung around and slew him. He turned to make another pass and found Jeshua standing over the form of his younger brother.

The remaining two robbers closed ranks. Before they could launch their final attack, Jeshua yelled, commandingly, "Enough!"

They checked their horses stopped in their tracks. They looked over Jeshua's shoulder, turned, and galloped off. Jeshua touched his brother, who seemed fine, only unconscious. He ran to Joseph who lay bleeding.

Joseph's eyes flickered open briefly, "Take care of your mother." His eyes closed for their final time.

Jeshua placed his hand on the wound, as his cry of anguish split the sky, but before he could speak a word, he heard, "*It's okay. He's with me. Leave him here. I will take care of you.*"

He gently removed his hand and turned towards Mishimar, only to find a familiar old man standing next to the body, holding the reigns of a now quieted Midnight.

"Uriel, where were you?" the ocean of anguish returned.

"It would have been much worse if I had not been here." Uriel looked towards James lying peacefully on the ground.

Jeshua, struggling with all of the pain, questioned, "But why? Why?"

"I have no good answer for you, other than there is a great evil loose in this world and he will fight to destroy you until the end," whispered Uriel gently.

Jeshua knelt down and closed Mishimar's eyes, kissing him on the forehead, as his tears fell. He got up and turned back to do the same for Joseph. Suddenly, a band of Romans rounded the corner at full gallop. They pulled up just short of Jeshua, their leader sliding out of his saddle in a single fluid movement. His eyes quickly took in everything.

He knelt, put his fingers to Mishimar's neck, and then recognized him. "Mishimar?" he exclaimed with almost as much anguish as Jeshua. He looked at James.

"He's okay, he was knocked unconscious when he was thrown from the wagon. He's my younger brother," interjected Jeshua into Anthony's questioning gaze.

"And?" as Anthony looked towards Joseph. Uriel was nowhere to be seen.

"My father, also slain." How could the boy still speak amidst the carnage and his obvious distress?

"And you?" Anthony questioned.

"I AM…fine," he spoke and something shuddered in them all.

Anthony looked around again and then his eyes stopped on Jeshua, "Who are you?"

"No one of any consequence, just the son of a carpenter." It seemed the sun peeked out from behind a cloud as the hint of a smile touched his tear-stained lips. "You knew my friend, Mishimar," Jeshua said, more a statement than a question.

"Yes, and I have met your parents briefly when they thought you lost at the Passover but found you in the temple with the teachers." He reached out a hand. "I am Anthony. I was a centurion when I first met Mishimar. He was on his way to find you in Bethlehem. Now I am Master at Arms for the king, but we were short-handed today, so I chose to lead this patrol."

"Jeshua," and he took his forearm in the Roman fashion.

"*Yes, this is the astonishing lad I remember from the temple,*" Anthony thought to himself. He turned to his men. "Right this wagon and let's carefully wrap these men in those blankets." He pointed, they dismounted at his command, and began to comply. Anthony removed Hane from the robber's chest with some effort and carefully wiped it clean. Even with those simple movements the sword softly sang in his hand. One of his men removed Hane's scabbard from Mishimar's body and handed it to Anthony. He replaced the sword in the scabbard and the song ceased. The soldier who had handed him the scabbard looked inquisitively at Anthony who simply put his finger to his lips, "Shush." He turned and presented the sword to Jeshua. "You'll see that his son gets this?"

"Yes, I will." Jeshua paused. "What will you do with the outlaw's body?"

"I should hack him to pieces and leave him for the animals," Anthony said disgustedly.

Jeshua walked over to the wagon, took one of the extra blankets, and walked back to where Anthony stood over the slain man. He handed him the blanket, knelt down next to the man and closed his vacant eyes. "Please see that he is buried properly," he said as he opened the money pouch he had taken off of Joseph, took out a coin, and handed it to Anthony.

"*Who is this young man, that he even pays for the burial of his enemies?*" Anthony thought in astonishment. But he only replied, "May my men and I accompany you home?"

"That would be wonderful, just give me a few minutes with my brother." James had finally regained consciousness, but with quite a headache. He cried uncontrollably for some time at the loss of his father and Mishimar, but as Jeshua held and consoled him, his sobbing finally quieted. He smiled weakly when Jeshua commented, "We'd all be dead if you hadn't warned us of the attack." The soldiers bundled James in a blanket and Anthony lifted him onto the wagon's seat and rode beside him. He offered to drive the horses, but Jeshua assured him that he would be fine and climbed up next to him. Anthony sent two of his men off with the robber draped over a horse, while the rest of them headed to Jeshua's home with Midnight tethered to the back of the wagon.

PART THREE

About Eighteen Years Later — It Begins

Chapter 20
There Was a Man Named John

He stood chest deep in the cold pool caused by a bend in the river. What a perfect place, on such a perfect day. Children swam upriver, women washed clothes, the river curved near enough to the road that people should hear him if he projected his voice and he could do that. His mother had often chided him at home to use his "inside voice," as he had no compunction about using his "outside voice." He felt ready, like all of his life had led up to this day. His name was John, not Jonathan, just John.

He took a deep breath, "Great change is coming, great change! You must prepare your heart and life, you MUST get ready!" The words came to him as naturally as breathing. All the time in the wilderness, all the practice listening and responding to His voice now paid off. He could almost see the words painted on the hills and written in the nearly cloudless sky. "He is coming. The one we have waited for so long is coming, and he is bringing the kingdom of heaven with him. Prepare your hearts for the rulership of the great king. Get ready, get ready!" People began to listen, lined up on the shore, responding to the words, His words. He knew they responded to something more than just him. He was nothing, nothing but a long-haired wild man in a camel-skin garment.

He had paused long enough. He began again, "What must you do, what must you do to be ready?" He let his gaze scan the crowd, "Confess your wrong doing, your sin, your straying from His ways. Confess out loud, that all may hear. Then come to me, here in the water, and I will baptize you. Down into the water you will go, your sin still clinging to you, but up you will come, clean and forgiven. Come!" He gestured to the crowd. A young woman stepped into the water, she could hardly be twenty. She waded to him and he asked, "What have you done?" She told him. "Then in the name of the Lord God of Israel, I wash it all away!" And he dunked her in the water. When he brought her back up, her countenance transformed, she virtually glowed. Smiling, she turned and hugged him, and joyfully splashed her way to the shore. She reached a young man, spoke urgently to him then he dashed into the water and headed for John. They exchanged words, John plunged him beneath the water, and he too came up transformed.

Many people now stood hesitantly on the shore. He began again, motioning to them, "Come, do not delay. The time is short, he is coming. I baptize you with water, but he will baptize with fire. There is no time to wait." A number of them stepped into the water, men, women, even children. They formed a line, waiting a turn to have their sins washed away.

Each day the crowds grew larger. Some of the religious leaders even came to see if the rumors they had heard were true. "*What should I say to them?*" he asked, then called out loudly, "So, who warned you to flee the wrath that is coming? You think that you are children of Abraham....that he is your father....Huh!" he said somewhat scornfully. "That's nothing to brag about. God could raise up children of Abraham from these stones." He had picked one up from the river bottom. "You are more likely children of the Serpent!" He gained momentum. "If you would have your sins washed away, first do those things which show that you have repented!" He turned to the entire crowd, "I tell you, the axe is laid to the root of the trees. Every tree that does not bring forth good fruit will be cut down, cast into the fire, and burned. What would this good fruit look like, you ask? If you have two coats and your neighbor has none, give him one of yours. Do the same with your food."

Some publicans and tax collectors stood there, and they asked him, "What must we do?"

John replied, "Take only what tax is required, extort no more for yourselves."

When they heard his response, many of them left to go make things right.

Some soldiers called out, "What about us?"

His answer rang in the air. "Do no violence, except that which is required by the situation, do not wrongfully use your power and position to benefit yourself, and be content with what you have."

A number of the soldiers conferred with one another, stripped off their armor and weapons, lay them at the feet of a fellow soldier, and stepped into the water.

Someone else shouted, "Are you the Messiah?"

He flinched like someone had slapped him. "No!" he called back emphatically. "I am just a voice, crying in this wilderness, 'Prepare the way, He's coming,' and He is coming. I am not worthy to kneel down and unlace His sandal. I baptize you with water, that your sin be washed away. He will baptize you with the Holy Spirit and with fire. He will cleanse the threshing floor, gathering the wheat to Himself and throwing the chaff into the fire which is unquenchable. So, again I say, prepare yourself, be ready for His coming."

Someone yelled, "Then are you Elijah?"

He replied, "No I am not!"

"Are you the Prophet, or one of the prophets?" another shouted.

"As I have already said, I am only a voice, calling for you to prepare your heart and life. I urge you to change and be changed." He baptized another person. "Come, come quickly, while there is yet time."

One of the younger priests looked to his brothers and said, "He may not be the Messiah, but what he says rings true." He stripped off his robes and entered the water. An older teacher of the Law did the same, though the others scoffed at them.

John smiled, and returned to pleading for more of them to come, as he baptized them one by one.

Chapter 21
Towards the Water

The years right after Joseph and Mishimar's death proved difficult, but Jeshua stepped into his father's shoes humbly, quietly, and confidently. Though it put a cramp in his studies his attitude did not show it. While not quite as carefree since he worked extra hard to keep food on the table, he was still always a joy to be around. James also jumped right in to help at the shop. Though younger, he did everything he could, and learned quickly like his older brother. The younger boys seemed to have little or no interest in carpentry. Elizabeth helped in the house and spent her free time bashing the boys in swordplay. Hannah, of course, did more than her part. They had all worked together and prayed their way through the tough times and now things felt pretty stable.

Hannah had the boys in the backyard with wooden swords, putting them through their basic paces with the help of her son Simon. Simon's natural leadership and teaching ability made the boys eager to follow him, but they rarely saw him at home. He had joined a secret society determined to resist the rule of the Romans. They called themselves the Zoe, the Greek word for life and also a play on their real name "Zealots of Esrael." Some of them used violence to take their rights back by force. Simon still hoped to be a voice of moderation in their midst, a planner rather than an executioner. One of their leaders, Theudas, considered himself someone special, maybe even the Messiah, and had led almost 400 men on an attack of the palace. The Roman army slaughtered him and about twenty others and the rest of them dispersed. That made times for the Zealots unsettling, both internally for their society and externally as the Romans turned over every rock to root them out.

Mary and Elizabeth came home from the market with their arms full of groceries. The boys, some young men now, ate like horses, but they still enjoyed eating together as a family.

"Elizabeth, would you call everyone in for lunch please?" Mary asked as she finished preparations.

"Yes, Mother."

"*She is such a joy. I am so blessed,*" Mary thought. "And inspect them as they come in. Make sure they have all washed." Elizabeth would have done it anyway.

Hannah and her trainees had taken a break.

"*Perfect timing,*" Elizabeth thought. "Wash up, lunch is ready," She announced and then walked quickly to the shop. Jeshua and James were sanding, seemingly having a competition to see who could create the biggest cloud of dust. "Lunch, and don't forget to wash up and change your tunics." She smiled at them both.

They stopped and smiled back. They checked each other's work, hands sliding smoothly along the sides of the bed frame. The bed frame looked like a piece of art. They smiled again, to themselves and one another, nodding in acknowledgment of the good work. They shrugged off their dusty tunics, walked outside to the well, washed in the no longer very clean water the soldiers of the wooden swords club had left for them, and donned their normal tunics before entering the house. They reclined at the table and Mary looked to Jeshua, who looked to James.

"Little brother," he said smiling again, "would you say the blessing?"

James looked to the empty seat at the end of the table like Jeshua usually did, "Thank You for Your provision, including this food. You are more than enough for us. Amen!" And they all added their own Amens.

Meals were always a wonderful time with Mary and Hannah's families together, even if sometimes chaotic. They all chatted, sometimes over the top of each other. Today Jeshua and Hannah sat to Mary's right as she began, "There was quite a buzz at the market today. It seems there is some wild man preaching and baptizing out in the wilderness at the river Jordan. Some say he is the Messiah, but he denies it."

"Who is he then?" asked Jeshua.

"He says he is just a voice, calling those to get ready for the coming One. When they confess their wrongs, he baptizes them to wash away their sin," Mary responded, looking intently at Jeshua.

He looked away and then up, as if listening to something or someone else. "We should deliver the bed frame later this afternoon. Can James watch the shop tomorrow?" He looked at James, who sat on Mary's left. James nodded his agreement.

"That should be fine," she replied. Jeshua still looked distracted.

"He may have to watch it for some time." His gaze still fixed on something in the distance.

"Why, Jeshua?" Mary questioned, softly, an unsettled feeling in her stomach.

"This may be the beginning," he said, simply.

Her heart felt a sharp, small prick and she feared to ask him more. "All right," she managed to breathe.

From behind Hannah looked at her quizzically. Mary shrugged her shoulders and conversation seemed to stall there.

After lunch, life resumed. Jeshua and James walked back to the shop. Along the way Jeshua asked James to hook up the wagon while he put the finishing touches on the bed frame.

"Sure," James replied. Jeshua never commanded, just made a request, but James never questioned him. He would have obeyed him anyway, but working with him was so wonderful that it was never difficult. He had learned so much. Jeshua called the best out of him, so James worked hard out of gratitude. He went off to fetch the team.

Jeshua wiped off the frame with the linseed oil cloth. It picked up the last of the sanding dust while also providing a satin finish and preservative to the frame. He smiled, "*James, you do exceptional work. Father would be proud.*" He must be sure to tell him. The shop would be in good hands, very good hands. He did not know how long he would be gone, just that he needed to visit the wild man at the river and wanted to have things prepared in case he could not come right back.

James walked in, "Ready."

"Good, so is the bed," and he stooped to pick up his side. James grasped his and they hoisted an end into the wagon. Jeshua moved around to the opposite end while James climbed into the wagon, lifted that end, and they slid it in. James threw him the rope and they lashed it down. They worked really well together. Jeshua would miss that, if his premonition proved correct. Another season of change had arrived. They stopped by the house to tell his Mother and Hannah before they left on their delivery and both of them blessed their going.

They rode in silence for a while and then James broached the subject. "What was all that about at lunch?"

"James, how does God speak to you?" Jeshua had an uncanny way of asking questions that went right to the heart of things.

"I'm not sure," he responded.

"Ask Him a question right now," another request, not a command.

"*What is Jeshua talking about?*" he thought, and before he could even verbalize the words, he would have sworn he heard, "*Listen to him.*" "I think I'm supposed to listen to you," he said out loud.

"For me it's not always the same, but I'm pretty sure I know when He is speaking. When mother was talking about the wild man baptizing, I knew I was supposed to go see him tomorrow. That's why I asked if you could watch the shop. I also think I might not be coming back for a while." It seemed so simple and yet not that easy to verbalize.

"Not coming back for a while, what does that mean?" James wondered if he should worry.

Jeshua picked up on his concern. "You don't need to worry, James. It just pays to be prepared." "*Now is the time,*" he heard. "You know, James, Papa would be very proud of you. The work you do is exceptional. In fact, everything about you is exceptional." James turned away, a bit embarrassed. "It's true, James." The way Jeshua said it, so rock solid, seemed to directly deposit the weight of those words into James's character. Jeshua had such a way with words, and yet it was more than the words. He had an uncanny way of speaking the Truth.

James managed to muster, through his embarrassment, a shy, "You really think so?"

"Most definitely!" came back the response, quicker than his next breath, as they arrived at their destination.

Chapter 22
The Jordan River

In the mid-morning, a few beautiful, billowy, white clouds floated across the sky alternately obscuring, then revealing the sun. John stood in the water up to his chest, a line of people waiting for him to baptize them. Occasionally he would stop and call out to the crowd, encouraging more to come, proclaiming the time was short. Jeshua stood on the bank watching the spectacle, finding it not unruly, but wonderful.

He heard the Father say, "*Join the line,*" and he did. It seemed John treated each person as unique. To Jeshua that underlined the reality of what transpired. The Jewish people had not seen this type of spiritual awakening for a long time. John prepared people for the coming of the Messiah. Two people waited between Jeshua and John.

Jeshua heard John ask, "What do you have to confess?"

The man began to weep. "I am a tax collector. I have defrauded many, but I heard you speak last week. I have gone and tried to make it right as best I can. What else must I do?"

John gently responded, "Simply as the scriptures exhort, 'To do justice, to love kindness, and to walk humbly before Him.'"

"I will," he sniffed.

John, a hand on his head, said, "Then I baptize you in the name of the Lord, God of Abraham, Isaac, and Jacob, and wash your sin away." He plunged him beneath the water. The man did not come right back up. John waited until he slowly rose from the water, a profound change to his countenance.

He embraced John, "Thank you, thank you, thank you," and then let him go.

The woman stepped forward. John spoke to her, "You do not need to tell me what you have done," as if he already knew. "Will you leave that life behind?" She nodded and she too began to weep. "Then I wash it all away, in His name," and he plunged her beneath the water. When she came up, she looked afraid to embrace him. He seemed to understand and held out his hands. She took them in hers. "Go, and walk in the power of a cleansed life." She nodded and released his hands.

Now Jeshua stood before him. John looked up into his eyes and rocked back on his heels as if he had just been struck with a thunderbolt. When he finally found words he pleaded, "No! Not you, I need to be baptized by you!"

Jeshua smiled knowingly, "This is the right thing to do."

John still could not bring himself to do it. Jeshua stepped beside him, took John's hand, placed it on his own head, and looked to him.

"*Please,*" he seemed to say. John took a deep breath and plunged him under the water. When Jeshua came up, he embraced John, "Thank you, I know how difficult that was." He turned and started to walk off.

The clouds had hidden the sun for a moment. They parted, and as the sun came out again, a dove flew down and lit on Jeshua's shoulder. John had the distinct impression that the dove was the Holy Spirit, and he heard a voice from the heavens, "This is my Son. I love him, and am so pleased with him." When the voice stopped, John realized he had held his breath. He inhaled deeply and watched as the man, the Messiah, walked to the shore. He said to himself, "*That's him, that's him.*" And he found himself weeping.

Jeshua looked back to where John stood, still stunned, looking at him, with a line of people waiting to be baptized. Jeshua motioned to the line, John followed his gesture, and that snapped him out of it. The next person stepped forward, and when John looked back towards Jeshua, he had gone.

Jeshua stooped, picked up his outer robe, rope belt, and head scarf from where he had left them. He draped them over his arm. In the warm sun his clothes should dry out pretty quickly. He began walking to the right, along the shore, enjoying the beautiful day. The words still rang in his heart, "*You are My son. I love you, and I am very pleased with you.*" He paused, noticing the wilderness off in the distance. "*Come,*" echoed in his heart. He walked into the wilderness under the strong compulsion of his Father's call.

His garments had dried. He folded his outer robe, placed it on a rock, and took a seat. He looked out across the landscape, "Why am I here?"

"*It is a time of waiting,*" came the answer.

"What am I waiting for?"

"*Soon we will not have much time like this, time alone, just the two of us. Can you wait for Me?*"

"Yes, I can, Papa." All his life he knew that Joseph was not his father, but sometimes it hardly seemed true that he had no human father, that he was conceived by the Holy Spirit, and that God was his Father. Here and now it seemed the most natural thing in all the world, and he relished the truth of it. "So, what would you like to talk about?" he asked Him.

"*There is much we need to discuss,*" came the reply. "*Would you like to take a walk with me, we can talk along the way?*"

"Yes, I would like that."

So they began walking, talking, and the Father shared what He could at this point with the Son. Because Jeshua had left his rights to deity in heaven, when he became a man, he would have to live as just a man. However, he was clean and connected to the Father, like Clay, the first man, had been in the beginning. Nothing prevented the fulness of their intimacy.

God said, "*It will be simple, but it won't be easy. You need to only do what you see me doing, and say what I give you to say.*"

"Hard for a man, but perhaps not so hard for a son?" responded Jeshua.

And God chuckled, "*Yes, I think you've got it.*"

Late that afternoon, Jeshua said, "I should probably look for something to eat. I haven't had anything since breakfast and we talked right through lunch."

The silence stretched out for a moment, like God was thinking. "*I have a request.*"

Jeshua responded, "You have but to ask."

"I would like you to fast for a while."

"Really, for how long and why?"

"*You fast before the Day of Atonement as an act of purification and preparation and you fast before Purim to remember Esther's fast because the enemy wanted to destroy My People.*"

"Yes, we fast at those times."

"*You do not need to be purified, but you do need to be prepared for what is coming. The enemy is coming and his intent is always to steal, kill, and destroy.*"

"Then I will fast as long as it takes," Jeshua concluded.

"Do you remember when Elijah fled from Jezebel to Mount Horeb?"

"Yes, I do."

"*How long did he fast?*"

"I believe for forty days and forty nights."

"*Yes, it was,*" God responded simply.

What had He said about this being simple, not eating, but not easy, for forty days? Jeshua smiled to himself, fascinated.

"*You probably should get some rest.*"

A good idea, the sun had set, and the desert rapidly cooled off. He folded his headscarf and used it to soften a rock for his head. He went to sleep thinking of Jacob and Bethel.

Chapter 23
A New Centurion

Markus found it both difficult and wonderful to have Anthony as a father. He did leave a lot to live up to, yet he emphasized excellence not performance. He would often say, "Whatever you put your hand to, do it with all your might. Be the best that you can be. No one can do what you can do and only you can do it well." For this his men loved him, followed him, fought for him. They would have marched into Hell itself for him, not because he asked them, but because he would have led them there. Honest, humble, strong, just, and merciful, he sounded like a saint, but more down to earth.

Markus felt especially glad that Rebecca was not his actual sister. He had grown up practically worshipping her. Why would he not adore her? She fought masterfully with the sword, and could outwrestle him two times out of three. She cooked superbly, excelling at Julian's young-woman, now a full-woman disguise, and listened to all his chief confidences. What more could he ask for? He put all that at risk the day he realized he loved her. His feelings had grown beyond friendship. Now what should he do? Well, he talked to her about everything else. Why not this?

So one evening out in the back yard, sitting alone by the fire next to her, he took a deep breath, "Rebecca, I can talk to you about anything, right?"

She smiled, she could sense his nervousness. "Pretty much, yup."

He gulped, "What if I told you I no longer wanted to be your friend?"

She had a pretty good idea what came next. "You no longer want to be friends?"

He turned away, "What if I wanted to be more than friends?" There, he had said it.

She looked at the back of his head, "You need to say it to my face, Markus."

He slowly turned and faced her. "What if I wanted more?" He left it there.

She smiled. "Then I think you need to have a chat with your father."

She could see the fear wash across his face. He had not thought about that. "Will you come with me?"

"No, Markus, that is a man-to-man thing. You have to do that one on your own." She looked like she enjoyed this a bit too much, but he was a man, so, time to be a man. He squared his shoulders, stood up, and marched into the house.

He did not catch his father totally off guard. Both Anthony and Julian had noticed Markus treating Rebecca differently, looking at her differently, and had talked. They knew what would soon happen.

Markus stood there, looked him straight in the eye, and said it. "Father, I think I am in love with Rebecca."

Anthony, also enjoying this but too disciplined to show it, replied, "You *think* you are?"

"I know I am." He tried to stand tall.

"And how many other women have you known?" He did not plan to give him an inch.

"Enough to know they all pale in comparison to her. She is incredible!"

"So, what are you asking?" Anthony tried not to smile too much.

"I guess if it's okay," he did not know the protocol, "to court her."

"You guess?" Anthony almost let a laugh break through.

"Father, you aren't making this any easier." He tried not to show his exasperation.

"And you were expecting it to be easy? What will be difficult is seeing so much of her and still keeping your head in the game," he explained.

"What game are you talking about?" Markus sounded confused.

"Markus, it's a metaphor for being able to fulfill all your other commitments, obligations, and responsibilities, while still walking around like a lovesick cow."

Julian had walked up to his side and squeezed his arm. She cut in, "He'll be fine," and she winked at her son. "Send in Rebecca, we need to talk to her also."

He escaped back outside, "They want to talk to you." Boy, he felt relieved to escape that conversation.

"And?" she asked.

He shrugged his shoulders, afraid to hope too much. "They just said that they wanted to talk to you."

"Should I be worried?" she played him a bit.

"I don't know?" He started getting flustered again. "They just said...."

She got up, "Okay, okay, no problem," and walked inside.

She found both of them reclined at the table. They gestured for her to sit too.

"I think he likes me," she smiled at her adopted parents. They smiled back.

"I'm afraid it's worse than that," Anthony started. "Will it be a problem?"

She chuckled, "I suppose you could get him transferred to some outpost in Egypt." They really liked her and wanted this to happen, especially under their supervision. She continued, "I think that if I could handle the soldier's advances in the bath, I can probably take care of myself with your son."

Julian and Anthony looked at one another. "Good point," Julian conceded. "Our only concern is that we don't want either of you to get hurt."

Rebecca looked to the ceiling, "I think we are all big enough to get through that, although I doubt that we'll have to." She looked to the empty spot at the end of the table. Elijah's place, they called it. "Let's ask Chayeem." In some aspects she acted almost like their spiritual elder. They prayed, Anthony called Markus in and they all prayed, and left it in Chayeem's hands.

Life did not change that much, other than Markus seemed to relax around them all. It felt nice to have it all on the table, out in the open. They took this new dimension of their relationship slowly and navigated it carefully. And then a few weeks later, Markus came home glowing. He waited until they all assembled together for supper and announced, "Today, in front of all the men, I was promoted to centurion. I will be assigned my own one hundred men tomorrow." That called for cheering, hugs, and even a discrete kiss on the cheek from Rebecca.

Chapter 24
The Tempter

It had been forty days, Jeshua was tired, and he was extremely hungry. He was walking along a mountain path. "*What is that incredible smell?*" he thought as he walked around a corner and there someone sat on his outer garment that seemed to be covering a rock, eating some figs. The words sang softly in his heart, "*That's him.*"

He looked up, "Oh, I didn't expect you. This is a pretty deserted place. Can I offer you a fig?" He held one out to him.

"No thank you. I'm fasting." Jeshua reply.

"Really, this isn't one of the regular fasting periods, is this for something special?" There was something odd, almost musical about his voice. Otherwise he appeared a rather good-looking, fit man in his early thirties.

"Yes, something special." Jeshua responded.

"Ah, fasting for something special, and what are you trying to cajole God into?"He didn't sneer, but even his tone was somewhat offensive.

"It's personal." Jeshua said shortly.

"Oh, I'm sorry, I didn't mean to pry," he seemed almost genuinely sorry that he might have offended. him. "So, why fast out here, in the wilderness?"

"Fewer distractions, and less temptation," Jeshua smiled behind his words.

At the word "temptation" the man raised his eyebrows. "That makes sense.

"Why are you out here?" Jeshua asked him.

"I spend most of my time in the marketplace, thought I'd get a bit of exercise, and the solitude is nice too." He added, "What do you do, when you're not fasting in the wilderness?"

"I'm a carpenter, just a carpenter." This almost seemed like some kind of a sword fight, them trading blows: thrust, parry, and counter-attack.

"Wait a minute," the man exclaimed, "I think I recognize you. You were that lad of twelve, sitting amidst the teachers, in the temple, during Passover. Your questions and answers were truly amazing."

Jeshua was caught flat-footed for a moment. "You were there?"

"Oh, yes." He said, "I have followed your progress quite closely. Well, as close as I could get. Your question about Job and the Accuser, that was quite an enlightening one." There was an edge to his voice.

"And what did you think of my answer?" He was back into the battle.

"That the Accuser was made a fool of? Ridiculous!" His edge was sharpening. "If you could have anything to eat right now, what would it be?"

"That's simple, my mother makes the best bread I have ever eaten," He said easily.

"If you were the son of God, couldn't you just command these stones to turn into bread and they would?" Ah, the Accuser was now accusing.

He took a deep breath through his nose, he could almost smell his mother's bread, he said, "When the people of God were in the wilderness, He fed them with manna, bread that they did not know. Why did He do that?" The Accuser shrugged his shoulders. "He did that so they might know, that man does not live by bread alone, but by every word that comes from the mouth of God."

His opponent flinched noticeably, he must try something else. In the blink of an eye, they were standing on the pinnacle of the Temple itself. "If you were the son of God couldn't you just step off this pinnacle and trust where He has written, "I will command my angels to guard you in all your ways, they will lift you up so that you can't even bruise your toe on a stone."

Jeshua smiled. It wasn't what he had said, but what he had left unsaid. The next thing David had recorded in that passage was. "*You will tread on the lion and the adder, the young lion and the serpent you will trample under your feet*," but all he said out loud to him was, "It is written that you shall not put the Lord your God to the test."

The Accuser flinched again, his strategy showing its weakness. He needed something even more potent. What if he could get him to take a short cut? Suddenly they were back on the mountain, at its very top. He showed him a vision of all the kingdoms of the world and their glory. It was an amazing spectacle. "All of this is mine. I will give it all to you if you simply fall down and worship me."

Jeshua pulled back, "Worship you?" He was insulted. "No! It is written, 'You shall fear the Lord God, serve, and swear by Him alone. Be gone, my enemy!'"

As the Accuser left him, he whispered under his breath. "I will return at a more opportune time!"

Peace restored, Jeshua removed his cloak, set it on a rock, and sat exhausted. He sighed deeply, glanced off to his left, and there was a familiar old man, striding towards him with a plate of steaming, freshly baked bread from home, a pitcher of cold water and cups for them both. Jeshua smiled weakly.

Uriel said strongly, "Well done!" and set the platter on another rock. As Jeshua stood weakly, Uriel swept him into his arms and kissed him. "And you thought Job made a fool of him," as he let him go and filled the cups. "I'm sorry I was not allowed to aid you sooner, but you really didn't need me."

"I wanted you though," He spoke, his mouth full of bread.
"*We are both here!*" sang in his heart again.
"I know, I know," He said in return.

Chapter 25
Political Intrigue

The Roman Emperor Agustus removed Herod Archelaus and installed his brother Herod Antipas as ruler of Galilee and Perea. To reward the sorceress Mekah, his faithful counselor and companion, Archelaus sent her to his brother. She soon had as free a reign of Antipas' palace as she had enjoyed in Archelaus'. It took some time, but she eventually found a secret place for the black altar she had dedicated to Chemosh, then he too had free access to all of the palace. Mekah convinced Herod to divorce his first wife and instead marry Herodias, the wife of his brother, Philip. Mekah also brought with her the Master Janus with his harem and his two favorite courtesans, Ahlam and Marie from Magdala. Herod gratefully appreciated the sorceress' counsel during those very troubling times, but knew nothing of the considerable profits which the ministrations of Janus and his harem poured into his treasury. Passion and deception gained a foothold, which developed into a stronghold, and all of the palace began to experience the effects.

In contrast, John the Baptist's ministry of spiritual awakening created its own stronghold. People continued to flock to hear him and to respond to him in droves. He now had many disciples baptizing along with him, and the lines stretched from the crowds on the shore, out into the water, all the way to each of the baptizers. The baptized rose out of the water, free from their sin and sinfulness, to walk in a newness of life they could hardly have imagined moments before. They shed tears of pain and repentance, soon replaced by the joy and laughter of freedom, healed relationships, and repaired lives.

However, some still scoffed, mostly people from the religious and political arenas. The priests and Pharisees would call out, "Are you the Christ?"

Again and again he would deny it, saying, "No! I am only a voice calling out in this wilderness for you to change your lives. Come, and wash your sin away!"

But they would ridicule him, "By whose authority do you do this?"

Often he did not even need to rebuke them. The crowds would respond and shout the hecklers to silence.

At a moment like this, he saw Jeshua coming back from the wilderness, flush from defeating the enemy, having been refreshed by heaven's angel. He recognized him instantly as though the dove still rested on his shoulder. He stopped baptizing, stepped to the disciple on his right, wrapped his right arm around the disciple's shoulder, and pointed with his left hand, saying, "Look, there he is, the lamb of God who is taking away the sin of the world."

"What?" answered his disciple.

John continued, drawing him to the disciple on his left. "I said, 'There is one coming after me whose sandal I am not worthy to unlace.' It is he!" and he pointed again. "He will baptize with the Holy Spirit!"

They stood in awe as Jeshua walked away. Finally, the spell broken, they returned to their baptizing.

The next day Jeshua returned, walking the shore. He walked slowly as though waiting for something or looking for someone. John saw him. Again he turned to the disciple on his right and the one on his left and proclaimed, "There he is, the lamb of God," and he stopped baptizing.

The two disciples did also, left the water, and followed Jeshua.

When Jeshua realized that they followed him, he stopped, turned, and asked them. "You are looking for something?"

One of them said, "Teacher," then paused, trying to gather his thoughts and finally blurted out, "Where do you live?"

Jeshua smiled, "Come along with me and I will show you."

They walked with him to where he stayed and spent the rest of the day with him.

One of them, Andrew, went and found his brother, Simon. When he had found him, he said, "Brother, we have found the Messiah, the Promised One," and he brought him to Jeshua.

Looking at him, Jeshua said, "Simon, son of John, I will call you Peter." They spent the evening with him.

The next day, Jeshua planned to leave Galilee, but before he did, he found Philip and simply said to him, "Follow me."

Philip came from the same town as Peter and Andrew. This brief encounter so impacted him that he went and found Nathanael and declared to him, "We have found him, the one of whom Moses wrote in the Law and the prophets! He is the son of Joseph in Nazareth, and his name is Jeshua."

Nathanael, however, did not find that impressive. He did not even ask for further explanation, he just sneered, "Nothing good comes out of Nazareth."

Unfazed, Philip replied, "Come and see for yourself."

Nathanael thought to himself, "*Hmmm, it will only cost me a short walk to prove the foolishness of this,*" and he went with him to meet Jeshua.

When Jeshua saw him coming, he said loudly for all to hear, "See here," pointing to Nathanael, "here is an Israelite who is single-hearted and honest to the core!"

This struck Nathanael nearly speechless, "How could you know me? We have never met."

"Ah, Nathanael," he spoke gently, "before Philip found you sitting under the fig tree, I saw you."

Now he could not speak, thinking, "*Philip was right!*" When he finally regained his voice, he stammered, "You are the son of God, the King of Israel."

Smiling, Jeshua replied, "Do you believe in me because of what I just said? You will be a party to things much greater than that, even to the angels of God ascending and descending on the Son of Man."

Chapter 26
It's Just a Wedding

Just another wedding held in the town of Cana? No, something special. The families had invited Mary, Jeshua's mother, as well as Jeshua himself, who brought his new disciples with him. While they celebrated and feasted, Mary noticed that the host family had run out of wine. In all the planning and preparation, someone had fundamentally miscalculated and now they could do nothing. Some would see it as a bad omen for the marriage itself. Mary mulled over all this when it seemed Chayeem spoke to her heart, "*Your son.*" She thought, "*My son? What about my son? What could he do about the situation? I don't think we have much money to spare, but maybe he knows...*" With that in mind, she went up to him and mentioned, "They have run out of wine."

He responded oddly, "What does that have to do with me, woman?"

She startled, a bit taken back and said nothing, though she thought, "*Why are you calling me woman, not mother?*" Maybe she had heard wrong or misinterpreted what she thought she had heard. She felt that little pin prick to her heart again.

He seemed to listen for just a moment and then continued with, "It is not my time yet."

She felt a little exasperated, thinking, "*I was going to ask you if we had the funds to buy them some wine. Are you saying you don't have time to do that?*" Then she heard in her heart, "*Tell the servants to do whatever your son tells them to do.*" She turned to the servants and said, pointing to him, "Do whatever he tells you to do." It sounded like a command, even though the servants did not belong to her.

Jeshua almost responded to that, when suddenly he saw what the Father was doing. Six large stone jars stood there, each of them capable of holding twenty to thirty gallons of water. He told the servants, "Fill the jars with water."

That took a while. By now pretty much everybody knew that the wine had run out, but they had lots of water for purification, as they had seen the pots filled to the brim.

He told one of the servants, "Draw some water from one of the jars and take it to the Master of the Feast."

The servant did just that, addressing the Master, "Excuse me, I have been told to bring this to you."

He had interrupted a conversation between the Master of the Feast and one of the other servants who had returned from the market with an answer to the question, "What will it cost to purchase enough wine to complete this wedding feast?" He had not been pleased with the answer, nor with being interrupted. "What is it?" he said sharply.

The servant still held out the ladle of water. The Master looked down at the ladle. The servant just kept holding it out. The Master took it from him, smelled it, took a drink, and his eyes widened. "Where did you get this?" The servant nodded toward the stone jars. "Well, start serving it and call the bridegroom over here at once." The servant left to comply, first telling his fellow servants to start serving the guests the water that had now turned into wine, and then went to send the bridegroom to the Master of the Feast, who drank another long taste from the ladle.

When the bridegroom approached, the Master questioned him, "Where did this wine come from?" Before he could answer, the

Master continued, "At every other wedding I have ever officiated, they put out the good wine first, then when everyone has drunk their fill and can no longer discriminate, they put out the lesser wine. You, however, have kept the very best for last. I have never tasted any wine equal to this." The bridegroom just smiled and went along with whatever he said.

The wedding continued joyously. All the while, the servants and Jeshua's disciples knew that they had just witnessed a miracle. What had begun as water had become wine, and such a wine! The disciples' faith in Jeshua began to grow.

Chapter 27
Their First Passover

Although Jeshua and his family had celebrated Passover in Jerusalem whenever possible after Joseph's death, this year Jeshua went with his disciples. He found things had decidedly degenerated from what he could recall. There had always been sacrificial animals available for those who needed them, those who had to travel far, or were unable to provide one of their own. Now, it had turned into a business. As they walked around they found vendors charging exorbitant prices for the animals and requiring local or temple currency to purchase the animals while charging large fees to convert money. What could the people do? They needed a sacrifice for their sin, and if it cost a lot of money to purchase the sacrifice, they would pay what they must for forgiveness.

As they continued to walk around, Jeshua became more obviously distressed. Finally, he stopped and turned to Peter, "Give me your belt!" Peter removed the rope he wore around his tunic. Jeshua turned to Andrew, "Yours too!" Jeshua also took his own and braided the three ropes into a short whip. He marched to the top of the steps, turned to the crowd and shouted,

"STOP!" with such command that immediately everything and everyone did.

He did not seem to be bellowing, but with such force behind his words that he might as well have been he continued, "My house is to be called a house of prayer for all the nations, but you have made it into a den of thieves and robbers! Take these things out of here!" He began to drive out the sheep and the oxen, turning over the money-changers tables, scattering coins all over the ground. He opened the cages of the doves and released them, as he continued to shout, "Out, out, leave my house!"

The disciples stared at him in awe, perhaps with a bit of terror. They had only know him a short time and had never seen him act like this. They did not know what to do. Should they join in, should they clean up after him? What should they do? As he continued to clear the courtyard they began to pick up tables and stack them to the sides. They did the same with the movable animal pens. When he had finally completely emptied the area, he stopped, turned around and walked back to his disciples. Peter and Andrew had found brooms and swept the money into piles, while others scooped it into money sacks that lay on the ground. They stacked the sacks with the tables. Jeshua unbraided his whip and gave Peter and Andrew back their belts.

He tied his own back around himself, "Thank you," he said. He looked somewhat flushed and winded.

The priests and Pharisees had come out of one of their assembly halls and stood at the top of the stairs. They barely controlled their indignation. One of them stepped forward and gestured to the courtyard as he spat out, "Show us some sign of who gave you the authority to do that?"

Jeshua smiled, "If you were to destroy this temple, I would raise it back up in three days."

"Ha!" the priest continued, "it took forty-six years to build this temple, and you would do that in three days?"

As the disciples stood by and pondered all of this, one of them whispered to another, "It is written that 'the zeal for my house will consume me,' I think we have just witnessed that."

Simon the Zealot, Mishimar's son, had been standing in the wings, watching this entire spectacle. He had seen the cleansing of the temple, Jeshua's confrontation with the priests, and he thought to himself, "*He is much more than the man I grew up with. This is a man I could follow, will follow!*" Beginning that day he joined himself to Jeshua and his disciples.

With Simon stood another Zealot, Judas Iscariot, who was also impressed by the zeal of this man called Jeshua. "*Jeshua,*" he thought to himself, "*the Lord saves. Will this be the one who delivers us from the Romans?*" and he too joined himself to the disciples who followed him.

Indignant, the priests and Pharisees turned and left. Jeshua walked up to the steps and sat on a lower one. The people began to refill the courtyard, came up, gathered in front of him, and he began to teach them. "To what will I liken the kingdom of God, it is like..." and he continued for a few minutes. The people hung on his every word, when suddenly he stood up and walked into their midst. A young man stood there leaning on his crutch.

He looked at the young man, listening, "*Ask him for his crutch,*" and then he said, "May I hold your crutch for a moment?" The young man looked into Jeshua's eyes, shifted his weight to his good right leg, and handed him the crutch. Jeshua than spoke in a commanding whisper, "Put your weight back on your left leg." Still looking in Jeshua's eyes, the young man did, and as he did it his leg strengthened and healed. As astonishment spread across the young man's face, Jeshua handed the crutch to an older man standing next to him, and embraced the young man.

"Thank you, thank you!" he stammered. The crowd watched, stunned into silence, as Jeshua released the young man, who began walking around, looking at his now normal left leg.

Jeshua walked deeper into the crowd and stopped in front of a young blind woman, who held on to a friend.

To the friend he asked, "Her name?"

Hope began to dawn in the friend's eyes, "Deborah."

He took a deep breath, "Deborah, let go of your friend and reach out to me." She did. He took her hands and brought them to his face. She felt his face in order to see him. He lifted her hands away from his face, "*Breathe on her.*" He took another deep breath, and breathed gently into her face. While the wind of his breath rustled her hair, she opened her eyes, and gasped. She began to weep. He said, "He loves you," waited a few moments until she quieted, then he gave her back to her friend with her sight restored. The astonished people murmured softly among themselves, "Who is this man?"

Chapter 28
Nicodemus at Night

Later that evening as it darkened into night, a Pharisee named Nicodemus came to Jeshua. He came at night, partly for fear of being seen, but more importantly to have Jeshua all to himself without the crowds who had begun to follow him everywhere. He also wanted to ask an intensely personal question. Andrew took him to Jeshua and left them alone together.

Nicodemus sat next to him and began quietly and reverently, "Rabbi, I know that you are a teacher sent from God Himself, because no one could do what you have been doing unless God is with him."

He had not even finished his question when Jeshua responded, "I tell you a simple truth, before you can even see the kingdom of God, you must be born again."

Startled, Nicodemus took a moment to regain his composure. "*How had he known the question in my heart?*" He responded "But how can a man be born a second time? Can an old man," he spoke of himself, as he desperately wanted to see the kingdom of God, "enter his mother's womb and be born anew?"

Jeshua continued, "Unless you are born of both the water and the Spirit, you cannot enter the kingdom of God. That which is born of the flesh is just flesh, but that which is born of the Spirit is spirit. Do not marvel that I say you must be born again. The wind blows where it will, you can hear it, but you cannot see where it comes from or where it is going. Everyone who is born of the Spirit is like that wind."

Confusion written all over his face, Nicodemus almost pleaded, "I don't understand, how can this happen?"

Sadly, Jeshua asked, "You are a teacher in Israel and yet you do not understand this? I tell you the Truth, I speak of what I know and bear witness to what I have seen, yet you do not receive my witness. If I tell you these earthly things and you do not believe, how will you believe if I tell you of heavenly things? No one has gone up into heaven except the one who has descended from heaven, the Son of Man. Just as Moses lifted up the serpent in the midst of the plague and all those who looked to it were delivered, so the Son of Man must be lifted up, and all who believe in him will receive eternal life."

Nicodemus still shook his head, finding this too much to take in at one time. He had thought his question so simple.

Jeshua continued, "God so loves this world, that He gives His only Son, that whoever believes on Him should not perish, but have everlasting life. He does not send His Son into the world to condemn it, but to save it. He who believes in the Son will not be judged, but he who does not believe has judged himself already, because he has not believed in the name of God's one and only Son. Here is how the world is judged: the light has come into the world and men, because of their evil deeds, have loved the darkness rather than the light. The one who does evil hates the light and will not come into the light because it exposes his evil deeds. The one who speaks and does the truth, willingly comes into the light in order that his works might be displayed as godly."

Nicodemus rose shakily to his feet. He suddenly felt very old. "Thank you, you have given me much to think about," and he began to leave.

He had only taken a few halting steps when Jeshua called after him. "You must do much more than just think about these things. You must believe in the One who has said them," and he let him depart into the night.

Andrew entered carrying a cup of hot goat's milk. "Well?" and handed it to him.

"For some, learning opens their eyes to see what they hadn't been able to see before, while to others, it seems to dull their hearing to perceive the Truth, even when it is sitting plainly before them. We will see which one he is," he said gently.

Chapter 29
Teaching Disrupted Again

While being a courtesan to the rich and influential had advantages like clean beds and customers, usually. The profession itself remained the same, stroking men's egos with pleasure. Whatever Ahlam had been looking for when she had begun this journey, she had not found it and still searched. She sat mulling over the nagging emptiness of life, her life. She had comfort, a measure of safety, plenty of nice things, but she lacked an illusive something. Maybe it was purpose, a powerful reason for being. Janus cared for her, almost like a father, and now she had Marie to look after, but what was the meaning of it all? One day just followed the next. There must be more.

She heard a soft, but insistent, knock at her door. A client this early in the day would normally be unusual, but it was not. As a priest, he needed to be more circumspect than most. They had seen each other before and she thought she knew what to expect. She was dreadfully wrong.

In the middle of things a flood of scribes and Pharisees suddenly poured into her bedroom. They seized her, gagged her, bound a robe around her, and carried her from the house into a large mob of people. They dragged her along with them, barely allowing her to keep her feet. As she looked around, she saw many of her regular customers caught up in the malevolent passion of the moment. Fear rose in her throat threatening to choke her. Her place of business lay near the temple and the momentum of the crowd carried her in that direction. "What could this mean?" The roughness of her handling and the jostling of the crowd knocked off her gag and loosened her bonds, but fear held her tightly in place and she could only weep. She could feel her tiny life swallowed up in the murderous rage of this crowd.

Jeshua had come to the temple that morning, and a crowd gathered around him. He had taken his usual seat on the temple steps. Many of the crowd also sat, so he began to teach them, as he often did.

Suddenly, around the corner came a mob of people. Led by the scribes and the Pharisees, they dragged a woman with them. They brought her to Jeshua, then thrust her forth to stand alone. She wept softly. Slowly Jeshua stood to his feet.

"Master," coming from their spokesman it sounded like a thinly veiled taunt, "this woman was taken in adultery, in the very act!"

Jeshua thought, "*And how did they accomplish that, collusion?*"

The spokesman continued with exaggerated deference, "In the Law, Moses commands us to stone such a woman to death, but what do you think we should do?" He gripped a stone in his hand ready to begin the gruesome spectacle and said this to test Jeshua. Jeshua had made a mockery of the Pharisees, driving their money changers and animals out of the temple, defiantly saying he would rebuild the temple in three days. They intended to expose him as a fraud, but they needed some concrete evidence against him. With this woman they saw their chance. The Pharisees knew Jeshua had escaped other verbal traps, *"But let's see him get himself out of this!"* The words screamed in the Pharisee's head.

Jeshua looked at the crowd, then at the woman, then knelt, and began to write something on the ground. He listened to his Father as he wrote "You shall love the Lord your God with all your heart, soul, mind, and strength..." As he did this, they continued to pester him for an answer. Finally, he stood up and said quite calmly, "He who is without sin may cast the first stone." He knelt back down, listened some more, and slowly continued to write, "and you shall love your neighbor as yourself."

The oldest of the Pharisees, even more revered than their spokesman, stepped forward, a rock in his hand. Ahlam saw all of this through her tears. She knew what came next. She prepared herself as best she could. The Pharisee looked down at what Jeshua had written, the words Jeshua had said ringing in his ears. He hesitated, thinking, *"Surely, I should be the one to throw the first stone."* He looked again at what Jeshua had written. Guilt engulfed his heart, remorse for what he himself had done. With the picture of his own sin emblazoned on his mind he let the stone fall from his hand.

Ahlam flinched at the sound of it striking the earth. The Pharisee turned, walked silently out of the courtyard, and left the temple. The eyes of the crowd followed him as he left. The spokesman stepped forward, fiercely grasping his stone, only to find his heart similarly gripped by the guilt of his own sin. He dropped his stone and left. Ahlam flinched again as it hit the ground.

One by one, each of the others stepped forward to experience their own form of regret and let their stone join the Pharisee's. After a while, Ahlam quit flinching as the stones clattered to the ground, hitting one another. Soon all the mob, even those he had been teaching had gone, leaving him alone with the woman, who still braced herself for the impact of the first stone that would hit her.

He stood up and stepped towards her, and reached out to take her chin in his hand. Startled out of her fear, she looked into his eyes as he lifted her head. He dropped his hand, "Woman, where are your accusers? Does no one condemn you?"

Why did he call her, "woman" she wondered. Surely even he had heard of Ahlam, the famous palace courtesan. He could have called her any number of other things. Perhaps he did not see her as just the object of men's desire, a toy to be used and cast aside. Perhaps he saw her as simply a woman, a lost, hurting woman. A spark of hope glimmered in her soul.

She looked around while she dried her eyes on the sleeve of her robe. No one stood around her any longer, no one to condemn her. She stopped looking and dropped her head again. He remained. He could condemn her.

He reached out, lifted her chin once again, and she looked into the eyes of the purest, most powerful love she could have possibly imagined.

"Neither do I condemn you," he said. "Go, and sin no more!"

The spark burst into a flame, "Go and sin no more? Was that even possible? Could I really begin a new life, from this moment on?"

As he let go of her chin, and then brushed the back of his fingers against her cheek, he simply nodded, "Yes," she felt more power in that unsaid word than in all the armies of heaven.

She turned to walk away, filled with a love and a purpose she had not dared to believed existed moments ago. The hope of a new possibility-filled future motivated her with a love beyond words.

Fifty steps away, she turned back to look at him. He still stood there, looking at her and smiling. The next time she turned around and looked, he had gone.

Chapter 30
Tax Collectors and Sinners

Jeshua taught in many ways: sitting, standing, walking, and in many places: in the Temple, along the sea shore, in the synagogues, out in the hill country. The disciples had become accustomed to his seemingly irregular ways. He would hear something or see something and off he would go. He had finished a time of telling stories and now they walked along the road. They passed the place of taxation and Jeshua noticed one of the tax collectors. Tax collectors worked for the Roman government, the enemy of the people. Besides collecting taxes for the government, tax collectors often added on a special fee which they pocketed for themselves. For those two reasons the people hated them. To say to someone, "You are worse than a tax collector" insulted their integrity beyond forgiveness.

Jeshua noticed a tax collector named Levi, who through his extortion had become quite wealthy. A long line snaked away from his tax booth. Jeshua just stood there observing. "*What is he looking at?*" Andrew thought to himself. "*Is he waiting for something? Maybe he's testing us?*" The disciples started getting a little restless, just standing there. Jeshua never seemed restless or in a hurry. *"Maybe that's what we're supposed to be learning. Just relax, listen to the Spirit, and follow His lead."* Jeshua stepped into the line.*"Now what's he doing? Are we supposed to get in line too? Is he going to pay his taxes?"* But the disciples stood off to the side and watched. The line slowly moved until only one person waited between Jeshua and the tax booth.

A stranger walked up to Andrew as he stood by the rest of the disciples, and pointed to Levi, "That fellow is a crook! My neighbor's farm is about the same size as mine. I know what he paid for his taxes, so I brought a little more than that with me last week. He told me I had to pay so much more, that I had to go back home and sell my plow horse. How am I supposed to farm without my plow horse? I hope he chokes on all that money!" and he spat on the ground.

The man in front of Jeshua finished paying his taxes and left.

"Next." Levi called out with little enthusiasm. "Name?"

Jeshua heard, "*Use his name, Levi*" and responded, "Levi."

Levi looked up, startled, "That's my name."

Suddenly time stood still as Levi looked into Jeshua's eyes.

"Follow me." Jeshua spoke softly for Levi's ears alone, but the tone sounded like a command.

"What?" Levi responded, astonished, then hesitated, "Now?" He still looked into those eyes that seemed to read his very soul.

Jeshua nodded, then turned and walked back to his dumbfounded disciples, who muttered to each other in hushed tones, "*What is he thinking, that's a tax collector.*"

Then Levi did the unthinkable. He rolled up his ledger and collected his things into a bundle, then stood up, slung it over his shoulder, left his tax booth, and joined Jeshua and his disciples. Jeshua put his arm around Levi's shoulder and off they walked, the rest of the disciples trailing bewilderedly behind them.

After about a half an hour of walking, Jeshua, who had been conversing with Levi in hushed tones turned around and announced, "Levi has asked us to have lunch with him. I have agreed. So, it's off to Levi's house."

Levi owned quite a house, fenced and gated, with a beautiful garden in the front and a large formal courtyard in the back. A crowd of people already gathered around a sumptuous banquet. The central table seemed designated for Levi and whomever he brought home with him that day, as no one occupied it. Jeshua, Levi, the disciples reclined at this table, and a number of slaves began serving them food.

Peter stood at the entrance to the courtyard chatting with one of Levi's security guards, when a number of scribes and Pharisees attempted to enter the courtyard. The guard stopped them. While most of the crowd followed Jeshua out of curiosity, these followed him like a plague, seeking to find a way to discredit him.

One scribe saw Peter and recognizing him, grumbled, "Why does your master eat with tax collectors and sinners?"

Jeshua got up, walked over to them, and spoke to them even though the guard still stood between them. In a voice loud enough for them all to hear he said, "Those who are well do not need a physician, only those who are sick. I have not come to call the righteous, but sinners to repentance."

The scribe responded indignantly, "We and even the disciples of John the Baptizer fast often and pray, but you and your disciples are here feasting and getting drunk."

Jeshua smiled, "Do the wedding guests fast while the bridegroom is with them? No, but they will fast when he is taken away from them."

The scribes and Pharisees looked at one another, uncomprehending.

He continued with an example, "No one will use a piece of a new garment to patch an old garment. If he does, after he has sewed it on and it is washed, the new garment patch will shrink and tear itself away from the old garment, leaving it worse than it was in the beginning. In a like manner, if you have made a new batch of wine, you will not put it into old wineskins, less as it ferments and expands, it bursts the old wineskin and spills, spoiling the wine and destroying the skins. Rather, new wine is put into new pliable wineskins so that while the wine expands, so will the skins." Finally, he said, "And after drinking finely aged and fully fermented wine, no one desires to drink unfermented grape juice. These are the things you should ponder, rather than complain about with whom I eat." And with that, he turned on his heel and walked back to the table.

Flustered and frustrated, the scribes and Pharisees turned around and stormed out into the road. Jeshua sat down and rejoined the conversation with his disciples and new friends.

Later that afternoon they went back to walking the roads and the crowd reassembled. Another tax collector, this one a chief among them called Zacchaeus wanted to see Jeshua, but could not because of the size of the crowd. His height prevented it. Cleverly, he took a short cut in the direction they seemed to be going, climbed a sycamore tree, and waited for Jeshua to pass by.

When Jeshua came to that place, he looked up into the tree and said, "Zacchaeus, come down, I must stay at your house tonight."

Zacchaeus nearly fell out of the tree, so joyously did he welcome the opportunity. He sent some of his servants on ahead to make preparations. He then recognized one of the disciples walking with Jeshua. "Levi?"

"Yes, Zacchaeus, it is I," Levi smiled.

"Are you…." he gestured to the other disciples standing there.

"Yes, I am one of his followers," Levi responded proudly.

"But you are a tax collector like myself," Zacchaeus stammered.

"I would never compare myself to you, Zacchaeus, you are a chief among us. Do you think it strange that he would allow tax collectors to follow him? Earlier today at my house Jeshua said, 'I have not come to call the righteous, but sinners to repentance.' I think we both qualify." His smile grew wider.

Zacchaeus turned to Jeshua, "Is this why you are coming to my house? That I too may follow you?" Jeshua wrapped his arm through Zacchaeus', "Let's go there and see."

As they left, many who knew Zacchaeus grumbled, "Humph, he has gone to be the guest of an even greater sinner. What's wrong with him?"

That night, after dinner, Zacchaeus stood and declared to Jeshua and those gathered, "My Lord, I give half of all that I have to the poor, and to those I have defrauded, I will restore what I have taken, fourfold."

Jeshua also stood, put his arm around Zacchaeus, and declared, "I tell you all, salvation has come to this house today, for this is also a son of Abraham. The Son of Man has come to seek and to save the lost!" Jeshua smiled again as he looked into Zacchaeus' eyes, "and I think I have found one. Perhaps he will follow with us?" The dinner guests all raised their glasses and cheered. Jeshua and Zacchaeus sat down and all continued to eat, drink, and enjoy lively discussion.

Judas turned to Simon and whispered, "I can't believe that he is letting tax collectors join us. What kind of rabble are we becoming? It's bad enough to have fisherman, but now tax collectors? Next he will be adding prostitutes to our group, foreigners, or even Romans!"

Chapter 31
Just Getting a Drink of Water

They had already walked twenty exhausting miles that morning on their way back to Galilee. Now the blistering midday sun beat on their heads and the heat rose from the ground in waves. To make matters worse, Jeshua insisted they go through Samaria. The Jews hated Samaritans and the disciples' antagonism showed. They stopped at a well outside the town of Sychar, deserted in the scorching heat. A single tree grew there and Jeshua sat beneath it. He sent the disciples into the town's market to purchase some food. While he rested there, a woman came to draw some water. That she came alone in the middle of the heat of the day said something about her character and standing in the city.

As she approached the well, Jeshua asked, "Would you give me a drink?"

Startled because she had not seen him in the shade of the tree, she approached before complying and noticed he was a Jew. "Why would you, a Jew, ask me, a Samaritan woman, for a drink?" This double breach of protocol appalled her. Normally, a Jew would have no dealings with a Samaritan, especially not with a woman.

He responded, "If you knew the gift that God had for you and to whom you are speaking, you would ask me for a drink and I would give you the water of Life."

Sarcastically, she replied, "The well is deep. Where will you get this water of life? You have no way to bring it up! Our father Jacob gave us this well, even drank from it himself, as did his sons. Are you greater than he, or do you produce living water from thin air?"

Jeshua countered with, "When you drink from this well, it is only to thirst again. The water that I give wells up inside of you unto eternal life, and you will never be thirsty again."

Now she became curious. "Well then, give me some of this water, so that I will never again be thirsty or have to come back to this well for water."

He heard, "*Have her go and get her husband. She has had five and the current one is not her husband.*" "Go," he said, "get your husband, and bring him back with you."

Her manner shifted, She suddenly held herself unnaturally still. "I do not have a husband," she could barely get the words out.

"That is true," he continued, "you have had five husbands and the man you are currently with is not your husband."

Stunned, she stammered, "Are you a prophet? I think you are a prophet."

The disciples returned from town and saw Jeshua talking with the woman. Astonished, they kept their distance, afraid to ask why he would talk to a Samaritan woman.

Seeing she now had an audience, she diverted the conversation to a safer topic, guaranteed to provoke heated discussion among any group of men. Perhaps she could slip away during the debate. "You Jews say the only place to worship is in Jerusalem, but our fathers worshiped here, on this mountain."

He smiled, lovingly, "It doesn't matter where you worship, in Jerusalem or on this mountain. You do not know what you are doing, but I worship Him because I know Him. Now is the time for true worship and for worshipers to worship the Father in Spirit and truth. He is looking for those who will so worship Him. He is spirit and we must worship Him in Spirit and truth."

Her eyes and heart opened. "When Messiah, the Anointed One comes, he will tell us everything."

His response opened them further, "You are talking to Him. I AM he."

She dropped her water jar, turned and ran into the town.

One of the disciples picked up the jar the woman had dropped. At least it had not broken. "Jeshua, we brought you some food," Peter offered.

He politely refused, "No thank you, I have food you know nothing about."

They wondered, "*Did the woman or someone else bring him something to eat?*"

As though hearing their thoughts, he answered, "My food is to do the will of Him who sent me. My drink is to accomplish His work."

They questioned among themselves what he meant.

He continued, "You think there are still four months until it will be harvest time, but I tell you, look to the fields, they are already white unto harvest. The reaper is already receiving his wages for gathering the fruit of eternal life, that both he and the sower may rejoice. The saying is true, 'one sows, the other reaps.' I send you to reap what you did not sow. Others have done that labor for you."

When the woman reached town she ran to her people, saying, "Listen, listen to me! You must come and see this man at the well. He told me things there was no possible way he could know about!"

"What did he tell you?" one of them questioned.

"He told me that I have had five husbands and that the man I am currently living with is not my husband," she replied.

"He could have learned that in town," another retorted.

"He hasn't been into town," she explained.

"Maybe he stopped at one of the outlying farms," suggested another.

She remained undeterred, "Come, I think he's the Messiah." They had to admit, something had definitely happened to her. Her newfound fearlessness and excitement intrigued them. A crowd of people began to follow her back to the well, some curious, some reluctant.

A few already believed because of the woman's testimony, "He told me things there was no way he could know about." When they came to Jeshua at the well, they asked him, "Would you stay with us for a while?"

He accepted their invitation, " I would be glad to."

He stayed with them for two days and many more people believed in him. They said to the woman, "We began to believe because of what you said, but now we have heard him for ourselves and know that this is the Savior who has come into the world.

After two days, Jeshua and the disciples continued their journey to Galilee, where many welcomed them. The word spread concerning his cleansing of the temple and how he taught with an authority and clarity they had never before witnessed.

Chapter 32
The Boldness of John

The two of them stood chest deep in the water. The breeze from the west almost made it seem chilly. The crowd had thinned out.

Jude stepped over to John. “It looks like the people have decided there is a bigger show in town.” Then he added apologetically, “not that we are a show, mind you.”

John smiled, unfazed, “I know what you meant, and took no offense.”

Jude continued, “They do say he is baptizing many more than we are now.”

John looked up at the few billowy clouds in the sky, “Which is just the way it should be. He must increase and I must decrease.”

They heard them before they saw them. The few people scattered, John and Jude looked towards shore, and a whole troop of cavalry rode over the hill. Their leader, a centurion by the looks of him, dismounted with a fluid motion as his steed stopped.

He called from the shore, “You are John, the one called The Baptizer?”

John turned to Jude and smiled, "My name is John, and I have been baptizing people, washing away their sins, so I guess that might be me."

The centurion responded, "We have come to take you back with us."

Jude spoke defiantly, "Well, come out and get him, we'll baptize you while you're out here."

John put a hand on Jude's shoulder, "What can I do for you, Centurion?"

"My name is Markus," he said, "and not having to come out there and take you by force would be helpful."

A small crowd regathered. Many considered John a prophet and they muttered at the presence of soldiers coming to arrest him.

John's voice carried above the noise of the rabble as he raised his hand. "There is no need for violence, Markus, I will come to you willingly." He began wading towards the shore, Jude with him. The other soldiers dismounted. One held the reigns of the horses, and the rest formed ranks around their centurion. When John reached the water's edge and Jude stepped out with him, all the soldiers' hands went to the hilts of their swords. Markus raised a restraining fist indicating, "*Stop!*"

"May I ask why I need to go with you?" John stood dripping on the shore. Jude walked up the bank, grabbed two bundles, and came back to him.

Markus stepped out of his soldiers' formation towards John, "You have said some things against the king and his wife."

"Ah," John nodded, "I thought that might require a response." He seemed awfully calm despite the situation. "I only spoke the truth, that it was unlawful for Herod to have his brother Philip's wife as his own." Jude handed John a towel from the bundle and he began to dry himself. The soldiers' hands twitched on their hilts anticipating a weapon.

Markus slashed his hand down, palm back, another "*Halt!*" gesture. "Yes, I'm afraid I must arrest you for saying that." Jude stepped protectively next to John. The crowd had moved closer too. "You need to tell this man and the people to stand down. I don't want anyone to get hurt."

John put a restraining arm in front of Jude, looking towards him, then raised his hand to the people. "It's okay, I will go with them. I will be fine, my time has not yet come." He spoke about his death.

Markus turned to his troops, "Mount up!" As they complied, he mounted his stallion effortlessly and reached an arm back down to John, who had put on his robe.

John grasped Markus' forearm and before he could blink, found himself swung up onto the horse, sitting behind Markus. It was a sign of great respect that he was sitting there. Normally, a criminal, even before his conviction, would have ridden behind one of the soldiers.

Markus turned and spoke over his shoulder as they rode away, "This is not the first time I have seen you."

John smiled, "I know, I recognized you too. I assume most of what was said and done on the beach was for the crowd and your soldiers."

"Yes, they all need to learn that we are not barbarians just because we are Romans." He laughed quietly.

"Yes," John added, "with power comes a great deal of responsibility."

"Do you remember baptizing me?" Markus asked.

"Ah," he thought a moment. "I do…there was a group of you and one of you watched over all your weapons and armor while I baptized the lot of you. You weren't a centurion then."

"No, I wasn't. It was before my promotion. I do think I need to warn you of something though." Markus moved from a fond memory to something quite serious.

"Certainly, what is it?" John continued to exude calmness.

"Herodias hates you quite bitterly for what you have said." Markus had perfected the ability to speak over his shoulder in a voice that only carried to his passenger. His men had no idea what they discussed. "If she had her way, you would be dead already."

"Hmmm," John mused. "I hoped it would move her in the other direction, towards repentance and a change of heart."

"Not likely. You also need to know that there is a powerful sorceress in the court, named Mekah. She has the ear of the king, but even more so of the queen. I think Herod respects you, and yet it is extremely difficult to keep everybody happy." Markus was being quite forthcoming.

"And what do you think of me?" John asked.

Markus paused, "I know you are not the Christ, you have made that quite clear, but you are preparing the way for him. Do we Romans need to fear his coming? Will the Jews try to overthrow us?" He spoke with genuine concern.

"As I have said to others before, 'If you do justly, love mercy, and walk humbly before our God,' you have nothing to worry about from Him. He has come to save the world, not condemn the Romans. Beside which, I have enough difficulty discerning my own way in this world, let alone to try and figure out His."

"Thank you, this has helped a lot." Markus sounded truly grateful.

"And thank you for the information," John replied, also grateful.

At the palace, Markus dismounted, helped John to the ground, dismissed his troops, and took John personally to the dungeons. As they walked through the doors a guard roughly grabbed John.

"Pollux, release him!" Markus commanded. Pollux could not have been more startled if Markus had slapped him, and complied immediately.

"I'm sorry, I thought…." He searched for words, as if he had not even seen Markus there, just the prisoner before him.

Markus commanded again, "You're dismissed. I will take him to the jailor."

"Yes!" and his fist slapped his chest in salute.

As they walked down into the dungeon, Markus said apologetically, "The accommodations aren't the best, but I assure you that I will do what I can."

"Don't worry, I'm used to a life that is pretty rustic," a smile still in his voice.

They met the jailor. "Amulius, this is John the Baptizer. I'm not sure for how long he will be detained. Have you got something somewhat decent for him?"

Amulius chuckled, "This isn't an inn, but I'll do my best."

Markus himself weakly smiled, "I'd appreciate it, I am in your debt."

He continued to chuckle, "A good place to be, I'll wager." To John he said, "Can I get you some supper?"

John also smiled, "Yes, but don't worry too much about it. I am used to locusts and wild honey, remember."

The jailor grimaced, "I think I can do better than that," then chuckled again.

As Markus turned to leave, he addressed John, "I'll tell the king that you are here." John just nodded, unconcerned.

Markus left and Amulius asked, "So, why have you been arrested?"

"Herodias was not too pleased about my calling her marriage to Herod unlawful," John responded.

"Oh, you're *that* John the Baptizer." He seemed to chuckle a lot. Maybe in this kind of profession he found it necessary.

"There are others?" John joined his chuckle.

"No, I don't think so. We don't get a lot of news down here, but I have heard of you. Let me get your supper and then perhaps we can have a bit of a chat?" He turned to leave.

To his back John responded, "I'd like that, Amulius." When he returned they had a good chat that pleased John. There seemed to be hope for Amulius' soul.

❖

John had been dozing when late that evening he heard boots and voices coming down the stairs. He opened his eyes to see torches approaching. A few feet from the bars stood the king.

John bowed his head for a moment, looked back up, and said, "Your majesty?"

"Bring the light closer," Herod commanded. The soldiers did so. "You're John the Baptizer who my centurion brought in from the Jordan river?"

"Yes, your Majesty. Your centurion brought me in earlier today." John stood tall but relaxed, a few feet from the bars.

"Come closer so I can see you," the king commanded.

"I'm not much to look at, but I am rather clean, having just come from a few dunkings in the river." The trace of a smile graced his lips.

"Do you know why you are here?" The king spoke sternly, but his voice belayed something else, fear maybe.

"I believe it has to do with my saying your marriage to your brother's wife is unlawful."

The king found such calmness unnerving. "You would say that to my face?" he spat out.

"Well, you asked me, and it is the truth." John's calmness persisted.

"Do you always tell the truth, even when it could cost you your head?" Herod seemed curious.

The "cost you your head" comment sent a shiver down his spine, but he took a quick breath, "To the best of my ability.... regardless of the consequences."

"And what could you possibly hope to accomplish as some wild man out in the river Jordan baptizing peasants?"

John thought to himself "*Was that an honest question?*" He found it difficult to tell. "Well, it seems to have granted me a personal audience with the king." He tried desperately not to smile.

"You're right! It did do that!" and the king turned abruptly and headed back up the stairs, with the soldiers hurrying to catch up.

PART FOUR

Heal Their Diseases

Chapter 33
Synagogues

Jeshua and his disciples returned to Nazareth where he had grown up. On the Sabbath they attended the synagogue. He stood up to read from the holy scriptures. Some of the attendees murmured, "Is this not the son of the carpenter? Isn't his mother Mary, and his brothers James, Joseph, Simon, and Judas? Are not his sisters also among us?"

Another spoke up, "Why should he stand to read? He is illegitimate, should he even be allowed in here?"

The ruler of the synagogue stepped forward, scroll in hand. "I have known Jeshua since he was a boy." He handed him the scroll, "Listen to him!"

The ruler had given Jeshua the scroll of the prophet Isaiah. He unrolled it, looking up at the ceiling of the synagogue as he did. He looked down again to the scroll and began to read, "The Spirit of the Lord is upon me, because He has anointed me to bring good news to those with nothing; to bind up those whose hearts are shattered, to bring freedom to those enchained, opening their prison doors; and to proclaim that the Lord's favor has finally come." He rerolled the scroll, handed it back to the ruler, and sat down. All the eyes in the synagogue fastened on him, as he said, "Today, this scripture is fulfilled, right here." and he pointed at his feet.

One man jumped up incensed, "Who does he think he is?" Others looked at each other and wondered about the words he had just spoken.

Another demanded, "It is said you perform miracles! Do some here, so that we may see them!"

Someone from the back yelled, "You eat and drink with tax collectors and sinners. Why are you here?" he sneered.

But Jeshua responded, "You want to see me do miracles here in Nazareth? Let me share with you a Truth, a prophet is not accepted in his own town. Do you remember that there were many widows in the land of Israel at the time of Elijah, when the windows of heaven were shut up and there was no rain for three and a half years? There was a great famine and yet Elijah was sent to a foreigner, a widow of Zaraphath, to feed her. What about all the other people? Also, there were many lepers in Israel at the time of Elisha, yet none of them were healed and cleansed except the Syrian general, Naaman."

When the people in the synagogue heard his words, a number of them rose up in wrath. They grabbed him and dragged him out of the synagogue, out of the city to a cliff, intent on throwing him off of it. Suddenly they halted. Their eyes glazed over and they could no longer move, like they froze where they stood. Jeshua looked over his shoulder, back towards the synagogue. There stood an old man. "*Uriel,*" Jeshua thought. The old man walked up to Jeshua, removed the hands that still grasped him, and put his own arm around Jeshua's shoulder, turning him around. Together the two of them walked calmly through the immobilized crowd and back to the city. Suddenly, the crowd awoke. They looked around. Jeshua was nowhere to be seen. "Where did he go?" many shouted. Their anger still burned, but now fueled with frustration. However, with no focus and direction it soon burned itself out and the mob dispersed.

❖

On another Sabbath, Jeshua entered a synagogue in that city. The ruler recognized him and asked if he would like to address the people. He smiled, nodded his thanks, and began to teach. In the middle of a story, Jeshua noticed a man sitting in the congregation who kept his hand inside of his robe. Jeshua wondered why this man had caught his attention. "*His hand is withered,*" he heard. Jeshua thought, "*Ah, another test.*" He asked what he should do and only heard, "*Wait.*" He looked around and realized the scribes and Pharisees watched to see what he would do. Would he heal a man on the Sabbath? They still searched for an accusation, something to hold against him.

Realizing their intent, he called to the man, gesturing to him, "Rise up, and come out here into the middle of the floor."

Reluctantly, the man did so.

Jeshua looked around, gesturing at them all, and said, "I ask you, is it lawful to do good on the Sabbath? What about evil? Is it right to save a life or destroy one?" He looked above him briefly, and heard, "*Have him stretch out his hand,*" so he said to the man, "Stretch out your hand." As the man obeyed, his hand grew whole, and looked just like the other.

Astonished, the man looked at his hand, the palm, the back. He flexed his fingers as tears filled his eyes and he fell weeping to his knees. Through his tears he looked back up and into the eyes of Jeshua to mouth the words, "*Thank you!*"

One of the scribes stood up, "You can't do that! It is not lawful to do that on the Sabbath!" The rest of the scribes and the Pharisees seethed with fury. They got up, stormed out of the synagogue, and began discussing among themselves how they might destroy this man who so flagrantly violated the Sabbath. All, that is, but one of them who lingered behind. His name was Joseph and he came from Aramathea. He walked back to the man who had finally scrambled from his knees.

Joseph asked, "May I see your hand?" The man showed it to him. "How long had it been withered?" he asked. He learned that the man had been born that way. Puzzled and shaking his bewildered head, Joseph looked at Jeshua. Jeshua just smiled and nodded to him. The healed man ran to Jeshua and embraced him.

On yet another Sabbath, Jeshua again taught in a synagogue, "*There is a woman here, bound with a spirit of infirmity for eighteen years,*" he heard. He looked around and finally found her. She crouched doubled over and could not straighten up. "*Her name is Hannah. Lay your hands on her and free her from this thing.*" Jeshua called her, "Hannah." She looked surprised to hear her name. With difficulty she turned in his direction. She caught his eye and thunder rumbled deep in her soul. She almost lost her balance. She started to hobble towards him, but he raised a hand for her to stop and walked quickly to her side. He stooped down, took her face in his hands, and looking directly into her eyes said, "You are freed from this thing." Her face still in his hands he slowly stood. As he did, she straightened with him. No words could express the joy she felt. She simply wrapped her arms around him, embraced him, and kissed him tenderly on the cheek. He gladly received the unusual display of affection. He held her a moment, then released her. She turned to go and met the angry stare of their rabbi standing in her way. He served as the ruler of this synagogue and looked livid. She stepped to the side.

Indignant with what Jeshua had just done, he spat out, "Do you not know the commandment? There are six days in which to work. Heal on those days! This is the seventh day, the Sabbath, and no work should be done on this day!"

Jeshua took a slow deep breath, listening as he did, and then answered him, "Do you not untie your donkey and lead him to water on the Sabbath?" he paused. "You hypocrite! The Accuser had bound this daughter of Abraham for eighteen years. Should she not be loosed on the Sabbath?" The rabbi stood there dumbfounded. His angry face changed and became colored with shame.

Hannah walked by him, her head held high, and the rest of the congregation burst forth in praise to God for what Jeshua had just done. Some whispered, "We have never seen anything like this before. Who is this man?"

The disciples also stood by and questioned among themselves, "Jeshua makes a distinction between the Law of God and the traditions of men. How are we to know the difference? The Pharisees would tell us that they are both based soundly on the scriptures, but are they? We need to ask him."

Judas turned to Simon, "This is why we follow him! He stands up to them, confounds them with his words and deeds. No one can stand against him. Surely he will deliver us from the Romans as well." Simon just raised his shoulders and shrugged.

Chapter 34
Who is Blind Here?

Jeshua and his disciples strolled along the road. As they passed a blind beggar sitting along it, Jeshua paused and heard, "*He is blind since birth.*" He pointed to the man and declared, matter of factly, "This man has been blind since his birth."

The disciples looked at one another. Peter spoke, "Rabbi, who sinned that this man was born blind? He or his parents?"

"Peter, if he was born blind it could hardly have been because of his own sin." Jeshua smiled.

Peter piped up again, "Then it was his parents," he said confidently.

"No," Jeshua continued, "This blindness was not the result of his parents' sin. This blindness was not the result of sin at all. This man is blind in order that the works of God might be displayed in him." He continued, "We must work the works of Him who sent me while it is day. The night is coming and then we will not be able to work at all. As long as I am here in the world, I am the light of the world."

He turned to face the man, knelt down where he sat, and heard, "*Spit on the ground.*" He did. Again, he heard, "*Make mud of the spittle.*" He did that too. "*Apply the mud to his eyes.*" He told the man, "I am going to be putting some mud on your eyes. Please allow me to do so." Jeshua anointed the man's eyes with the mud. "*Now tell him.*" He said to the man, "Now, go, wash the mud from your eyes in the pool of Siloam."

The man started to scramble to his feet. "Can someone take me there?"

Jeshua looked to Andrew, "Would you please take him to the pool?"

"Certainly," said Andrew. He wrapped the man's arm through his own, and off they went. When they got to the pool, Andrew stopped him. "We are going to kneel here." He helped him kneel, unwrapped the man's arm from his own, and guided the man's hand into the water. "There you go, wash away." Andrew stood, took a few steps away from the man and into the nearby crowd. The man scooped up the water to his eyes, again, and again, and again, until he no longer felt any mud on them. When he opened his eyelids, he nearly fell over. He could see! Initially, the light shown so brightly he felt like he looked into the sun itself. He sat back on his haunches and just stared and blinked. Eventually the shapes made sense. Now he found it difficult to see through his tears, and he had no words, either. He wiped his face dry on his tunic, got up, and started to walk back to where he used to sit.

Along the way, some of the people said, "Isn't that the blind man who used to sit and beg down the road?" Some others said, "No, it can't be. It is just someone who looks a lot like him."

He heard them and he responded, "Yes, I am the man. I used to sit," and he pointed, "down there and beg."

They questioned him, "But you were blind from birth, how is it that you now can see?"

He answered, "The man they call Jeshua, he put mud in my eyes and told me to wash it out at the pool of Siloam. I did, and now I can see."

They said, "Where is this man, Jeshua?"

He said, "I don't know. I left him there when I went to the pool." and he pointed again.

They took him to the Pharisees, because it was the Sabbath. Jeshua had healed him on the Sabbath and work on the Sabbath broke the Jewish law.

The Pharisees asked, "What is your name?"

Afraid of them he answered, " Ahvram, my name is Ahvram."

One of them continued, "We understand that you were blind. How is it that you now can see?"

Ahvram replied shaking, "He put mud on my eyes. When I washed it off, I could see."

Another of them said, "Surely this Jeshua is not from God. He doesn't keep the Sabbath."

Another said, "But if he were a sinner, would he be able to do such a miracle?"

They began to argue among themselves. One of the elders raised a hand to silence them and then he asked Ahvram directly. "What do you say about him? It was your eyes that he healed."

He still trembled, "He must be some kind of prophet?"

Their argument continued. "Maybe he wasn't really born blind?" They decided to call his parents, taking Ahvram out of the room to an antechamber while they did. When they him brought back in, his parents waited there. They also looked terrified.

An elder Pharisee asked, pointing to Ahvram, "Is this your son?" They nodded. "Was he born blind?" They nodded again. "How is it that he now can see?"

Ahvram's father spoke, "This is our son, yes. He was born blind, yes. How he now sees or who healed him? We don't know. You can ask him, he's of an age to speak for himself." They feared the leaders. Rumors said that if anyone confessed Jeshua as the Messiah, the leaders would cast them out of the synagogue. So they said, "*Ask him, he is of age,*"

The Pharisees began to get angry. They said to Ahvram, "Give God the glory, we know that this man is a sinner."

Ahvram suddenly found courage welling up in his soul."Whether he is a sinner or not, that I don't know. All I know is one thing. I was blind! Now I can see!"

But they did not listen, they responded, "Tell us again. What did he do? How did he open your eyes?"

Ahvram stood taller, took a deep breath, and told them, "I have already told you, but you seem unwilling to hear me. Why would you want to hear it again?" He smiled, "You don't want to become his disciples too, do you?"

That did it. One of the other elders snapped, "You are his disciple! We are disciples of Moses! We know God spoke to Moses, but we don't even know where this man comes from."

Boldness now flowed through Ahvram's veins. "What an amazing thing! You don't know where he comes from? Who cares! He opened my eyes! God doesn't listen to sinners! If you worship God and do His will, then He listens to you. Not since the beginning of time have we heard that someone has opened the eyes of a man born blind. If this man Jeshua were not from God, he could do nothing!"

The elders were incensed, "You were born completely in sin! Take him out of here!" and they cast him out of the synagogue.

When Jeshua heard that they had cast him out, he went and found him. Jeshua said to him, "Do you believe in the Son of Man?"

Ahvram responded, "Who is he, that I might believe in him?"

Jeshua responded, "You have seen him. I AM he."

Ahvram fell at his feet. "I believe in you!" and he worshiped him.

Jeshua continued, "I have come into this world for judgment, that those who do not see may see, and those who think that they see may realize that they are blind."

A few of the Pharisees stood nearby them and heard Jeshua speak. They questioned him, "Are we blind?"

He responded, "If you were blind, you would not be guilty. But because you still think you can see, your guilt remains." Most of them turned and walked away, but one knelt and began to weep. Jeshua stepped forward, laying a hand on his shoulder. "You are not far from the kingdom of heaven." He lifted his hand and left him there.

Chapter 35
Four Good Friends

His popularity soared. He found it more and more difficult to go anywhere, do anything, without crowds surrounding him. They had returned to Capernaum and the house they stayed in quickly filled to capacity. No one could sit, they barely had room to stand. Many of the Pharisees and teachers of the Law had come. Jeshua shared with the people, telling them stories about the kingdom of God.

Years ago Justin had fallen from a ladder while working at home and broke his neck. Paralyzed from the neck down, he felt lucky to still be alive, but his future looked pretty hopeless. He knew nothing could cure something like this. Yet he practiced contentment and his four buddies loved him for it. He rarely complained, usually said a kind word, and almost always smiled whenever people came around.

His friends had all heard the stories about the new rabbi, Jeshua. Most of what people said about him surely could not be true. It sounded too wonderful, too amazing. People said that he healed the sick, made the lame walk, even made the blind see. He taught through simple yet profound stories. The people loved him and flocked to him. The religious leaders feared him, mostly because of his popularity. He had not raised anyone from the dead yet, but most people thought he soon would.

Adam, Jerud, Eliezar, and Shem had met at Justin's house. They had just finished feeding him. They liked to help whenever they could and relieve some of the responsibility from his parents that caring for a paralytic took. It took a lot.

"Any big plans for the day?" Jerud addressed Justin. "Horseback riding?"

"No," he smiled, "I think we'll save that for later in the week."

"We could take you fishing," Shem chimed in. "We need some ballast in the boat until we catch all the fish."

"That might be fun," Justin still smiled. "I need more practice bailing with my tongue."

Eliezar turned more serious, "What do you think of this fellow called Jeshua, that new rabbi?"

"He is making quite a stir." Justin added, "Mother and Father were just talking about him. Most of it seems too good to be true."

"I think he's the real thing," Adam answered, adding, "a friend of Hannah's daughter was healed by him."

"Really," Justin sounded intrigued now. "What was the matter with her?"

Adam replied, "She was deaf, and now she can hear just fine."

"What did he do?" Justin feared getting too excited about this.

"Hannah said that he didn't even touch her, but told her to take a deep breath, then exhale. While she did, he said 'Be opened,' and then she could hear."

Adam thought he would take a chance. "What if we took you to see him?"

Justin hesitated, reluctant, "I don't know, what do you think?"

They each responded, "It couldn't hurt." "It's worth a try." "He's healed a lot of other people." "What have we got to lose?"

"Okay, I guess if you guys are up to it, so am I, but I'm not too hopeful."

Adam jumped in, "Well, we're all up for it," and the others chorused their agreement.

Adam and Jerud left and got the bed they used to carry him around. The four of them picked him up, and transferred him to it, then off they went.

Carrying a paralytic through a bustling small town creates an interesting adventure, but at least they got Justin out of the house, always a good thing. They had him well roped to the bed, so that amidst the jostling he would not get dumped on the ground. When they reached the house where Jeshua stayed they ran headlong into a huge crowd. They asked those on the edge of it and heard that only standing room remained inside. Adam walked up and peeked inside to confirm.

"Yup," he said, "standing room only."

Justin replied a bit dejectedly, "I guess this was just a wild goose chase."

The four looked at one another, then Adam said, "The roof!"

The other three looked at each other, wide-eyed, and said, "Yes!" They headed for the back of the house and the stairs to the roof.

They set Justin down, checked the security of the ropes, and jokingly said, "Hold on tight." He just shook his head from side to side in disbelief. Off they went, up the stairs. The bed tilted precariously, but they made it without incident.

"Now what?" Shem said to Adam. "This was your idea."

Adam walked across the roof. "I would estimate Jeshua is sitting right about here. What if we took off the tiles, untied Justin, and used the ropes to lower him down on his bed?"

Shem, again, "Have we got enough rope?"

"We might have to drop him the last couple of feet, but he won't feel it." Adam joked, at least Justin hoped so. "No, I think we have enough rope. If not, we can add our belts. Are you ready for this, Justin?" Justin did not want to say "no" after all they had already done. They got the ropes ready first, then took off the tiles without making too much of a mess below, and lowered him down. Perfect, just enough rope, and right in front of Jeshua. Jeshua looked up, saw the four of them leaning over the hole they had made, and shook his head back and forth,.

"*Incredible,*" he thought. Their faith pleased him and so did the action it had precipitated.

Jeshua saw Justin's sin as a large bundle sitting on his chest, preventing him from getting up. He said, "Justin, your sins are forgiven."

Justin thought to himself, "*He knows my name,*" and then, "*Oh no! He knows of my sin, too.*" He struggled under the deep conviction of the enormity of his sin, but you could only see it in his eyes. The struggle continued, but he was after all still paralyzed. As tears filled his eyes he closed them and mumbled, "I am sorry, I am so, so sorry!" and something new began to dawn in his soul. *Jeshua said my sins ARE forgiven, not they could be or would be, but "ARE!"*

The scribes and teachers of the law thought, "*What? This is blasphemy! Only God can forgive sin.*"

In his spirit, Jeshua perceived what the scribes and teachers thought and said to them, "Oh, the things you are thinking. Which is easier to say to this man? 'Your sins are forgiven,' or 'Rise, take up your bed and walk?' But in order that you may know that the Son of Man has the authority on earth to forgive sins…." He said to Justin, "Rise, take up your bed and walk."

Justin's mind whirled, "*Is this really possible?*" but it seemed the incredible weight had lifted from his chest. "*My sin, it's gone,*" he thought. Suddenly he felt as light as air. He looked down at his hand, raised it to his face, and dried his tears on his sleeve. He brought the other hand to his face and just looked at it. He brought his knees to his chest, rolled on his side, and got off the bed. He stood up, turned to face Jeshua, and mouthed, "Thank you!" He could not speak out loud as the tears reformed in his eyes. He blinked them away, reached down, picked up his bed, looked up at the beaming faces of his four friends, and announced, "Let's go ride some horses!" His friends, looking down, nearly fell through the hole in the roof. They quickly turned and scrambled down the stairs to meet him outside.

The crowd parted for Justin and his bed. The people exclaimed, "We have never seen anything like this before!" In amazement they began giving glory to God. As voices crescendoed, caught up in the moment, Jeshua abruptly stood, and followed Justin out of the house. He caught even the disciples off guard. They quickly got up too in order to follow him, but the way through the sea of people had closed behind him. When they finally reached the door, they could see him nowhere. Off in the distance they could see Justin and his four friends practically dancing home in joy, but as for Jeshua, nothing. They asked some of the people where he had gone and received blank stares in response. For the moment, he had simply gone. Meanwhile, the scribes and teachers of the law argued among themselves. They could not mistake what they had all seen, but they could not believe what they had heard.

When the rest of the people finally realized that Jeshua had left, they too began to disperse in ones, twos, threes, most of them sharing the wonder they had experienced. The disciples went back into the house and began cleaning up after the crowd and the roof rubble. They drew lots. Two of them set about repairing the roof while the other disciples, and the women who traveled with them, set up for supper. He would come back when the time came for him to be back. They would just have to wait, do what they thought he would want them to do in his absence, and get ready for the rest of the evening.

Jeshua spent the evening alone in the mountains with his Father. These extended times alone together happened too rarely. Sure, they were always together, but only in the middle of everything that was always going on, people, people, people and their incessant needs. He loved them, yes, wanted to serve and help them, yes, but occasionally he needed times like this: just him, his Father, Uriel, and a star-filled sky. They talked about many things, but also just spent time in each other's presence, enjoying the love and the silence. When he returned, the disciples had fallen asleep. He went to bed himself, refreshed.

The next morning he woke them early and announced, "Let's have a quick breakfast, then we are all going into the mountains for a few days."

Chapter 36
Markus' Slave

Markus had quickly established himself as a centurion. He exhibited most, if not all, of the same qualities that had made his father's men follow him to the ends of the earth. He inspired loyalty, expected obedience, and rewarded good behavior. He dispensed equally, as the situation required, both justice and mercy. His men loved him for it. He inherited a large residence, then quickly wooed and married Rebecca. With the house came two slaves: a kitchen slave, Judith, to help Rebecca with household duties, and a personal slave, Rex, to look after his own needs. They both worked hard and within a short time they asked for an introduction to Chayeem. They became more like family than slaves and at the appropriate time Markus and Rebecca planned to set them free from servanthood.

❖

Jeshua and the disciples had disappeared into the mountains, escaping the crowds that incessantly followed them, but it had only taken a few days for the crowds to rediscover them. Jeshua sat near the top of a hill with the people spread out below him and he taught them. Even the children sat enraptured for hours listening to his clear and simple stories, pregnant with meaning. Sometimes the people did not want to go home at night, and the disciples felt like shepherds having to drive their sheep to another place to sleep. Jeshua and the disciples would then eat a light supper that the women provided, and often the disciples would ask him to explain one of his stories. Eventually, they would fall asleep under a starlit sky. They enjoyed these wonderful times.

As they returned to Capernaum, they heard a group of horses riding hard behind them. They stepped out of the road to let them pass, but the leader, a centurion by his dress, pulled up his horse and dismounted in a single fluid motion. His men soon stood beside him.

Jeshua heard, "*He has a request of us,*" and stepped out to meet him. "Centurion, what can I do for you?"

"You are Jeshua?" he questioned.

"I AM!" The hair stood up on their necks as though an unseen wind blew from behind them.

The centurion took a knee, fist to his chest as though addressing a king. Looking at the ground, he began, "My name is Markus. My slave fell from the roof of my house while repairing it. He lies paralyzed, suffering grievous torment."

"*Go with him and heal his slave.*" Before Markus could say any more, Jeshua interrupted, "I will go with you and heal him."

Markus froze at the unexpected response. A Jew who entered a Roman house became ceremonially unclean, but Jeshua had not even hesitated. Markus' father had spoken about Jeshua and he himself had heard lots of rumors concerning his healing and compassion and so had ventured to come to him, but this? He finally found his voice, and looked up, "I am not worthy that you should come under my roof." He paused, searching for the right words. "Just say the word and my servant will be healed." He paused again. "I am a man under authority and have soldiers under my authority. If I say to this one, 'Go!' he goes. If I say to another, 'Come!' he comes. If I say to my slave, 'Do this!' he does it."

Now Jeshua looked stunned. He marveled, "In all of Israel, I have not found faith like this!" He paused to look around him, "I tell you all, many will come from the East and the West to sit with Abraham, Isaac, and Jacob in the kingdom of heaven, while those who think they are sons will be cast out into utter darkness where there will be weeping and gnashing of teeth." He turned back to Markus, "You may go home. As you believed, it has been done. Your slave is healed."

Markus bowed his head again, "Thank you." He abruptly stood and commanded his men, "Mount up!" which they did immediately. Nodding again to Jeshua, they rode off. When Markus and his men returned to the house they found the slave up doing his duties. When he asked what time he had been healed, the slave replied with the very hour Jeshua had said so. The entire house echoed with joy, as Markus sat them all down and shared what had happened in his encounter with the rabbi, Jeshua. He began to wonder whether Jeshua could be the one who John the Baptizer had been talking about, the one who was to come. They all began to wonder.

The disciples and Jeshua started back on the road heading home to their house in Capernaum. The crowds, of course, waited. Word quickly spread that he had been sighted and seemed to be coming home.

Chapter 37
Healing a Heart

Rumors and mutterings around town often criticized Jeshua for eating and drinking with tax collectors and sinners, but he ate with others as well. One evening, a Pharisee invited him to dinner and he accepted.

Leah worked as a woman of the roads. Although she belonged to Janus, as did Ahlam and Marie, she served the common man rather than the rich and famous. This she did, however, with a rare enthusiasm that proved quite popular. She developed her own extensive following. Recently though, she found her passion for her profession waning. She felt an emptiness like she lacked something, something important. When she heard about the wandering rabbi, Jeshua, the stories intrigued her. "*I must meet him,*" she thought to herself. She heard that Simon the Pharisee had invited him to supper and she knew how to enter through the back entrance of his house. "*I have been there before,*" she mused. "*I think I will become their evening's uninvited guest.*" Before she left her house, she spied her alabaster jar of ointment.

Saving it for the day when she would retire from her profession, she added to its expensive contents whenever she could. She had filled it about half full at this point. For some reason she snatched it off of her dressing table and hid it in the folds of her robe.

When she entered the dining room, she saw them all reclined at the table. Jeshua faced away from her, his feet towards her. Simon looked wide-eyed at her, speechless. Jeshua turned to look at her. His gaze arrested her and nearly unhinged her with its intense compassion. She could hardly breathe. Tears welled up in her eyes, she unbound her hair, and knelt at Jeshua's feet. She began weeping soundlessly at his feet, then on his feet. He reached out, touched the top of her head, and she wept even more. She covered his feet with her tears, washing them. She then dried them with her hair, kissing them. Finally, she reached into her robe, removed the alabaster cruise of ointment, broke it open, and began to massage it into his feet. The perfume of it filled the air and Jeshua closed his eyes, overcome with emotion.

Simon said to himself, "*Humph, if this man were a prophet like some claim him to be, he would know what kind of a woman this is touching him. She is a grievous sinner!*"

Jeshua heard the words of his heart, also clearly written on his face, and said to him. "Simon, I have something to say to you."

Simon gulped audibly, "By all means, say it," a dangerous response to give to a prophet, but he no longer considered Jeshua a prophet.

Jeshua accepted the invitation. "A money lender had two clients. One owed him five hundred denarii, the other fifty. Neither of them could pay off their debt, so he canceled both debts. Which of his debtors will love him the more?"

Simon thought for a moment and then answered, "I suppose the one for whom he canceled the larger debt."

Jeshua responded, "You have answered correctly." Turning to Leah, he continued, "Do you see this woman?"

Simon flinched, "*Of course I see that woman! She's a woman of the road, a notorious sinner,*" but he said nothing.

Jeshua turned back to Simon and began again. "When I came into your house, you gave me no water to cleanse the dust of my travels from my feet, but she has washed my feet with her tears and dried them with her hair." Simon blushed. "You gave me no kiss of greeting, but she is still kissing my feet." The blush deepened. "You did not anoint my head with oil, but she has anointed my feet with costly perfume." His shame increased. "Simon, I tell you, her sins, which are many, are forgiven, for she has lavished her love on me, but the one for whom little is forgiven, will love only a little." He turned to Leah, "Your sins are forgiven."

Simon and the others reclining at the table started to get up from it enraged, "*Who does he think he is? He can't forgive sins! Only God can do that!*"

Ignoring them and still looking at Leah, he said, gently, "You may go in peace. Your faith, demonstrated in your love, has saved you."

She went to replace the stopper on the ointment and realized she had used it all. She left the empty jar where it lay, a token to the expense expended for what she now possessed. She stood and walked out, rejoicing over the inner peace and joy she had longed for, and the one who had given it all to her. Under her breath, she whispered his name, "Jeshua."

PART FIVE

Deliver Them from Evil

Chapter 38
Salome

Mekah stayed bowed down, her face to the ground. On the black altar the bowl of goat's blood still smoldered. "*How could it burn so long*?" she thought to herself. Its pungent smoke made breathing difficult, but she continued to mumble her incantations, hoping to summon Chemosh. Suddenly it all cleared, the room filled with the most brilliant of lights, and a tangy aroma replaced the smoke. While not particularly pleasant, at least she could breathe again. She slowly raised her eyes the barest fraction to see a nearly luminescent pair of sole-to-calf sandals, worn by the most magnificent pair of legs she had ever beheld. She feared to raise her eyes any higher, but a strong hand grasped her chin and lifted her face to his, as he bent down, kneeling on one knee. He kissed her full on the lips so passionately that she fainted. She awoke on her back, disheveled, and panting deeply.

Above her stood Chemosh, clearly a god. She had seen him before, but never like this. Such raw, savage power emanated from his being that her heart raced wildly, her breathing labored. He reached a hand down to her. "*Should she even dare to touch his hand?*" but he left it extended. Slowly, trembling, she reached out. He grasped her hand and easily pulled her to her feet. She bowed her head again, "My Master."

When he spoke, it seemed to contain all the music of the cosmos, but in a minor key. "You are familiar with Herodias' daughter, Salome," he stated, not asking. "Bring her here to me."

"Now, my Lord?" she asked.

A broad smile graced his face, "Most definitely! I will await your return." An ornate throne appeared next to him and he sat down.

Mekah knew all the secrets of the palace, many of her own making. She arrived at Herodias' chambers without encountering any guards. She did not announce herself, she just entered. Herodias was in awe and at the same time terrified of her. She knew the power Mekah held over the king, that Mekah had persuaded the king to marry her, and that if it came to a real showdown, Mekah ruled the land, under the direction of Chemosh, of course.

Mekah stood at the end of Herodias' royal purple-draped canopy bed. She slept or feigned sleep. Mekah waited and listened. "*No, she is asleep,*" she thought. She whispered an awakening incantation and Herodias' eyes blinked open, wide awake. She sat up, "Mistress Mekah, what can I do for you?"

"I need to borrow your daughter for a while," she spoke with an air of command.

A shiver ran down Herodias' spine, "Certainly. She sleeps in the next room."

Actually, as Mekah knew, Salome hid behind the curtain, clandestinely listening to their conversation. "Thank you," Mekah replied graciously, and walked into Salome's room without betraying her hiding place. She turned and waited for Salome to reveal herself. Salome peeked out from behind the curtain. Making sure Herodias could not see, Mekah motioned her to come out. Salome obeyed instantly on unusually silent, bare feet. Mekah was impressed.

Mekah motioned her to the small ornately carved ivory table that graced the room, and sat in the second chair. She spoke to her in hushed tones, so as to remain unheard outside of the room. "Have you ever met the god Chemosh?" she whispered.

Salome smiled innocently, "Only in my dreams."

"And what was he like?" Mekah inquired.

"He appeared as the most magnificent and powerful man I have ever seen," she replied passionately.

"Has he spoken to you?"

"Oh, yes." She hesitated, "He said that you would lead me into my destiny," she continued humbly.

That impressed Mekah even more. This was going to be easier than anticipated. "Would you like to meet him?"

"In person?" Mekah felt her genuine excitement. "Now?"

"You have bathed?" Salome wore her bath robe.

"Yes, I had just finished before you arrived to talk with my mother," she shyly responded.

Mekah walked over to her closet, "Let's see, what should you wear to meet a god?" as she looked through the clothes.

Salome stepped to the closet and selected a gown.

"Who is this young woman?" she murmured to herself. "Okay, you'll wear that one."

As she began to dress herself, Salome questioned, "What does," and she recited the awakening incantation that Mekah had just used on Herodias, "mean?"

Mekah stepped back abruptly, like cold water had just been thrown in her face. More than impressed, Salome's perfect recall astonished her. "It is a spell of awakening." "*Perhaps I have the makings here of an apprentice?*" Genuine delight spread through Mekah's abdomen. She pondered this for a moment, then when Salome finished dressing, she offered Salome her hand, "Come."

Salome reached out and took Mekah's hand. A shiver ran down Mekah's spine. Mekah uttered another spell towards Herodias' room so softly that Salome could not hear it and Herodias was sound asleep when they passed back through it. Again, they encountered no guards as they returned to Mekah's room and faced the door covered in sacred and occult symbols. She muttered another word, again careful not to let Salome hear, "*If she learns that quickly, I must be careful.*" The door opened and they entered the chamber with its black altar.

"Reach out your hand." At this point it would have been difficult for Salome not to comply, but she responded without hesitation. "You know that I will never hurt you?" She lied, but hoped Salome could not yet tell that.

"Yes, Mistress Mekah," and she smiled. Maybe Salome could already detect her lies.

"I am going to lightly cut your palm." She did it quickly, painlessly. "Ball your hand into a fist and squeeze some blood into this bowl." She held out the bowl from the altar. Salome complied. Mekah muttered another incantation. The resulting concussion and explosion of light knocked Mekah to the ground. When she recovered, Salome stood just in front of Chemosh. He moved his hands to the sides of her face and breathed on her. She inhaled deeply, while Mekah fainted. When she regained consciousness, Salome now stood at Chemosh's side as he sat on his thrown.

Chemosh addressed Mekah, "I want you to take her to Janus and have Ahlam teach her to dance."

"My lord, Ahlam has left the company of the courtesans," she said hesitantly.

"What!" The air reverberated with his indignation. "How can this be hidden from me?" he shouted to no one in particular. He closed his eyes, put the thumb and forefinger of his right hand to the top of his nose, and seemed to think for a moment. He snorted, "It means nothing! Take her to Janus and have his best dancing girl teach her to dance. Quickly!" He and the throne vanished.

Mekah held out her hand to Salome, who looked down at it and stepped to Mekah's side. She seemed to have emerged through some rite of passage and now considered herself much more than Mekah's potential apprentice. "*Yes, I will have to be careful with this one,*" she mused. Together they walked to Janus' quarters.

Chapter 39
The Dance of Death

John had fallen asleep. "*For how long have I been asleep*?" he wondered. He felt tired, hungry, dirty. He had tried imagining that he just fasted in the wilderness, but it did not help much anymore. Even his imagination felt tired and he figured that he did not have locust dipped in wild honey waiting for him. "*What woke me?*" he mused. His hearing had become more acute as the cell's conditions starved his other senses. "*Ah, soldiers coming. It must be mid-week. Time for a visit from the king.*" He tried to straighten his robes the best he could.

Herod's guards surrounded him as they descended the steps. Once they had convinced themselves that the dungeon held no threat to the king's life, Markus dismissed them back upstairs. He alone stayed with the king.

The king approached the bars. "My lord," Markus cautioned his first responsibility, "not too close, my lord." He held the torch in one hand, his sword in the other. He did not really believe that John could threaten the king, but his training held.

"He's not going to bite me, Markus," chuckled Herod. "Put the torch closer to the bars if you need to keep him back."

He did move the torch closer towards the bars, but just so they could see better. "Forgive me, my lord, but your safety is my first concern."

"I know that, Markus, and I appreciate that." Herod turned and John's gaunt appearance shocked him.

He had bowed, "Your majesty," he spoke as he swept his hands away from his body.

A twinge of concern marked Herod's words, "Are they not feeding you enough, John?"

John smiled, "I think your food is designed to sustain life, not necessarily to promote health, your majesty. I'm fine."

"It is my birthday, today. Could I bring you anything special?" He seemed to show genuine concern.

Now John chuckled. "No, thank you, in my present condition, I'm afraid your rich food would make me sick."

Herod stopped for a moment, thinking, "*Should I ask him?*" Deciding he asked, "I am hearing rumors about a new teacher, a rabbi named Jeshua. Do you know of him?"

"Yes, I do. I baptized him in the river." He spoke humbly.

"And what was he like?" Herod seemed interested.

"He is like no one I have ever met before." Awe radiated from his words.

"Some are saying he is your promised deliverer. What do you say?" Herod's voice held a little bit of an edge now, making John cautious, uncertain of its meaning.

He looked Herod directly in the eyes, "I think you would have to ask him."

Herod stepped back a step, the moment over. "Are you sure you don't want something from my party?"

"No, thank you, but you should probably ponder the brevity of life and how much time you have left." "*There, he had said it.*" John turned, stepped back into the darkness of his cell, and sat down among his rags.

Herod shook off John's last comment and headed back up the stairs.

❖

The party had already begun when Herod, the special guest, arrived. As he walked regally to his place of honor at the head table, many of those attending cheered and applauded. He stood before his place and raised his hand for silence. It took a while, as many of the attendees had been drinking for some time.

Finally he spoke, "Thank you all for coming. I would say 'Let the party begin,' but it looks like many of you started without me." Some laughed at that. He continued, "I will be taking down the names of those who have been that rude." The room silenced. "You could have at least waited for my wife and daughter," he pointed to the doorway and they entered.

Herodias always dressed elegantly and she had spared no cost this time, but Salome had mastered the art of simplicity. When she entered behind her mother, her subtly modest short dress brought them all to their feet and left them there. Salome's discrete beauty made Herodias' extravagance pale in comparison.

When the royal family sat, the rest of the assembly followed suit and the festivities began in earnest. Markus stood near the king, in his place as Herod's most trusted centurion. Mekah, the sorceress, no longer sat at the head table. She found it easier to rule things from a distance. Next to Mekah sat a man who Herod did not recognize.

With a wave of his hand Herod motioned Markus to him and spoke to him over his shoulder. "Who is that warrior sitting with Mekah?"

"They announced him as a visiting prince from Persia. I did not catch his name. Shall I find out?" Markus whispered.

"No, just keep a discrete eye on him. There is something about him that I find unsettling." Herod turned back to the acrobatic troupe performing for everyone's benefit.

"As you wish, my lord." Markus resumed his post.

Across the hall sat Janus. He had obviously brought a few of his dancing girls with him, all young, beautiful, and hardly touching the food and drink. At what seemed like just the right moment, he stood, gestured to the musicians, and his girls glided onto the floor. Their dancing mesmerized and impassioned. When they finished, the audience sweated.

The warrior sitting next to Mekah stood up and stepped out onto the floor. An aid brought him two swords, and Markus immediately drew his own. No weapon came into the presence of the king except those of his guards.

Mekah rose gracefully to her feet, "My lord. There is no threat to your person. Kambroze, one of the Persian princes, is my guest." She motioned for him to continue.

He strapped the two swords on and bowed deeply before the king. When he withdrew the first sword, its beauty dazzled and it made a mesmerizing sound, as if made of light. He drew the second. The contrasting plainness startled the onlookers. The swords seemed the complete opposites of each other. He struck the plain dark one against his metal wristlet and it resounded with a deep "Doooom" as it sucked the sound out of the room.

Markus thought to himself, "*Does he have one of the singing swords? If so, then what is the other sword, and who is he, really?*"

Kambroze began his own dance, the dance of the two swords, equally wonderful and as full of acrobatics as all that had preceded it. Even more amazing, when he finished he had hardly broken a sweat. That impressed Markus as much as the swordplay. This Persian prince would be an extremely formidable opponent, if he ever became one.

Before the applause ended and Kambroze had a chance to sit back down, Janus stood to his feet again. "We have another special treat today. I have had the recent privilege of having the princess as a dance pupil, and tonight is her debut." He gestured towards the head table.

Salome stood, excused herself from her royal parents and took the floor. She gestured to the musicians herself. The exquisite music coupled beautifully with her simple and graceful dance. The music began to build majestically as did her movements of lithe gestures, bends, and astonishing leaps. Both the music and her dance crescendoed to a climax that left the audience speechless. As the final note faded and Salome folded fluidly into a kneeling posture before her father the king, the audience sat stunned and silent. Before anyone could regain enough composure to cheer or applaud, the king stood, deeply moved.

He spoke softly, yet commandingly, "Whatever you want, up to half of my kingdom. It's yours."

Salome looked at her mother, who looked at Mekah. Mekah nodded, Herodias nodded, and Salome spoke distinctly, so all could hear, "The head of John the Baptizer on a silver platter."

An audible gasp ran through the hall, even Herod could not speak. Tears began to form in his eyes, but because of his oath, he could not refuse her. He turned to Markus and barely whispered, "Bring me his head," and sat down.

Markus had to shake himself out of his own shock, but he turned and left the banquet room, gathering a couple guards and picking up the executioner along the way.

The musicians began playing something more subdued and the murmur of the people resumed, many noting the glee on Herodias' and Mekah's faces. Kambroze finished a whispered conversation with Mekah, then he too left the banquet.

As John conversed with Chayeem, he heard them coming. He knew what came with them. They stood at the door of his cell. John spoke from where he sat on his blankets, "I assume you have come for my head?"

Markus responded shocked, "How could you possibly know that?"

John simply pointed up. "Here, or somewhere else?"

"The execution chamber is just down the hall," replied Markus sadly.

John looked at the chains and shackles in Markus' soldier's hands. "You won't need those, I will go willingly."

Markus nodded permission to the guards. They unlocked his door, and they all walked to the execution room. In the middle of the room, well-lit with torchlights, stood the chopping block. One of the guards had grabbed a blanket. Almost reverently, he folded it, and lay it on the floor as a place for John to kneel.

"I should have taken the king up on his birthday dinner," John smiled. "I do have one request: that you, Markus, would dispatch me into the arms of Chayeem."

Tears filled Markus' eyes and he muttered, "I don't think I can do that."

John looked at him squarely, "Yes, you can," and knelt at the block. Another guard reached out and offered him a hood. "Not necessary." John embraced the block. As Markus lifted his sword, John said, "Too bad you don't have one of the singing swords." He even smiled, "I will greet Chayeem for you." He did not even close his eyes.

With a cry of anguish from his broken heart, Markus chopped off John's head.

They wrapped it in a towel, placed it on the platter which they had brought, and Markus dispatched a guard to return it to the king. He probably should have delivered it himself, but he wanted to properly take care of John's body. They staunched the blood flow from his neck before they lifted him to a linen-covered table. They wrapped him tightly, reverently, and carried him back to his cell. Markus then numbly dispatched a courier to John's disciples telling them they could come and collect the body.

Chapter 40
Crumbs and Cannots

Deeply exhausted, Jeshua, the disciples, and the women who traveled with them dragged themselves into the house and flopped down around the table. The women nearly stumbled into the kitchen hoping to prepare a simple meal. Philip entered last, as he had stopped to draw some water. At least they had that for starters. He filled their cups.

They had not used this house before, so hopefully they could stay hidden from the crowds until they could rest a little. The aroma of freshly baking bread soon spread through the room, bringing smiles to their fatigued faces.

Soon, Joanna brought a plate of steaming bread, "Be careful, it's fresh out of the oven." She set it in front of Jeshua. They all sat up, preparing to grab some, when Jeshua raised his hand. They stopped.

He picked up the plate and said, "Thank you, Father, for always providing for our needs, even for this daily bread." He set the plate back down, picked up some bread quickly and tore it in two. He then passed the plate. He would take his last.

Suddenly, they heard a knock at the door. Philip got up first to answer it, ushering a small foreign woman into the room. She appeared to be Greek, probably Syrophoenician.

She fell at Jeshua's feet and began weeping. Jeshua began to turn from the table to give her his attention, but heard, "*Wait,*" and paused, still facing the table.

She finally collected herself, wiped her eyes on her tunic and said, "Lord, son of David, have mercy on me. An evil spirit grievously torments my daughter," she cried.

One of the disciples, Judas, whispered, "Send her away, she's a foreigner."

Jeshua looked at Judas, but heard his Father, "*Say this.....*" and he responded to the woman, "I have been sent to the lost sheep of the house of Israel," while still looking at Judas.

"Please, Lord," she said as she began weeping again and touched his feet, "help her."

He heard, "*now this...*" and said, "It is not right to take the children's bread and give it to the dogs." And while not spoken harshly, even Judas appeared taken back by the rebuke.

She looked at him through her tears, "Yes, Lord, but the dogs will eat what little crumbs may fall from their master's table."

Jeshua sighed deeply, then smiled, satisfied. "Your faith is great, you have your request. Your daughter is delivered."

She bent over and kissed his foot. "Thank you, Lord," she scrambled to her feet, bowed to him, and left. Judas sat there shocked.

And Jeshua said to him "In a certain city lived a judge who neither feared God nor respected man. A widow came to him pleading, 'Give me justice over my adversary.' But he refused her. Regardless, she continued to come to him daily until he finally said to himself, 'Although I do not fear God nor respect man, I will give this woman justice, so she will quit bothering me with her persistent request.' Are you hearing what this judge said? Will not my Father grant justice speedily to those who cry to Him day and night?"

Judas looked down at the table as Jeshua continued, "Will I find faith when I come?" Judas looked up and mouthed the words,

"*Forgive me, I judged her wrongly,*" and Jeshua added, "People are not our enemy, but principalities, and powers."

The next morning after breaking their fast, while they still lounged around the table, Jeshua got to his feet, "Peter, James, and John with me." He strode out the door.

Surprised, the three of them jumped up without grabbing a cloak, a stick, or anything, and hurried out the door following him. The rest of them got up from the table bewildered, asking among themselves, "Should we follow him too?"

"Andrew, you and Bartholomew, follow them. Then send back Bartholomew to tell us the direction they've gone," said Philip. "The rest of us will catch up with you soon." Andrew rushed out the door, followed closely by Bartholomew. Philip stuck his head in the kitchen. "Jeshua, Peter, James and John have just rushed off somewhere. I'll send Bartholomew back to tell you where they've gone when I know more." He waited for a response from the ladies.

Joanna turned from the dishes, wiped her hands on a towel, walked over and kissed him on the forehead, like a child, "Thanks." She turned back around to rejoin Suzanna, who stood up to her elbows in dishwater, smiling. Philip still stood there, dumbfounded for a moment until he heard his name called from the other room, "Philip?"

Bartholomew had returned, panting heavily, "It appears the four of them have headed off into the mountains. Andrew is trying to follow them at a discrete distance. We will have to hurry to catch up."

They finally caught up with Andrew in the foothills of the mountains, and saw the beginnings of a crowd. "He wants us to stay here. He kept going and took Peter, James, and John with him." They settled in there in the foothills and waited. As the crowd grew in size, the disciples engaged in a question and answer time with them. They had been with Jeshua long enough that they could at least answer some of the inquiries. A mother brought a sick girl to them, carrying her in her arms. She set her at their feet. They all looked at one another.

Andrew stepped forward, "What seems to be the matter?" he asked.

"She has had a fever for days. Nothing seems to help." the mother said.

Andrew knelt down, laid his hand on her forehead, confirming that she did have a fever. He distinctly heard, "*Rebuke it.*" He looked around, but no one had said anything. He looked up, shrugged his shoulders, and said, "Fever, I rebuke you. Leave this girl!" The girl shuddered and her fever broke instantly. Her mother touched her forehead again, finding it cool now.

She picked up her daughter in her arms, "Thank you, thank you!" She turned and left them.

A young man brought his younger brother in his arms, set him down in front of them and said, "He is deaf and mute."

Philip stepped forward. "What's your name and how old is he?"

"My name is Judah and he's seven," the young man said.

"How long has he been like this?" Philip asked while he kept listening for that other voice.

Judah hung his head, "Ever since my father beat him a few years ago, he can no longer hear and has stopped speaking."

Philip heard, "*Forgiveness.*" "Judah, can you tell God that you forgive your father?"

The young man began to weep, knelt, and through his tears said, "God, I'm sorry I have held my father responsible for Jonathan's deafness....please forgive me." He was quiet a moment, took a deep breath, and continued. "Papa, I forgive you for hurting my brother."

"And Jonathan, can you do the same?" Philip continued.

Judah answered, "He can't hear you, he's deaf."

But Jonathan said, "God, I forgive my father, please forgive me, too."

Judah looked at Philip, at his brother, back to Philip, grabbed Jonathan and hugged him, then they both quickly hugged Philip and ran off excitedly.

A man came up behind them carrying his boy. "My son has seizures. Please deliver him! When the evil spirit comes upon him, it throws him to the ground, he shakes all over, foams at the mouth, and his pain is terrible."

Judas Iscariot stepped forward thinking, "*I've got this one.*" and said, "Let me have the lad." As soon as the boy lay in Judas' arms the boy had a fit. He flailed out of Judas' arms and fell to the ground. Judas shouted, "Come out of him, come out of him, you foul, unclean spirit," but the boy just writhed on the ground and kept screaming. Two of the other disciples tried to restrain him and it required all their might as he continued to writhe and scream. Quite a crowd formed around them. Finally the boy hit his head against a stone and knocked himself unconscious. His father picked him up and walked away, weeping. Judas looked at the others sideways thinking, "*How will I help lead the revolt if I can't even do this?*"

Jeshua, Peter, James, and John had neared the top of the mountain. "You three stay here while I go up a bit more and pray."

They did. He went up a little further, knelt, and began to pray. Suddenly his countenance and clothing changed. His face shone like the sun, his robe turned a dazzling white. The entire top of the mountain filled with glory and two other people joined him. Peter, James, and John wondered, "*Who are these two?*" They thought they heard Jeshua address them as Moses and Elijah. The three had a long conversation. When they finished, the three of them stood up. Moses and Elijah disappeared, Peter walked up to Jeshua and said, "This has been wonderful. We should build three tabernacles here, one for you, one for Moses, and one for Elijah." He looked for confirmation from Jeshua. As he said this, a cloud enveloped them all. Their sudden inability to see terrified the disciples, then a voice spoke from within the cloud, "This is My Beloved Son, listen to Him." When the voice stopped, the cloud dissipated, and they stood alone with Jeshua.

He told them that they should tell no one what they had seen until he had been raised from the dead. They just looked at one another, thinking, "*What on earth does that mean?*" As they came down from the mountain, they encountered the crowd and the man whose son had the seizures. He no longer had the boy in his arms.

"Master," and he began to weep, "my son suffers terribly. I came to your disciples, but they could not help us."

Jeshua responded, "This generation is crooked, with little faith. How long must I bear them, and be with them? Bring the boy to me." Tears shone in his eyes. As the man brought the boy to Jeshua, the demon took control of him, he escaped his father's arms, was dashed to the ground, and began to writhe in agony.

Jeshua rebuked the spirit, "Come out of him, and do not return!" With a loud wail the spirit came out, leaving the boy motionless on the ground.

Someone whispered, "He is dead."

Jeshua looked around and found the speaker, looked at him, knelt, and took the lad by the hand. The boy's eyes fluttered open, and Jeshua helped him to his feet. He then presented the boy whole to his father, who fell at Jeshua's feet with the child held tightly in his arms, and worshipped him.

When they got home, Judas asked him, "Why could I not cast it out? I said almost the very same words that you used!"

Jeshua responded, "It's not about the words. It is about listening and seeing what the Father is doing. You were unprepared. Sometimes you need to add fasting to your prayers and thereby sharpen your listening."

Chapter 41
My Name is Legion

As they walked alongside the lake back towards the town, Jeshua paused. He recognized some fishermen preparing their morning's catch for market. He asked if he could borrow their boat for a day. They felt privileged that he asked and enthusiastically said, "Yes!"

Jeshua said to the disciples, "Let's go across to the other side." So they left the multitude that followed them, piled in the boat, and headed out. Jeshua went to the stern of the boat where he found a cushion on the seat. He lay down, and fell quickly asleep. While he slept, the skies began to darken and before long a storm caught them. The winds blew, the waves grew, and it soon became so perilous that the disciples, even the seasoned fishermen, began to fear for their lives. Waves crashed into the boat filling it up faster than they could bail the water out.

Finally in despair Peter shook Jeshua awake. "Do you not care? We are going to perish!"

Jeshua shook his head to clear it from sleep and stood up. In a voice of command he said, "Wind, enough!' and it stopped immediately. "Sea, be still, be at peace." The disciples stared uncomprehendingly at the sudden complete calm. Jeshua looked at them, “Why were you afraid? Where is your faith?” Turning away, he lay back down on his cushion.

As they continued to bale out the remaining water, a different fear replaced their initial terror, one mixed with awe, Marveling, they murmured among themselves, “Who is this, that even the winds and the waves obey him?”

They reached the other side without further incident, landed the boat and stepped out onto the beach. There they faced a man from the tombs with an unclean spirit. No one could bind him, though often people had tried. They caught him, put him in chains and fetters, but he would just tear them apart or break them into pieces. This nameless man roamed the mountains, dwelt among the tombs, crying out, and cutting himself with stones.

Jeshua called the demon forth saying, “Come out of him.” but the spirit resisted.

The man fell at Jeshua’s feet and the demon said, “Jeshua, son of the most high God, why are you here? Have you come to torment me?”

Jeshua looked skyward and then commanded of him, “Who are you?”

And the spirit responded, “I am called Legion, for we are a multitude.” The demons began arguing among themselves, “If we leave we must wander amidst waterless places trying to find rest, but we will find none.”

Now a large heard of swine grazed on the nearby hill. While raising swine broke the Jewish Law, the Jews here had compromised their beliefs for economic reasons. Romans had no dietary prohibition against eating pigs. On the contrary, they paid handsomely for the opportunity. These Jews had established a thriving business raising, herding, slaughtering, and delivering swine to the Romans, unclean to themselves or not. Herders watched over about two thousand swine on this particular hill.

The demons perceived an answer to their dilemma and asked Jeshua, “Give us leave to enter into the swine.”

Jeshua answered, “I permit it.”

The demons left the man and entered the swine, driving them mad. The swine rushed down the steep bank into the sea and drowned. Most of the herders ran back into the town and told all the people what had happened. The furious townspeople went out to see the truth for themselves. They found Jeshua, his disciples, and the man who had been possessed. The disciples had pooled their clothing and given it to him so that he could clothe himself. He now sat next to Jeshua talking to him like a sane individual. The townspeople asked the herders who had stayed behind, "What happened?" They confirmed the story, as did all the dead swine floating in the bay. The peoples' fury turned to fear. They murmured among them selves, "What will we tell the Romans?" In the meantime they pleaded with Jeshua to leave them in peace.

"Yes, we will leave you," he said sadly, "but you will not have the peace you seek."

The formerly demon-possessed man earnestly pleaded with Jeshua that he be allowed to accompany them.

Jeshua smiled, "I have something better for you. I give you back to your friends and family. Tell them how much the Lord has done for you, about His great mercy and compassion."

Initially the man looked crestfallen as they pushed the boat back into the water and he had to say goodbye. However, as he stood watching from the shore, his heart began to gladden. He turned and headed home. His wife would regain her husband, his children their father. What greater mission could he have? Like Jeshua had asked of him, he would tell all he met of the great mercy and compassion of God, and of the freedom Jeshua had given him.

Chapter 42
Changing Her Name

When Ahlam returned from her impromptu meeting with Jeshua, she met privately with Janus and told him all that had transpired. His fondness for her bordered on that of a father's, and while he did not truly understand, he tried. She did not serve him as a slave, she worked for him as a free woman. His heart dropped when she told him she planned to leave. She wanted to start a new life. When he pointed out that she had only ever had this one occupation, she countered with hope. Not only that, she wanted to take Marie with her, which would nearly double his loss of income. He slowly shook his head, trying to come to terms with the loss in his mind, but his heart won out, and in the end he said, "Yes." He even gave her the substantial bonus that he had been squirreling away for this day. She cried in his arms for several minutes out of gratitude. She saw tears in his eyes too, as he finally broke her embrace and told her she must leave before he changed his mind.

Back at her lodgings, she woke Marie, told her a little of the story, but emphasized that they were leaving now. They had little that they wanted to take to their new life. They each quickly gathered their few things into a bundle, hoisted it over their shoulders, and left their old lives behind. They found an inn for the evening. After a meager supper, Ahlam spoke to Marie long into the evening explaining what had happened to her and trying to answer her questions.

In the morning, there he sat among the people, engaged in teaching them. Why did this always seem the most natural place to find him? Truth be told, everywhere he went seemed the most natural place for him to be. He seemed so comfortable being Jeshua. Ahlam held Marie's hand, tightly. Ahlam felt excited, Marie felt a bit afraid. What she feared she did not know, but something deep inside of her seem greatly troubled. What Ahlam had told her of him sounded wonderful. Marie felt something quite different inside. As they approached, Jeshua stopped teaching and stood up. The crowd stepped back. Ahlam's reputation still clung to her. Her near stoning had occurred only yesterday.

Jeshua held out his hands towards Ahlam, she dropped Marie's, and ran into his arms. He held her close, her head on his shoulder, stroking her hair. Some of those he had been teaching whispered to one another. He could hear their scathing words.

"Doesn't he know who she is?" they sneered.

He turned and looked at them sharply, but said lovingly, "I know exactly who she was, but is no longer." They reacted like he had snuffed out their candle or maybe more appropriately, like he had lit a candle in their dark places and suddenly they all could see. He took her chin in his hand, how familiar that felt, looked into her eyes, and stepped out of their embrace.

She gestured towards her friend saying simply, "This is Marie."

He heard distinctly, "*Mary,*" reached out his hand, and said, "Mary."

She blanched, nearly froze where she was. "My name is Marie," she corrected.

He had dropped his hand at her rebuke, but heard again, "*Take my hand.*" He raised his hand again, and said, "Mary, take my hand."

She started to scream at him, “My NAME is…” but found herself holding his hand. She looked down at it, up and into his eyes, bent over and began to retch. Not once, but seven times, each one longer, deeper, until the seventh one seemed to come from the very soles of her feet. Now she held his hand in both of hers, gasping for air. She finally quieted, looked up into his eyes again.

“Mary, they are gone. They are not permitted to return. You are free.” He whispered reassuringly. She felt wave after wave, after wave of something wonderful pour over her entire being. The crowd gasped when she crumpled to her knees, grasped his legs, and wept openly. He just stroked her hair until the sobs subsided.

She looked up at him, “May I follow you? I will go wherever you go!” The stark sincerity moved him deeply.

He looked off into the distance, as if he saw something, perhaps the future. “Yes, you most certainly may, but it will stretch the very boundaries of your heart.” He shared it, not as a warning, but rather as a profound truth.

She simply nodded and began to get up.

He smiled, “Come I will show you where we stay,” and held out one hand to her, one to Ahlam. They each took a hand and walked out of the courtyard, the disciples following him. Most of the crowd remained behind motionless.

PART SIX

Raising Their Dead

Chapter 43
My Daughter is Dying

Jairus ruled the synagogue and had for a number of years. People respected him for his piety, as well as for his scholarship. He taught because he loved the scriptures, loved people, and loved to share the scriptures with those people. His only child had recently turned twelve. Had she been a son, he would have prepared for his the coming of age ceremony, when boys were welcomed fully into manhood in the eyes of God and the community. Although only a girl, Jairus saw her quite differently. He saw her potential. While she could not attend synagogue school with the boys, he could teach her in the privacy of his own home, at night. So he did, and she equaled any boy he knew her age, except one.

Nearly twenty years ago, in the temple during Passover, he had seen a young man confound the scribes and Pharisees. His questions and answers had amazed them all. He had followed up on him and found that he was a twelve-year-old lad from Nazareth named Jeshua, the son of a carpenter. Now, that name emerged again. A new rabbi entered the scene, also named Jeshua. Coincidence or perhaps the lad had grown up? Some said this might even be the Promised One, the Christ, the Deliverer. He taught up and down the countryside, and stories said that God went with him to heal, the blind, the deaf, the lame, cured by a word, or a touch, or by seemingly nothing at all. Some people claimed he delivered them from evil spirits. Multitudes followed him everywhere he went. Jairus had hoped to meet him someday, but that possibility now seemed unlikely, especially once his daughter fell sick.

It had started with a fever, progressed into a general weakness, and now she just lay there wasting away. The physicians said they could do no more for her and they held out no hope for her recovery. They counseled him to pray. Then the thought occurred to him, "*What if what they are saying about Rabbi Jeshua is true and he can cure the sick?*" Immediately, Jairus left to find him. As usual, the town buzzed with the latest rumors and news about him. "*He is down by the seashore.*" He hurried in that direction.

When Jeshua and the disciples returned from the deliverance of the man with Legion, the multitude, as always, met them. As they walked along the sea, Jairus came and fell at Jeshua's feet.

"Rabbi, Rabbi, they say that you can cure the sick," Jairus began, almost weeping. "My little girl is dying. The doctors say there is no longer any hope, she will soon die, but if you come, lay your hands on her, she may be made whole once again and live." Now he wept openly.

Jeshua knelt down, lifted Jairus' head, and looked into his tear-stained eyes. "Come, let us go to her," and he helped him to his feet. The entire multitude turned like a school of fish and headed towards the town. He asked, "What is her name?"

Jairus regained some of his composure. "Her name is Judith," and a faint smile crossed his lips. "It means praise."

"Yes," Jeshua sighed and smiled, "and you will soon have much to praise about again," and he quickened his step a bit.

❖

Travail had filled Annah's last twelve years. She knew she neared the anniversary of the day she began to bleed, but she could not remember the exact day it had all began. It had started out as only a little bleeding, and she still had good days. Well, if she spoke the truth now, she would say she had bad days and worse days. She did not have much wealth, but she had spent all her meager savings trying to get well.

One physician had said, "Do this exercise three times each day, morning, noon, and night." Another, "Drink this potion first thing every morning." Another, "It is your diet, eat only vegetables." Another, "You need more red meat." And it went on and on and on, until she had wasted all her money on various cures still without relief. She had almost lost hope when she heard the rumors. A rabbi named Jeshua, wandered the countryside and people told amazing stories about him.

"I saw it," said one woman. "He put his hands over her ears, looked up to heaven, said something, and the woman could hear again."

Another, "I saw a blind man regain his sight."

"I heard a man with a withered hand had it restored whole, just like his other, by Jeshua."

The stories seemed almost too good to be true, but what if they were? What if he could help her? Unfortunately, the Law told her to stay away from people. A rabbi in particular would never touch her. Her bleeding made her unclean as well as anyone who touched her.

"I heard that a leper, named Simon, came to him, and said, 'If you will, you can make me clean.' And Jeshua reached out and touched him saying, 'If, Simon? Be clean!' And he was. His skin was restored completely like new," said another.

"*Then there is hope*," she thought.

"I heard he cured a centurion's slave with just a word," another whispered.

"*Then he doesn't even need to touch me. What if I touch him? Maybe if I just touch his cloak?*" Hope grew inside her. She found the crowd and followed. They headed to the home of Jairus, the synagogue ruler. His daughter lay dying, she heard. "*He's busy, I shouldn't bother him. He's helping someone else. Who am I that he should care about me?*" But she pushed those words aside in favor of her hope. "*It is said he has compassion on all, sinner and saint alike. I must at least try.*" She pressed onward. "*If I touch him I will be made whole,*" she told herself again and again. She could see him just ahead. She struggled to get closer. Finally, she got close enough. She reached out and touched the edge of his robe, stumbled, and fell to the ground. She felt it, something wonderful had just happened. Two paces ahead, Jeshua stopped.

He looked around, "Who touched me?" He did not accuse, he did not sound angry, just curious. He had felt the power, the virtue, go out from him and heard, "*Someone just touched you.*" He continued looking around. "Someone touched me."

The disciples laughed, "Master, with all the jostling around, in the middle of this crowd, everyone is touching you. Why are you asking who touched you?"

Jeshua replied, "No, this was different. I felt something different." And he turned around and finally saw the woman trembling on the ground, terrified, knowing what had just happened.

She crawled to his feet, head down, and confessed, "I touched you." She thought, afraid, *"Maybe he will take it back. Who am I?"*

He knelt down, raised her face to his, "Daughter, your faith has cured you. You may go in peace, knowing you have been made whole from that which plagued you all these years." And he kissed the top of her head, and began to stand.

At that very moment, one of Jairus' servants approached them. He whispered to Jairus who stood anxiously while Jeshua talked to this woman on the ground. "Your daughter has died. It is too late." He looked at Jeshua. "You can let him go, go about his other business." Jairus nearly crumpled to the ground.

Hearing the whisper, Jeshua finished standing, turned around, and spoke to Jairus, "You have no need to be afraid, only believe."

Jairus initially thought, "*What, my daughter just died? This was all for nothing.*" But he clung to Jeshua's words and hoped regardless.

Jeshua spoke to his disciples, "Peter, James and John with me, the rest of you, keep the crowd here." He put his arm around Jairus and herded him towards his home. Peter, James, and John looked at each other and then followed him. The rest of the disciples held the crowd at bay.

They quickly completed the short distance to Jairus' home, where they walked into utter chaos. People wept, wailed, and exhibited great distress. The ruler of the synagogue's daughter had died.

Not taking heed of the tumult, Jeshua entered the house and strongly declared, "Why are you weeping? The girl is not dead, she is only sleeping."

Those present knew she had died. Their weeping turned to hysterical laughter. One even said, "She's dead, you fool, his daughter is dead!" Their laughter increased, but he continued undeterred.

He turned to Peter, James, and John. "Put everyone out of the house except Jairus and his wife."

The disciples began doing just that, much to the chagrin of some.

"Who does he think he is?"

"We have a right to be here."

"Take your hands off me."

The crowd finally gone, the six of them went into the room where the child lay. Five of them stopped near the doorway, Jairus holding his wife, the two of them silently weeping, trying to comfort one another. Jeshua continued forward and knelt beside the bed, took her limp hand in his, leaned over her, and quietly whispered. "My Judith. My little one, it is time to get up." And he waited. He said nothing more. Her eyes fluttered open, she looked him in the eyes, and smiled. He put his other hand underneath her, "Little one, you've been asleep. It's time to get up, Pappi is here." He helped her sit up.

She took a deep breath, stretched, shook the sleep from her eyes, and finally turned to her father. "Pappi," she whispered, as Jeshua helped her to her feet. "I just had the most wonderful dream." And she ran to embrace him.

Jeshua looked at her parents, "Let's keep what just happened here between us, please?" Her parents shook their heads in assent. "Oh, you should probably give her something to eat," he smiled, "she will be famished. Her dream was quite exciting, and exhausting." He winked.

Jairus released Judith and his wife, and dropped to one knee in front of Jeshua. He reached down and took Jairus' hands in both of his own. Jairus bowed his head, "How can I ever thank you?"

Jeshua lifted their entwined hands, which brought Jairus' head up too, "Seeing you together," and he looked at Judith and her mother also, "is thanks enough." He let Jairus' hands go, and turned to his disciples, "My friends, shall we." They walked out of the room and back into another kind of chaos.

Chapter 44
Breaking Up the Procession

The multitude outside of Jairus' home hummed with anticipation, speculations, and questions. The weeping and wailing had ceased. So what had happened? Jeshua, however, walked through them like nothing of consequence had occurred, though he smiled from ear to ear. Peter, James, and John followed, a bit bewildered. "*What had they just seen? Was she dead, had she only been asleep? We have a lot of questions.*" Those would have to wait until later.

Mathiah had always been a wonderful son, " *I miss him so...*" Pricilla thought as they walked along. He had never caused any trouble growing up, not even during the turbulent teen years. He had such a heart to serve others, kept good company, and was so thoughtful and conscientious. His father beamed with pride when Mathiah began his full instruction into all the duties of the office of priest. Then tragedy struck. In what seemed like an accident, she had lost her husband. "He was simply in the wrong place, at the wrong time. He tried to stop a robbery, and they killed him." They had never apprehended the robbers.

She had hardly completed her year of mourning and now her son, her precious only son, had left her too. "*What is there left to live for?*" she thought as she trudged behind those carrying the bier. A quick, virulent disease struck him down. He had so much potential, but had not married yet. She would never hold any grandchildren, all hope wiped out, like a snuffed candle. Her despair hung about her like a cloud. She looked behind her at all those in the procession, many of his friends, a few family members, how could they understand her pain? She kept on, putting one foot in front of the other. At least she could make it through this day. She would worry about tomorrow, tomorrow.

Jeshua and his disciples, and the few women who traveled with them walked along the road through some of the nicest pasture land around, approaching the small town of Nain. The beautiful sunlit day energized their spirits. They cheerfully conversed as they strolled along the road. A large crowd followed them, but Jeshua and Mary from Magdala kept a few paces out in front of them all.

Mary had just asked Jeshua a question, when he heard, "*Look, up ahead.*" It seemed almost as if the Father pointed as they came to the crest of a small hill. A large funeral procession from the city climbed up the other side of the hill. Behind the priest, he saw six young men carrying the bier, followed by a single woman, and a large contingency of likely friends and family. He heard more, "*She is a widow, that is her only son.*" He felt a nearly incapacitating sadness. The crowd following him moved to the side of the road to let the procession pass. As it did, he joined the widow, under a familiar compulsion. Initially, she turned with shock, until she looked into his eyes, and hers filled with tears again.

He put his arm around her shoulder, she put her head on his, as they walked along. "Mother, there is no need to weep." She started to react when a flood of peace and strength overwhelmed her. He let go of her and quickened his pace to join those carrying the bier, while those behind began to murmur, "What is this? Who is he?"

When he got to the front, he turned around, standing in their way. They had to stop or run over him. When they halted, he reached up, touched the bier, and looked upward. A wave of silence swept over the procession and the crowd that followed him. The bearers looked at one another, but before any of them could speak, Jeshua broke the silence.

"Mathiah, are you listening? Rise." and he smiled.

The young man blinked, opened his eyes, sat up, and said, "Yes, what can I do for you?" In shock the bearers just stood there.

Jeshua reached up, offering him a hand, "Come down, join your mother, and re-brighten her life."

Mathiah practically leapt off the bier, grinning from ear to ear. "With pleasure," he replied. That broke up the procession. Everyone gathered around them. Jeshua and the disciples left them and walked on to the town. Many of the procession joined them.

"Who is this man?"

"They say his name is Jeshua, from Nazareth."

"And he raises the dead?"

"So it would appear."

"God is surely with him."

"He must be a prophet, like those of old."

"It is like God Himself has shown up, doing wonders."

And his fame spread even more through out all the countryside.

Jeshua turned to Mary, "What again was your question?" Through tears of joy at what had just transpired she repeated the question from moments before. It did not really seem that important any more. She smiled as he launched into his answer. It seemed important to him.

Chapter 45
More Than Just Friends

As they traveled through Bethany a certain woman named Martha stopped him. She had heard much about him, and seeing him walking her roads had asked a bystander to confirm, "Who is that man, the one who the crowd is following?"

The woman had seemed astonished, "You don't know? That is Rabbi Jeshua. I thought the whole world knew about him."

She had thanked the woman, then run on ahead, taking a short-cut, and got in front of him and the crowd. As he came around a corner, she had stepped out in front of him and knelt, "Rabbi Jeshua."

He stopped, lifted her to her feet, "Yes?" and heard, "*Go with her.*"

"My name is Martha. You would be doing me a great honor if you would have supper at my house," she said as she bowed her head again.

He smiled, "There are sixteen of us."

She gulped, but continued, "That would be fine."

He lifted her head, "Then, lead the way." He turned to the disciples and explained, "Martha has offered us supper," as off she went. He quickly caught up to her side. "So, why have you asked us to supper?"

She blushed, "I have heard much about you. I suppose I wanted to know if it is really true."

He smiled again. He enjoyed this, "And what have you heard?"

"That you do miracles, that God is with you. Is that true?" she replied.

"Yes," he replied simply.

She looked up at him, "Which?"

"They are the same thing." Then he asked, "What else have you heard?"

There conversation came easily and caught her attention so thoroughly that she almost missed the turn onto her road. "Oh," she said somewhat startled, "We're here." They turned, walked a short way further, then entered a beautiful, flowered courtyard. "Please, give me a moment to prepare. I wasn't sure that you would come." She left them there and entered the house.

Most of them sat on benches around a brick patio, but Jeshua remained standing, turned, and announced, still smiling, "This is going to be fun."

They laughed. "*More fun?*" They thought, "h*e is always full of surprises.*"

Martha returned a few minutes later, "Please, be welcomed into our home," and ushered them in.

She left them with her sister, who introduced herself. "I am Mary. Welcome. These are our servants, James, Chleo," and she stepped behind them, "and Anna, who will escort you to the dining room."

Jeshua entered first. James washed his feet, Chleo anointed his head with fragrant oil, Mary embraced him, kissing him on each cheek, and Anna led him into the next room, where a fourth servant had water for him to wash his hands. He did so, drying them on a towel provided by a fifth servant. Then he reclined at the table. When they all assembled around the table, Mary joined them at Jeshua's feet, reclining between him and Mary from Magdala. Jeshua began speaking about one of the stories he had been sharing about the kingdom of God earlier in the day as they had been walking.

John asked, “I’m not sure I understand what you meant when you said that, ‘the kingdom must suffer violence, and the violent must take it by force.’ Are you saying that we should be prepared for a battle?”

Jeshua appeared to think for a moment, then responded, “The world will hate you because it has hated me. That is true. However, in this comparison I meant to imply that some will find the kingdom only if they diligently strive to find it with violent fervor. As Jeremiah said, ‘You will seek me and find me when you seek me with all your heart.’”

Every once in a while Martha would poke her head into the dining room, give Mary a look, and then scurry back out. Mary continued to sit at Jeshua’s feet taking everything in. Finally, Martha could take it no longer. She marched into the dining room, up to Jeshua, bent down, and spoke in a whisper loud enough for all to hear, “Lord, don’t you care that Mary has left me to prepare and serve this supper alone? Tell her to get up and help me!”

Jeshua pulled Martha gently down to her knees beside him, “Martha, Martha, you are anxious and troubled about so many things. There will always be a lot of things, but only one thing which is really necessary, and Mary has chosen it. I will not take it away from her. Besides, we are in no hurry. We are just grateful for your hospitality. Thank you.”

It took a moment for the words to sink in, but when they did, her countenance changed. “Oh,” she paused, took a deep breath, “You’re welcome,” and got to her feet smiling, “and thank you.”

Jeshua responded, “And you’re welcome.” He looked at Mary and nodded towards the kitchen. She smiled, got up, and followed her sister into the kitchen. Just then, the two women’s brother, Lazarus, joined them. He walked around the table and sincerely greeted each guest, stopping last at Jeshua. “May I join you?” And he motioned to the empty cushion next to him.

"It is your house, Lazarus," Jeshua smiled. "Yes, I would be pleased if you sat here, next to me."

"I'm sorry that I am late, but I'm sure my sisters are taking good care of you," Lazarus sounded a little worried about the response.

"Ah, we are being treated like kings and princes." Then Jeshua looked towards the women who traveled with them and chuckled, "and queens and princesses. Thank you."

"The weight of the responsibilities of my business sometimes consume me," Lazarus added apologetically.

Mary and Martha entered with hot bread and soup, set it at the head of the table and paused. Lazarus gestured towards Jeshua, "Rabbi?"

Jeshua proceeded to sing the Aaronic blessing in his deep baritone voice.

> "The Lord bless you and keep you;
> the Lord make His face to shine upon
> you
> and be gracious to you;
> the Lord lift up His countenance upon
> you and give you His peace."

When he finished, a few wiped away tears, as Peter said, "Pass the bread, please." Jeshua picked it up, broke the loaf and passed it with the soup and ladle as well. Thus began a great friendship. Whenever possible, Jeshua and the disciples would spend time with Lazarus and his sisters in Bethany.

Months later, Jeshua and the disciples walked along a road in the midst of a crowd as usual, when James, the servant of Mary and Martha, approached them at a run.

He paused a moment to catch his breath, "Master, the one you love is sick." James sounded extremely distraught.

Jeshua stopped for a moment, listening, then replied, "His sickness is not unto death. Rather it is for the glory of God, that the Son of God might be glorified in it."

"So then, you will come quickly?" James still panted.

"You may go, and tell them what I have said." Concern etched Jeshua's face.

"Thank you," and off he ran.

Jeshua stayed away for two more days, even though he loved Martha, Mary, and Lazarus. Then he said to his disciples, "It is time, let us go to Judea again."

They tried to protest, "Rabbi, they want to stone you there. Why should we go back?"

But he answered them, "There are only twelve hours in the day when it is light enough to work and not stumble. If you try and work outside at night, you will trip over something and fall on your face." Then he said, "Our friend, Lazarus, has fallen asleep, and I go that I might wake him."

Peter said, "If he's fallen asleep, he will wake up without us." He did not realize that Jeshua spoke about Lazarus being dead. They thought he was just taking a nap.

Then Jeshua said plainly, "Lazarus is dead, and I am glad for your sakes that I was not there when it happened, but now I go to him."

Thomas said to the others, "Let us go with him. If we die, at least we all die together."

On the fourth day after Lazarus' death they approached Bethany. Because of the short thirty-minute walk from Jerusalem, many of the Jews had come to console Mary and Martha concerning their brother's death. When they heard news of Jeshua's arrival, Mary stayed at home, but Martha ran to meet him.

She knelt and grasped him around the knees, "My Lord, if you would have been here, my brother would not have died. Yet even now, I know God will do whatever you ask of him."

He placed a hand on her head, "Your brother will live again."

She began to weep, "I know that he will rise again in the resurrection, at the last day."

He put his other hand on her head, "I am the resurrection, and the life. Whoever believes in me, though he die, will yet live, and he who believes in me will never die. Do you believe this?"

She raised her tear-filled eyes and looked into his, "Yes, I believe that you are the One who is to come, our Messiah, the Son of God."

He helped her to her feet, "Go and fetch your sister."

She went back to the house, found her sister privately, and said, "He is here and he is calling for you."

Mary quickly got up and ran to where he waited, still outside the village where Martha had left him. When the Jews who had come to provide her some level of comfort saw her leave, they thought she went to the tomb to weep, and followed her. When Mary found Jeshua, she too fell at his feet. Weeping, she repeated what her sister had said, "Lord, my Lord, if you would have been here, my brother would not have died."

Jeshua looked at her, still weeping at his feet, and saw the Jews who had followed her also weeping. For a moment Death seemed all pervasive, blocking out everything. He heard nothing, nothing at all, just the emptiness of death. It moved him deeply and troubled his spirit. Then finally, he heard, "*Go to the tomb,*" and asked Mary, "Where have you buried him?"

She got up, and through her tears replied, "I will take you there," and she took his hand. Before she could drag him there, Jeshua began to weep himself.

Some of those standing by said, "See how much he loved him." Others said, "He opened the eyes of the blind, the ears of the deaf, cured the lame and the infirm, could he not have saved Lazareth's life also?" When they got to the tomb, Lazareth lay in a cave, covered by a large stone. It struck him deeply to the core as a similar image flashed across his mind.

He took a slow deep breath, "Remove the stone."

Martha replied, "My Lord, he has been dead four days, there will be quite a stench."

He looked her squarely in the eyes, "Did I not tell you that if you believed, you would see the glory of God?"

She spoke to her servant, "James, roll away the stone." He looked questioningly at Mary, who nodded in agreement. He and a couple of his friends grasped the stone, and put their backs into it. It moved an inch in its track, another, and then they rolled it up the small slope, and braced it.

Jeshua pulled back the head of his robe, looked to the heavens, and said, "Father, I thank you that you have heard me. I know that you always do, but for the sake of those standing here, I have spoken out loud, that they may believe that You sent me." Then he cried out loudly, "Lazarus,… come forth!" It seemed as time stood still, then Lazarus shuffled out of the cave, his hands and feet still bound, his face obscured by a cloth. In a softer voice, "Unbind him, he is free." They did so while Mary, Martha, and the crowd engulfed him. They smelled not even a trace of a stench on him. Rather as they embraced him, kissed him, wept over him, all they could smell was a fresh spring day, just after a light rain.

Jeshua stood to the side alone. He looked to the left of the tomb. In the shadow of the rock stood the dark Angel of Death, his fists clenched at his sides. The dark angel muttered, "You have not seen the last of me, you imposter."

To the right stood a familiar old man smiling. Uriel drew his sword and cut the air with a note of purest beauty and the dark angel vanished. It seemed as though the note had stopped time. Uriel sheathed the sword, the note dissipated, and time began again.

Uriel stepped to Jeshua's side, placed a hand on his shoulder, "Well done, again," and then walked away. Jeshua walked through the crowd to Lazarus' side, put a hand on his shoulder, and Lazarus turned his head toward him. Jeshua asked, "A little celebration?" and they all headed off to Lazarus' house.

Many of the Jews who saw Jeshua raise Lazarus from the dead believed in him, but others went to the Pharisees and told them what Jeshua had done. The priests and Pharisees gathered together and considered how they could destroy him, and Lazarus too. "If we do not act soon, all will believe in him, and the Romans will take away all that we have." The word then spread that they searched for someone to help them find him, that they might arrest him.

PART SEVEN

His Last Passover

Chapter 46
Another Anointing

Passover quickly approached. Pilgrims flooded into Jerusalem and the surrounding towns from all over the country. Guests filled Mary, Martha, and Lazarus' home in Bethany for the evening, so Jeshua and the disciples ate dinner at Simon the Leper's.

Leprosy, a completely debilitating skin disease, eventually resulted in the afflicted individual losing parts of their body. Not only that, but the Law labeled the person "unclean" and ordered them quarantined, isolated away from everyone, all the time. When Jeshua healed Simon, it cleansed his entire life from the inside out. Now, he and all that he owned had been made clean. He could welcome his friends and family into his newly cleansed home. Together they enjoyed a wonderful, while not lavish, supper.

Mary had walked out of the room and returned with an alabaster jar of ointment, pure nard. She stepped up to Jeshua's back as he still reclined at the table, broke open the jar and poured it over his head, massaging it into his hair. Its fragrance filled the room.

Judas indignantly said under his breath, "What a waste!" then louder to Jeshua, "You know that perfume could have been sold for nearly a year's wages? We could have given the money to the poor!"

he huffed. He did not say that because he cared about the poor, but because he had responsibility for and authority over their finances. As the keeper of the money pouch, he had begun skimming off of their funds, setting money aside to start the rebellion.

Jeshua replied, "You will always have the poor among you."

"Yes, but, Lord?…" Judas continued his question when Jeshua interrupted him.

"Leave her alone!" he said abruptly. "She has done something wonderful to me. She has anointed me before my burial. You will not always have me with you."

All the disciples looked at one another, "*What?*"

Jeshua continued, "I tell you a solemn truth, whenever and wherever the good news is proclaimed throughout the entire world, this story will be told about Mary, remembering what she just did for me."

Still indignant, Judas stormed out of Simon's house and into the road.

Now, the Pharisees and priests had long looked for a way to get Jeshua into their hands and arrest him. Judas went to them with a proposition, "What will you give me if I deliver him to you?" He thought, "*The rebellion fund is almost complete, and if I can force Jeshua into taking some political action beyond just cleansing the temple it might be the spark to start the rebellion against the Romans.*"

The chief priests responded, "We will give you thirty pieces of silver if you deliver him into our hands." From that moment on he looked for the right opportunity to betray him. When he got back to Simon's he found that they had all left for their lodgings. He hurriedly caught up with them.

When he did, Peter asked him privately, "Where did you go?"

He replied, "The whole thing with the perfume made me angry. I took a walk to cool off. I'm okay now."

Peter raised his eyebrows, but took him at his word.

Chapter 47
Entering the Gates with Praise

With Passover nearly upon them, their home had already filled up with out-of-town guests. Finally, they had a rare moment alone, lounging around the breakfast table as one of the slaves finished the morning dishes. They heard a knock at the front door.

Lydia called out, "I've got it," and walked to the door, followed closely by her husband, Isaac. When they opened it, a very fit looking older man greeted them.

"I'm sorry. We are nearly at capacity already. Would you mind sharing a room with some others?" Isaac asked politely.

The visitor stretched out his hand in greeting, "My name is Uriel, I'm not here for a room."

Isaac grasped his arm in the Roman fashion. "Then what can I do for you?"

Uriel smiled his disarming smile, "I have a rather strange request."

Isaac smiled in return, "It won't hurt to ask."

Uriel began, "You have a young donkey that no one has ever ridden?"

Isaac answered in surprise, "Yes, I do."

Uriel continued, "I would like you to go get him, tie him to the post here at the front door, and at about the third hour this morning, two men will show up to borrow him."

Even more surprised, "You're not serious, are you?"

Uriel's smile broadened, if it could, "Yes, I'm being quite serious. You don't have anything to worry about. You will get him back unharmed. When they show up and start to untie him, you can ask them what they think they are doing, and they will tell you, 'The Lord has need of him.' You can safely entrust your colt into their care."

Isaac reacted, "And why on earth should I do this?"

Uriel's tone turned somber, "Because the Lord really does need him, and you will be a part of something more wonderful than you could possibly imagine: the entrance of the King of Glory into Jerusalem." Then, before their eyes, he disappeared.

They looked at one another in astonishment and Isaac bolted through the door, saying over his shoulder, "I'll go get the colt."

Jeshua, the disciples, and the women had finished up their breakfast when Jeshua stood up. "I have a bit of a strange request of you this morning." They all began looking at one another, thinking, "*This should be interesting.*"

"Well, especially Philip and Andrew." he continued, and the two of them thought, "*Here we go again.*" Jeshua turned to them, "On our way to Jerusalem, I will ask you to go into a certain village. Next to the front door of one of the houses you will find a young donkey tethered, on which no one has ever ridden. You will untie it and bring it to me."

Philip piped up, "And if someone asks us what we are doing stealing their donkey?"

Jeshua smiled, "Oh. You will just be borrowing it, but you can tell them 'The Lord has need of it,' and they won't stop you."

Andrew spoke, "You're sure that they won't try to stop us?"

"No, they will happily let you borrow it." He, still smiling, treated it like a practical joke or something.

Andrew did not look convinced, "Just like that?"

"Yup, just like that," he said.

"Well, I guess if you say so," Philip seemed on board with the idea. "Then what?"

"You'll bring the colt back to me and I will ride him into Jerusalem," he answered. And that settled the matter. They finished cleaning up from breakfast, grabbed their cloaks, and headed out to Jerusalem. As they approached one of the villages, Jeshua said to Philip and Andrew, "Okay, we will wait for you here," and off they went. Sure enough, they found it exactly as he had said. A young donkey stood tethered in front of one of the houses.

As they began to untie it, a man stepped out of the house and asked them, "What do you think you are doing?"

They looked at one another, then back at the man, and said, "The Lord has need of it?"

The man responded, "Ahhh," smiled, "bless you then," and let them take it.

They brought the colt back to Jeshua, then the disciples spread their cloaks over it, and Jeshua sat upon it. They led the donkey all the way to Jerusalem. As they came down from the Mount of Olives, they encountered the multitude entering Jerusalem for the celebration. Many already rejoiced, singing the Songs of Ascent. When they recognized Jeshua, they turned their praises to God for all the mighty works that Jeshua had done: healing the sick, delivering the oppressed, giving sight to the blind, hearing to the deaf, voice to the mute, making the lame to walk, even raising the dead. Some even threw their garments on the road in front of him or cut branches from the palm trees and placed them on the road too, calling out in loud voices, "Blessed is the King, coming in the name of the Lord, bringing peace, and the glory of the heavens to earth." Some of the Pharisees in the crowd heard them proclaim him king and shouted to Jeshua, "Stop them, stop them! You will get us into trouble with the Romans!" but Jeshua answered, "If they cease their praise, the very rocks would cry out in their place."

As Jeshua drew near the city he began to weep, "O Jerusalem, Jerusalem, if you had only fully embraced this day and these things that are the makings of peace. Unfortunately, they are hidden from your eyes, and because of that, the days are coming when your enemies will surround you, pressing in from every side. They will tear you down to the ground, you and your children with you. They will not leave one stone unturned, because you missed the day of your visitation." He entered the temple, looked around, seeing everything once again. "Andrew and Philip, I need your belts." They removed the ropes that they used for belts as he removed his own. He braided the three of them into what resembled a whip and began to drive out the money changers once again. "Begone, you thieves, you robbers! You still do not believe that my house is to be a house of prayer for all of the nations!" This time he let the animals remain. They had not chosen their lot.

When he finished, he gave Andrew and Philip back their belts, and told them to return the donkey they had borrowed, which they did. He then went back to the courtyard steps and began teaching. The chief priests and scribes who sought to destroy him could do nothing, as the people had flocked around him and hung on his every word.

Finally, they could stand it no longer. One of the elders stood up, "By what authority do you do these things? Who gave you the right to do this?" and he gestured to the tables empty of the money changers.

Jeshua got up from the steps, looked up briefly, took a step, and stood before them, "I will ask you a question, only one question. If you answer it, then I will gladly answer yours. Was the baptism of John from heaven or from men? What do you say?"

The priests, scribes, and elders turned to one another and began arguing among themselves, "If we say John's baptism was from heaven, he will say, 'Then why did you not believe him?' But if we say it was from men, the people will stone us. They consider John a prophet." So they answered him, "We do not know."

Jeshua smiled at them, "Well, since you have not answered my question, then I will not tell you by whose authority I do what I do!"

Incensed, the priests, scribes, and elders turned, in mass, and left the courtyard.

Jeshua continued teaching until the evening and then he, the disciples, and the women who travelled with him, left and returned to Bethany.

Chapter 48
One Final Passover Supper

Judas Iscariot had slipped out of the house early that morning and met with the chief priests. "I don't know where we will celebrate the Passover meal, but I think I know where we will go afterwards. I will come and lead you to him." They gave him a down payment on the thirty pieces of silver that they had agreed upon. He thought to himself, "*His arrest will surely cause the uprising we desire. Then we can overthrow these oppressors!*" When he returned to the house, the rest reclined at breakfast.

Judas sat next to Peter, who whispered, "Where have you been?"

He lied, "I went out to pray. I believe that the time to rise up against the Romans is near. We must be mentally and spiritually prepared to fight."

Simon the Zealot, sitting on his other side, heard him, "What uprising is this?" He too looked for the overthrow of Rome and the rightful return of Israel's rule to the Jews.

Judas just smiled, "Watch and see. I believe the revolt will begin tonight."

❖

Thaddeus had just finished his breakfast when he heard a knock at the door. His servant who still collected the dishes looked at him. He smiled, and raised his hand, "That's okay, I'll get it." He went to the door, which he opened to encounter a fit looking older man.

"Good morning, my name is Uriel, and I have a rather unusual request of you."

He carried himself with such an aura of tremendous authority that Thaddeus instinctively straightened his robe and replied formally. "How can I help you?"

"You have a guest room, an upper room?" Uriel asked.

"Why, as a matter of fact, I do?" stammered Thaddeus.

"And it is unoccupied this evening?" Uriel continued.

"It is." Thaddeus still did not comprehend.

"My Master would like to use it this evening for the Passover meal. Would that be okay?" He asked with so much authority and yet it still seemed like a request.

"And who is your master?" His incredulity subsided as the conversation continued.

"His name is Jeshua," spoke Uriel, reverently.

The awe returned. "Jeshua, the Rabbi, under my roof?"

Uriel did have such a disarming smile, "If you would be so kind."

"It would be my pleasure," said Thaddeus genuinely.

"Take a pitcher to the well and fill it with water. Two of his disciples will follow you home and ask if their Master may use your upper room this evening for their Passover meal."

"Is there some reason not to just send my servant?" he asked.

Uriel's smile deepened. "I think you will enjoy the adventure," he replied.

Amidst his incredulity, "When should I leave?"

Uriel chuckled, "In about an hour," and disappeared.

Thaddeus did not think he could have experienced any deeper awe, but when Uriel simply disappeared from standing right in front of him, he almost fainted.

He heard his wife call from the other room, "Who was at the door, dear?"

He stumbled to the bedroom, "You are not going to believe this."

❖

They finished with their breakfast and lounged around the table, as they liked to do. They had cleared their plates and refilled their cups, and Philip went to the kitchen to help the women with the dishes.

Nathaniel asked, "Master, will we be celebrating the Passover meal here tonight?"

Jeshua looked up, as though he was listening, thinking, or both, and responded, "Peter and John, I would like for you to prepare for the Passover."

They looked at each other, and John asked, "Here, Master?"

He chuckled, "No, I have a bit of a quest for you." They looked at each other again. Peter raised his eyebrows. "I saw that, Peter," Jeshua continued. "The instructions for this quest are pretty simple. Go into the city. On your way, you will meet a man carrying a pitcher of water. He will not look like a servant, because he isn't. Follow him to his house. When you get there, tell him, 'The Master has need of your guest chamber. He and his disciples desire to eat their Passover meal there.' He will show you to a furnished upper room where you can make the final preparations for our arrival, later."

They looked at each other, like, "*Here we go again,*"shrugged and said, virtually in chorus, "Yes, Lord," and got up from the table. They grabbed their cloaks, left for the city, when they arrived, they found it just as he had said. Thaddeus had furnished the room for them. They made the rest of the necessary preparations. When the time came, Jeshua and his disciples arrived and found everything ready.

"You have no idea how I have longed to celebrate this Passover with you." Jeshua began, "before my suffering." Often during this last week he had mentioned his death in Jerusalem, but they had not understood him. They just looked questioningly at each other as he said it again. "I will not drink of the fruit of the vine again until I drink with you in the kingdom of heaven."

"*Ah, he is preparing us for the beginning of the revolt,*" thought Judas. "*He is about to establish the kingdom of heaven on earth,*" and he smiled slyly.

Jeshua realized that the Father had given everything into his hands that he would need for these next few days, that the Father loved him, and that soon he would be returning to Him. He took the bread after supper, and said, "One of you will betray me."

"*What?*" they all thought as they looked at each other, many of them thinking, "*surely it is not me, is it?*"

John leaned over and whispered to Jeshua, "Who is it?"

Jeshua turned to him, "The one to whom I give this bread." He dipped it in the soup and gave it to Judas, saying, "Go and do what you have to do, and do it quickly."

Judas received the bread, and the Accuser fully entered him. He got up. He caught Simon the Zealot's eye, winked, and nodded as he left the table. He said to himself, "*For all of time, I will be remembered as the one who set the wheels of the rebellion in motion.*" He went quickly to meet with the chief priests.

Simon the Zealot started to rise and go with him, but Jeshua caught his eye, and shook his head "*No!*" Simon sat back down. Since the formal celebration of the Passover meal had ended, the women joined the men at the table.

An untouched loaf of bread sat on the table. Jeshua took it, raised the bread, broke it, blessed it, and said, "I want each of you to take a piece and eat it, for this is my body which is broken for you." He passed half of the loaf to the right and half of the loaf to the left. He continued, "Do this to remember me." They each took a piece and ate it, but looked at one another with confused expressions. One cup at the table had not been touched during the Passover meal, the cup at the place set for Elijah, The ancient writings promised the return of Elijah, so this cup symbolized future redemption. It heralded the coming of the Messiah and the Kingdom of Heaven. Jeshua reached over and took Elijah's cup. He raised it, blessed it, and said, "This cup is my blood, the blood of the new covenant, shed for you and for many, for the remission of your sins. Each of you, drink of it also," and he passed the cup around the table. They all took a drink, as a sadness, a seriousness, and a deep awe descended on them. He completed this time with, "I will not drink of the fruit of the vine again, until I drink it anew with you in my Father's kingdom." The holiness of this moment gripped them all.

Then Jeshua stood and began to sing, in his deep baritone voice, and the very atmosphere changed as he did.

> "I lifted up my eyes to the hills and asked, 'Where does my help come from?'
> My help comes from the Lord, it is He who made the heavens and earth.
> He will not let my foot be moved; for He neither sleeps nor slumbers,
> but is the sustainer of all of His chosen ones.
> The Lord is my guard and protector; He shades me from the heat of the sun
> during the day and the full moon at night.
> The Lord will keep me from all evil and the evil one;
> He will fill me with the breath of life itself (Chayeem is His name)
> He will be with me wherever I go, there is no place that I can go where He will not be with me from this very moment and forevermore."

When he finished, they all seemed refreshed, and he said, "Come, let us go to the Mount of Olives." They stood with him and left the women to finish cleaning up.

Chapter 49
Captured in the Garden

Early that morning, Herod sent for his most trusted centurion. "Markus, the rumors are many. This Passover may be the most difficult we have ever faced. I am going to assign you and your men to the temple, to work in concert with the Pharisees, the high priests, and the temple guards to assure that order is kept. I have information that a revolt is planned, the popularity of the Rabbi Jeshua is at an all time high. Thousands greeted him just the other day as a king, when he rode into Jerusalem on a donkey. He drove the money changers out of the temple again. Things are getting out of hand."

Markus still stood at attention, "You can count on me, Your Majesty, but I would be surprised if the Rabbi Jeshua is involved in any kind of revolt."

Herod responded abruptly, "You can be surprised all you want, but since the death of John the Baptizer, things have been a powder keg just waiting for the right match to be struck. My information says he's the match."

"Yes, my lord." Herod's paranoia left no room for discussion. "How many men may I take with me on this assignment?"

"Take as many as you need."

Markus breathed a sigh of relief.

"Just err on the side of caution."

Markus saluted and left the king's presence to hand pick the best men for the task. They would need to be men who could keep their wits about them and be able to defuse difficult and potentially dangerous situations when tempers and emotions ran rampant. Fortunately, he had a number of such men in his command, probably because he inspired that kind of behavior himself.

After Jeshua sent Judas away from the dinner, Judas went to the chief priests, and told them, "I am prepared to take you to where Jeshua will be so that you may arrest him." In his heart he knew that this would be the spark that would set the revolution in motion. They would try to arrest Jeshua, and he would reveal his full power, maybe even have Moses and Elijah help him. Peter had told him secretly that they had shown up on the mountain. The chief priests and Pharisees would finally believe and join forces with Jeshua to drive out all uncleaness from all of Jerusalem, including the Romans. History would record this as the greatest, most holy Passover. He could hardly wait. In the meantime the chief priests gave him the rest of his thirty pieces of silver, a centurion, some soldiers, a few of the high priest's guards, and the high priest's personal servant. Judas led the way out of the temple.

As Jeshua and the disciples made their way to the Garden of Gethsemane, he said, "The Son of Man is about to be delivered into the hands of sinful men, who will mock him, beat him, crucify him, and kill him." Over these past three years he had often mentioned his death, but they seemed unable to hear him.

Peter responded, "We only have two swords with us," and he looked at Simon the Zealot and Thomas the Twin.

But Jeshua said, "They will be enough." When they reached the garden, he asked them, "Peter, James, and John, come with me. The rest of you please stay here and pray." He went with the three of them further into the garden and then said to them, "Stay here. Watch and pray, as I go over there," and he pointed. He walked about a stone's throw further into the garden, knelt on the ground, and began to pray.

Sorrow began to overwhelm him and his soul felt deeply troubled. In the gloom, he did not see the dark angel gloating in the shadows. He began to weep quietly, and the smile on the dark angel's face broadened. Jeshua fell slowly on his face as he continued to pray, "Father, Father, this is too much for me. If it is possible, let this hour, let this cup, let it all pass away from me. I don't think I can drink it. Please, take it away, please." He began to sweat under the stress, as he groaned beneath the weight of what lay ahead. He now breathed heavily, almost gasping. "Please, please...." Finally, he took a slow deep breath and said, "nevertheless, not my will, but Your will be done." He struggled to his feet and stumbled back to where the three disciples lay, asleep.

He gently kicked Peter's feet, "You are sleeping? At a time like this, you are sleeping? Can you not watch and pray with me for a single hour?" They struggled awake. He continued, "The spirit is willing, but the flesh is weak. Pray that you might not enter into temptation." He turned and stumbled back to where he had been kneeling and fell at the feet of a familiar old man who bent down and laid his hands on him, comforting him. Jeshua entered into the agony again, repeating similar words, "Can You not take this cup from me?" He paused, waiting, then said again, "Yet not my will, but Your will be done." He practically crawled back to the three, but the heaviness of sleep had overtaken them again. He almost whimpered, "You're sleeping again?" They awoke to hear his whimper, and did not know how to answer him. Jeshua returned to the agony a final time, and then just before he collapsed, Uriel grasped his shoulders and helped him to his feet. They held each other a moment until Jeshua's breathing became regular once again. Then together they walked back to where the three still slept.

Jeshua sat on a rock, his back against a tree, and said quietly to them, "Sleep on, take your rest, soon I will be betrayed into the hands of sinners." He gave them a few more moments, then

Uriel held out a hand and gently pulled him to his feet. He stood up refreshed, and as Uriel disappeared called to the others, "Arise now, my betrayer is at hand!"

At that moment, Judas entered the garden at the head of a rabble with lanterns, torches, swords, and clubs. He had told them, "The one I embrace and kiss will be the one you want to arrest." He knew the others would fight for him and that would begin it, the revolt that would free them from their oppressors. Jeshua stepped forward, the others gathered loosely behind him. Judas met him, "Rabbi," and kissed him.

"My friend, you would betray me with a kiss?" Jeshua said. Judas broke the embrace, and stepped out of the way. Peter reached out a hand to Simon the Zealot, who withdrew Hane from its sheath to produce a note of chilling beauty. He quickly passed the sword, hilt first, to Peter, who raised it. Two of the mob stepped forward to grab Jeshua. Peter's downward swing of the sword halted suddenly with a stark, "Peter!" from Jeshua, but not before Peter had cleanly sliced the ear off the high priest's servant, Malchus. Had Jeshua not interrupted him, he would have cleaved him in two. Malchus fell to his knees, a hand to his head where his ear had been, but had fallen to the ground. He bled profusely.

Markus, the centurion, and his soldiers had their own swords halfway out of their sheaths when Jeshua knelt beside Malchus, picked up his ear, blew on it, reattached it to Malchus' head, and the bleeding stopped.

From his position on the ground Jeshua looked at Peter sternly and continued, "Shall I not drink this cup that my Father has given me? Put away your sword." Peter handed it back to Simon as Jeshua finished, "All who take up the sword, will perish by it." Simon stepped back in shock at Jeshua's words and dropped the sword to the ground where he stood. He quickly removed the scabbard and dropped it too. Then he stepped back from them both as though he fled snakes.

Jeshua stood, helping Malchus back to his feet. The servant continued to feel his ear, still in awe that it had been restored, but the blood, still wet on his cheek, testified to its earlier removal. Jeshua asked, "Who are you seeking?"

Markus' sword had cleared his scabbard. He spoke clearly, "We seek, Jeshua, the Nazarene."

Jeshua, replied, "I AM..." and before he could complete the sentence, Markus, the soldiers, and the guards, all fell backwards to the ground. Judas smiled and took a step towards the fallen sword, but Jeshua repeated his question, "Who are you seeking?"

Markus had struggled back to his feet first, "You," for he had met Jeshua before when Jeshua healed his servant. Judas stepped back into the shadows.

Jeshua continued, "Then let these others go." Markus nodded and the disciples fled. Jeshua held his hands crossed in front of him. Markus stepped to him, bound them, and said sadly, "I'm sorry, but I have my orders."

Jeshua smiled faintly, "So do I." The soldiers and the rest gathered around him and they all left the garden. Malchus still held the side of his head as he began to stagger along behind them. He looked down at his other hand. At some time in the confusion he had picked up the sword, wiped it clean, put it back in its scabbard, and now carried it. "*I must give this to the centurion.*" he thought.

Bewildered, Judas still stood in the shadows. "*What had happened?*" All of his plans were starting to go awry. Had he misunderstood Jeshua's command to, "Do it quickly." He watched them depart, as his misgiving grew.

Chapter 50
A Mockery of a Trial

As they made their way back to the temple, Malchus caught up to Markus, and handed him the sword dropped by Simon the Zealot. Its name was "Hane," and it practically hummed in its sheath. When Markus took it, he felt a shiver of acknowledgment from the sword and in his own spirit. He recalled his father telling him the legends of the singing swords. His father said that Herod had remarked concerning one of them, "A sword fit for a god, let alone a king." This would make a powerful gift to Herod. Perhaps it would draw attention away from the arrest of this innocent man.

Judas stumbled along behind the mob, no longer needed. Things had not gone according to plan. The "*Put up your sword!*" still rang in his ears. Instead of beginning the rebellion, he had brought about the arrest of his master, an innocent man. Dark, jumbled thoughts swirled amidst his emotions of futility and regret. "*What have I done? What... have I done?*" At a distance, hidden in the shadows, Peter and John also followed the mob that had arrested Jeshua.

Jeshua walked silently between two soldiers who roughly grasped each of his bound arms. "*This is nothing compared to what lies ahead. Thank you for sharing that with me, Father, and thank you Uriel, that you are here somewhere,*" Jeshua thought to himself. They took him first to Annas, the father-in-law of Caiaphas, the high priest for that year. It had been Caiaphas who had told the assembly, "It is better that one man should die than all the people." The high priest knew Jeshua's disciple John, so he had been allowed to enter. John spoke to the servant at the door and she admitted Peter also. Peter stayed near the door, warming himself at a nearby fire, while John moved to where he could hear the proceedings.

The high priest asked Jeshua, "Tell us of your teachings and about your disciples."

Jeshua responded, "I have taught openly in the synagogues and the temple, wherever people meet. I did not speak in secret. Why do you ask me? Ask those who have heard me."

One of the guards struck him, "Is that the way to talk to the high priest?"

Jeshua spoke again, "If I have said something wrong, what is it? Why have you hit me? I meant no disrespect." Annas then sent him, still bound, to Caiaphas.

Markus had been waiting outside in his makeshift shelter. Gentiles, even Romans with authority were not allowed to enter Jewish counsels, not even for Jeshua's interview with Annas. Instead, he removed the wonderful blade from its scabbard. It still hummed in his hand. He grabbed a cloth and cleaned it better from the blood it had spilled. He took a small flagon of oil from his kit, and oiled the blade. The sword almost purred in his hands. It seemed genuinely pleased to be well treated. He resheathed it, took off his own short sword, and attached this longer sword to his hip. "*Interesting. As long as it is, it doesn't feel cumbersome. For some reason, it seems a part of me.*" He stepped out of the shelter and into the open courtyard, deserted for the moment. He drew the blade and nearly came unhinged at the power and pleasure of wielding it. He took a couple of slices with it through the air and it began to sing more loudly. He remembered his father had once swung one and it had sung for him too. He had said, "*A singing sword will usually only sing for the person to whom it belongs.*" Yet, on that day, although the sword had belonged to someone else, it had sung in his father's hand too. The owner had said, "Perhaps you will meet the sword again," and he had, many years later. Unbeknownst to Markus, he held that same sword, and unless the king claimed it, the sword now belonged to him. If the king did want it, it would be difficult to part with, but he lived, after all, under oath to serve the king.

He resheathed the sword just before the door opened. The temple guards held Jeshua by the arms again. "We must take him to Caiaphas." Markus whistled a muster command and his soldiers immediately presented themselves, some still buckling on their own swords. They took him to the door of the house of Caiaphas and knocked. A servant opened it.

"We have Jeshua," they announced.

The servant said something over his shoulder, turned back around, and said to the temple guards, "Bring him in." The Romans again remained outside. Inside, the council had assembled. They had gathered a number of witnesses to give testimony against Jeshua so that they might find reason to condemn him to death, but none of the witnesses' testimonies agreed.

One said, "He said he would destroy the temple, and build another in three days." But even on this they could not agree. Jeshua simply stood in their midst saying nothing.

Caiaphas suddenly stood and addressed Jeshua directly, "Do you have nothing to say to those who bring witness against you?" Jeshua did not open his mouth. Caiaphas continued to pressure him, "Tell us. Are you the Messiah, the son of God?"

Jeshua looked him straight in the eye as he said, "I AM!" and a shudder passed through them all. He continued, "and you will see the Son of man sitting at the right hand of God, and coming with the clouds of heaven!"

The high priest tore his garment. "We need no further proof! You have all heard this blasphemy! He must die for that!" and they condemned him to death. Some stepped forward, spat upon him, others hit him.

They blindfolded him, struck him again, and jeered, "Prophesy, if you are the Messiah, tell us who hit you?" and they reviled him.

Judas had followed them to Caiaphas' and because he was in the council's employ had been allowed to attend the trial, albeit from a distance. When he heard Jeshua confession and that they had condemned Him to death, he took the thirty pieces of silver and threw them to the floor. He cried out, "Take it back, take it back, I have betrayed innocent blood." That stopped things for a moment.

Then a priest responded, "What do we care?" Judas wept bitterly, left the chambers, and later hung himself.

One of the priests picked up the scattered coins. Another said, "This is blood money, we cannot put it into the treasury." So they counseled together and agreed to use the money to buy a field in which to bury strangers.

They sent Jeshua to Pilate to be condemned to death.

Chapter 51
Another Mockery

As the door opened, Hane began to hum again on Markus hip. No one else seemed to hear, but he could feel it distinctly. One of the priests emerged, “He has been found guilty of blasphemy and condemned to death. Take him to Pilate! We will follow you,” he commanded, not requested, but Markus understood authority, and he had been sent to help keep the peace.

He addressed his men, “With me! We take this man to Pilate,” and they formed ranks around him. They had obviously beaten Jeshua. Blood dripped from the corner of his mouth and bruises began to form on his cheeks. Spittle also shown on his head. Markus addressed him as he took a cloth from a pocket in his uniform and handed it to him, “Can you walk?”

Jeshua nodded, “I'm fine,” and took the cloth in his still bound hands, “Thank you,” he whispered as he wiped the spittle and blood from his face. Off they went towards Pilate's palace. The priests, a few temple guards, and some representatives from the council followed along in all of their finery.

When they neared the palace, the Jews halted in the outer courtyard. They would not enter for fear of being rendered unclean during the Passover. Pilate, escorted by his personal guards, came out to them, having been roused from his bed at this early hour. He saw the obviously bound prisoner in their midst. Pilate addressed them, almost mockingly, "What has this one done?"

The chief priest responded, "If he were not a criminal, why would we have brought him to you?"

Pilate shook his head, trying to rid himself of their nonsense, "Take him, and judge him according to your own Law." "*There, that should get rid of them.*"

The chief priest spoke again, "It is not lawful for us to put a man to death. That right is reserved to you."

That had Pilate wide awake, "Bring him inside."

Markus and his men joined Pilate's guards and escorted Jeshua into the palace. They did not enter the main throne room, surely this situation did not require that. They simply entered one of the judgment rooms and Pilate took his place up on the dais in an ornate chair. He addressed Markus, "Who is this man?"

Markus came to attention, as did his men, "He is called Jeshua. He is from Nazareth, and said to be a carpenter, but currently he is a wandering rabbi and teacher."

Pilate had heard of this man. "Some say you are the king of the Jews. Are you?" His voice no longer mocked. He sounded truly curious.

Jeshua took a step forward. Pilate's guards' hands' went to their swords, but Markus joined Jeshua, at his side, almost as a negotiator. Jeshua said, "Are you asking me this or has someone else told you to ask me?"

Pilate got up, stepped off the dais, and responded to Jeshua's face, "What do you think? Am I a Jew? Your own priests and people have delivered you into my hands. What have you done to deserve this?"

Jeshua answered him, "You have asked if I am a king. I was born and have come into this world to bear witness to the Truth. Everyone who is of the truth, listens to me."

Pilate laughed, "What is truth?" he said flippantly.

"Your majesty?" Markus said to Pilate, while Hane buzzed on his hip. He thought to say, "*You need to listen to this man,*" but Jeshua caught his eye and shook his head slightly, "*No.*"

Pilate looked at Markus, "Yes, Centurion?"

Still looking at Jeshua, Markus replied, "Nothing." And Hane quieted.

"Hold him here!" Pilate stepped between them and walked outside to where the chief priests and multitude had assembled. Addressing them, he announced, "I find no fault in this man."

The Persian prince, Kambroze, stood in the back of the crowd and called out, "He stirs up the people, teaching subversive things throughout Judea, from Galilee all the way here!" The people turned to see who spoke, but could not find him.

Pilate said to himself, "*Wait, he's from Nazareth. He is a Galilean. That's Herod's jurisdiction.*" He stepped back inside, "Take him to Herod!" and he left them.

Markus took control of the situation and led Jeshua out of the palace. As they emerged, he announced, "Pilate has sent him to Herod." With the help of his men he herded him through the multitude which reformed behind them and followed them to Herod's palace.

For a long time Herod had wanted to meet Jeshua. He had heard a lot about him, much of it from John the Baptizer before Salome forced his beheading. He hoped to see Jeshua do a miracle. Herod came out to his formal courtyard so the chief priests who had entered it would not become unclean. Herod asked him many questions, but Jeshua answered none of them. The priests continued to accuse Jeshua of many things, with great emotion, but they had no evidence to support any of their charges against him. Finally in exasperation, Herod turned to Markus. "Markus, what is going on here?"

"My Lord, this is all beyond me. They believe that he has blasphemed and deserves to die," Markus matter-of-factly stated.

Through all of this, Jeshua still kept silent. Finally Herod, tired of the entire charade, said "Take this imposter back to Pilate." Markus and his men formed ranks around Jeshua again and marched him back to Pilate. As they exited the palace, the rabble surrounded them.

They arrived back at Pilate's palace. Pilate's patience had grown thin at this mockery of justice. He knew now that the chief priests and religious leaders just wanted Jeshua out of the way, but he did not know what he could do to keep the peace. What a job he had, keeping the peace in this powder keg of a province.

He called the people together, including the chief priests and rulers, "You have brought this man, Jeshua, to me as one who has tried to lead the people astray, but I have examined him and find none of this to be true. I sent him to Herod and he found nothing either. Therefore, I will simply have him beaten." He went back into the palace and ordered Jeshua flogged. Markus thought to protest, but Pilate's soldiers outranked him here. They grabbed him roughly and dragged him off.

As Pilate prepared to address the people again, he received a note from his wife, "Have nothing to do with this righteous man. My dreams have been terribly troubled because of him." That worried him even more. Then a thought came to him. He had begun a custom a few years ago. To honor the feast, he would offer to pardon and release a prisoner. He currently had a notorious murderer in his custody, Barabbas, who had been arrested for starting an insurrection that had culminated in killing a number of citizens.

Pilate went back out and stood before the people, "You know that I have a custom of releasing a prisoner before your feast. Today I give you a choice." He had Barabbas dragged out still in chains. "Should I release Barabbas, or Jeshua? But when they brought Jeshua out, he had been beaten so severely that they could barely recognize him. The soldiers had woven a crown out of thorns and stuck it on his head, gouging it so deeply that blood covered much of his face. Pilate and many in the crowd audibly gasped when they saw him.

However, from the back of the crowd again came the now familiar persuasive Persian voice, "Barabbas, give us Barabbas!"

The chief priests and religious rulers quickly joined in, "Yes, Barabbas, release to us Barabbas!"

Pilate looked confused, "Then what should I do with this one you call the King of the Jews? I find no fault in him."

One of the priests spoke out, "He claims to be the Son of God. For that blasphemy our law say that he should die! Crucify him!"

And the rabble turned it into a chant, "Crucify him, crucify him!"

Pilate feared their growing animosity, but still tried to find some way to release him. "You want me to crucify him, when he is your king?"

Someone responded, "We have no king, but Caesar. If you do not kill him, then you oppose Caesar!" They practically started to riot.

To allow them to calm down, he took Jeshua back into the palace. "Who are you?" he asked, but Jeshua said nothing. "Do you not realize that I have the power to release you or to crucify you?"

From his blood-stained face, Jeshua opened an eye and looked directly at Pilate, "You have no power over me." Pilate tensed. Jeshua continued, "The only power you have is that which you have been granted by heaven. Those who have delivered me to you, it is they who have sinned."

Now truly frightened, Pilate went out to the people again and tried to release him, but they responded as before, "If you release this man, you are no friend of Caesar. He makes himself out to be a king, opposing Caesar!" He again brought Jeshua, bloodied and bruised, out for display, hoping that seeing his condition would sate their bloodlust. "Behold the man!" he announced.

But they responded, "Away with him, crucify him, crucify him!" So Pilate took a basin of water and washed his hands before them all as he said, "I am innocent of the blood of this man!" The crowd neared hysteria, "Let his blood be upon us and upon our children. Crucify him!" Finally, Pilate relented, released Barabbas, and ordered Jeshua's crucifixion.

When John heard this final pronouncement, he slipped away from the palace, ran quickly to tell the disciples and the women, and then to where Jeshua's mother lodged for the Passover. He told her briefly what had transpired. The sword that Simeon had prophesied about so many years ago, finally fully pierced her heart and soul. She nearly fainted, but Mary of Magdala had accompanied John. She embraced her and held her until her feet steadied. Then the three of them traveled together to where they knew Jeshua would eventually be delivered for his crucifixion.

Chapter 52
To Golgatha

Between the scourging, the other beatings, and the loss of blood, Jeshua could barely stand. The soldiers had to half drag him to a waiting chamber.

The commander of Pilate's soldiers directed one of his own men and Markus, "Go and get his cross!" The soldier grabbed a torch and led Markus to another chamber where many crosses stood lined up against the wall.

One of them seemed different, more recently hewn. Markus pointed towards it, "How about this one?"

The soldier replied apathetically, "It makes no difference, they are all the same."

Markus walked over and pulled it from the wall. Between the two of them they wrestled it back to where the other soldiers waited with Jeshua. The soldiers tried to straighten him up as the soldier with Markus laid the foot of the cross on the ground and Markus lowered it to rest the cross-beam on Jeshua's shoulder.

Jeshua stood up to embrace the weight of it, wrapping his arm around and over it. Then something strange happened.

Jeshua's eyes opened wide, a slight smile graced his blood-stained face. He looked up at the cross he held, and Markus would have sworn he heard Jeshua mutter, "Chayeem, is that you?" His stance strengthened. "*Yes, I am here, Jeshua.*" Markus thought he heard in response to Jeshua's question.

They led him out of the palace and onto the road that led to the place of crucifixion, called Golgotha, the place of the skull. Markus, his men, and Pilate's soldiers, all tried to maintain some semblance of order, but the word had spread like wildfire. Crowds lined the road already with a very mixed response, some weeping, others shouting, jeering, hurling insults. Jeshua's initially strong steps soon disintegrated into halting stumbles. His exhaustion and weakness overcame the initial joy that he had found embracing Chayeem. The soldiers resorted to brute force to keep the crowds at bay. Jeshua stumbled to his knees under the weight of the cross. In frustration, one of the soldiers pushed Jeshua and yelled for him to keep going. Jeshua collapsed to the ground, the cross crashing down on his back, pinning him down. Two soldiers picked the cross up off him. One of the other centurions grabbed a man out of the crowd, Cymon by name, and told him to carry the cross for Jeshua. An Egyptian, the son of an officer, Cymon knew he had no choice and complied. Markus lifted Jeshua from the ground, put Jeshua's arm over his own shoulder, and began to practically carry him as they continued along the road. Mekah and the Persian prince, Kambroze, walked disguised among the crowd.

Some of the lamenting women wailed as he passed by. Jeshua tugged on Markus' sleeve. He stopped. Jeshua turned to the women and spoke haltingly, "Do not weep for me. Weep for yourselves and your children. You did not know the day of the Lord's visitation and the days are coming when it shall be said, 'Blessed are the barren, those who have never given birth to or suckled a child.' Mourn and call for the mountains to fall on you, covering your wrong. If they do this to the green tree, what will they do to the dead and dry branches?"

Two robbers also accompanied them, carrying their crosses, to their own crucifixions. When they got to the place of execution, they took the cross off Cymon and released him. They laid the cross on the ground, placed Jeshua on the cross, and nailed him to it. The sound of the nails hammering into his feet and hands and his moans of agony rang throughout the surrounding countryside. Before they lifted him into the hole prepared for his cross, Jeshua whimpered, "Father, forgive them. They don't know what they are doing." They lifted him on the cross, and dropped it into its place between the two robbers. He cried out again in anguish. Pilate had a sign written and attached to Jeshua's cross above his head. It read, "Jeshua of Nazareth, King of the Jews" in Hebrew, Latin, and Greek.

When the chief priests saw it, they went directly to Pilate and complained, "Revise the sign to say, 'he claimed to be King of the Jews' only," but Pilate replied sternly, "No! It remains as I have ordered!"

"But, lord?" they pleaded.

"No! Who are you to question me? As I have ordered it, it will remain!" then to his soldiers, "Remove them from my presence!" and they did.

The crowds had now gathered at the cross. Many of them began hurling insults at Jeshua, "You said you would destroy the temple and rebuild it in three days. Well then, save yourself, come down from the cross!"

The chief priests followed suit, "You saved others. Can you not save yourself?"

The Persian prince called out, "The sign says you are the king of the Jews. Prove it! Come down from the cross!"

The soldiers took Jeshua's clothing, tore them apart and divided them among themselves, except for the cloak. It had been woven without seam, so they cast lots to see who would get it.

Jeshua said, "I thirst."

A soldier offered him sour wine to drink from a nearby jar.

One of the two robbers mocked him, "If you are the Christ, save yourself and us."

The other robber rebuked the first, "Do you not fear God? We are receiving the just penalty for our deeds, but he has done nothing." He looked at Jeshua, "Remember me when you enter into your kingdom."

Jeshua stood a little taller with painful difficulty, "I tell you a sacred truth, today you will be with me in paradise," and he slumped down again.

❖

Markus stood nearby with the guards, both his and Pilate's. He walked slowly to the cross. Jeshua showed more difficulty breathing. Crucified men usually died from suffocation, hanging on the cross, because of its design. However, it was a slow and agonizing process. As Markus neared the cross, Hane buzzed on his hip.

Jeshua opened his eyes, "Hane?"

Markus responded, "You know my sword?"

Jeshua struggled to respond, "Yes. He is one of the seven. I met him on the hip of another, when I was but two years old. Give him to your son when he comes of age."

Markus smiled weakly, "I have no son," he confessed.

Jeshua replied briefly, "Yet." Then he stopped, and fought for his breath. Hope and awe flooded Markus' heart.

About this time, Mary, Jeshua's mother, Mary from Magdala, and John attempted to come closer to the cross, but the guards kept them at bay. Both of the Marys wept. John barely held himself together, but he wanted to be strong for the women.

Markus turned in time to see and hear the three of them confronting his soldier. He called out, "Crispus, what seems to be the problem?"

Crispus had his spear extended horizontally, trying to keep the mob back, including the two Marys and John. "She says that she's his mother, but she doesn't look that old."

Markus stepped closer, then responded, "You may let her pass. She is his mother." He had seen her before.

Crispus asked, "What of the other two?"

He answered, "Yes, them too. They are no threat." Crispus let them pass.

They approached the cross. They all looked up to him hanging there. He looked at his mother, then at John, "Let her become your mother." Then back at Mary, "Let him become your son." From that moment, John counted her as his mother, and took her home to live with him.

At barely noon the sky suddenly darkened and it became like night. The soldiers had to light torches, and it stayed that way for the next three hours.

Jeshua finally cried out, "Eloi, Eloi, lama sabachthani?" which means, "My God, my God, why have you forsaken me?"

Chayeem whispered, "*We are still here.*"

Some of those standing nearby thought he called out to Elijah and said, "Let's see if Elijah comes to release him."

Jeshua whispered, hardly able to breathe, "Into Your hands I commit my spirit." and then "It is finished," and died.

At that very moment, the veil of the temple tore from the top to the bottom, and the earth quaked. Mekah, back in her demonic temple, worshiped prostrate before the black altar. The severe quake toppled the altar, pinning her to the floor, and the roof collapsed to bury her alive. The Persian prince, who had been in her presence, turned away and suddenly disappeared.

Markus, having seen all of these things, stepped up to the cross, laid his hand on Jeshua's bloodied feet, and said, "Surely this was the Son of God," and wept silently. The women standing there joined him. The Marys, some of the disciples, others of the multitude beat their breasts in grief at his death. The soldiers just stood there in shock and awe. Because it was the day before the High Sabbath and the bodies could not remain on their crosses Pilate sent word, "Break their legs, that they might die quickly."

The soldiers broke the legs of the robbers who hung on each side of Jeshua. When they came to Jeshua, it appeared that he might already be dead. In order to comply with Pilate's wishes,

Markus asked Crispus, "Give me your spear." Crispus gave him the spear and Markus plunged it into Jeshua's side. Out came blood and water, proving that he had already died. The sky began to lighten again.

Chapter 53
In a Borrowed Tomb

Joseph of Arimathaea and Nicodemus, both Pharisees, secretly followed Jeshua and looked for the coming of the kingdom of God. They went to Pilate and asked an audience with him. He came out to speak with them.

Joseph bowed and spoke for them both, "Your Majesty, I am Joseph of Arimathaea and this is Nicodemus. We would like the right and authority to take and bury the body of Jeshua from Nazareth."

Pilate looked shocked, "He is already dead? I just sent word a short while ago to break his legs and the legs of the two robbers."

"When they went to break his legs, he had already died and they didn't need to. You can send and have this confirmed, if need be," Joseph continued.

"But you are Pharisees. Your chief priests and rulers had me crucify him. Why do you want his body?" Pilate sounded skeptical.

Nicodemus spoke, "He is no common criminal and we did not agree with what the council did, but regardless, he should be buried according to our Law. Would you please allow us to do that?"

Pilate asked, "Where will you bury him?"

Joseph spoke again, "I own a new tomb that has never been used, hewn out of solid rock. I will bury him there. It will be sealed with a large stone."

Pilate had his scribe write a certificate of release of the body, affixed his seal to it, and gave it to them. "Give this to the centurions in charge. There is one of mine and one of Herod's. They will escort the body to the tomb with you."

When they got to Golgotha, they found that most of the crowd had dispersed to prepare for the Sabbath. Only John, the Marys, and a few of the other women still mourned. Joseph and Nicodemus gave the certificate to Markus and Pilate's centurion and the two of them supervised the removal of the cross from its hole, its laying down, and the removal of the nails from his hands and feet. Markus ensured utmost care and reverence from his soldiers. Joseph and Nicodemus had brought a hand cart with them. They draped it in linen, had the body laid on it, then carefully wrapped the linen around the body, with some myrrh and aloes, and bound it. The centurions, some soldiers, and the women accompanied them to the garden where they laid him in the tomb. Once they had laid him to rest and exited the tomb, the soldiers rolled the great stone over its opening. Making sure to secure the stone, the soldiers left, and all the rest went to their homes.

After the sabbath, the chief priests and Pharisees gathered together at Pilate's palace. He came out to speak with them accompanied by his centurion and some guards. "Now what do you want?"

The chief among them spoke, "When that deceiver was still alive, he said that he would arise from the dead after three days."

Pilate laughed, "You've got to be joking. He said he would rise from the dead?"

The priest did not laugh, "Yes! Therefore, we would like you to assure that his tomb is secure, and deploy soldiers to guard it. We fear his disciples may try to steal the body and say that he has risen from the dead. This would be worse than all the other claims he made when he was alive."

Pilate turned to his centurion, who said, "It would take a small army to remove the stone covering the tomb. It took four of my men to roll it down the hill and into its current place."

Pilate's patience with all of this had run thin, "Affix a seal to it and assign some men to guard it." He addressed the priest, "How long do they need to be there?"

The priest almost audibly sighed in relief, "Only a few days, at the most a week."

Pilate addressed his centurion again, "Find some men who will be content doing absolutely nothing for a few days," and he dismissed him. Speaking to the priest, "There, are you finally satisfied?"

"Yes, lord. Thank you." Pilate went back inside while the chief priests and Pharisee departed back to the temple.

Before the sunrise, on the first day of the week, Mary from Magdala and the other Mary decided to go to the tomb with some additional spices. His initial burial had seemed so rushed, they wanted his final resting place to be as special as he. The sun had just risen when they felt the earth tremble. It nearly knocked them over and they looked at each other, shocked and afraid, as half a dozen soldiers ran past them engulfed in their own fear. They entered the garden and smelled the smoke of the soldiers' campfire.

As the echo of the soldiers' running feet faded away, Mary from Magdala had thought, "*They would have been able to help us roll back the stone.*" They rounded the corner to encounter an extremely fit young man in a dazzling white robe. Their fear turned to awe and terror.

"There is no need to be afraid," he said. "You are seeking Jeshua, the Nazarene, who was crucified. He is not here, he is risen from the dead. Look, see the tomb?"

Sure enough, the tomb stood open, the stone rolled to the side. They dropped their spices and fled back to their lodging.

Mary from Magdala found Peter and John, "They have taken the Lord from the tomb. Where they have taken him, I don't know."

Peter and John each grabbed their cloak and ran out of the house. Mary followed after them. John arrived first, ran past the smoldering fire, and looked into the tomb. He could see the linen cloth lying there folded up, but he did not go in. Peter, however, when he arrived, went right into the tomb. He, too, saw the linen wrap folded up, there on the slab where Jeshua had lain, but the napkin that had been on his head now lay rolled up and set neatly in a place by itself.

Peter exclaimed in wonder, "This doesn't look like his body has been stolen. What grave robber would fold up the linens he had been wrapped in and roll up the cloth that had covered his head?"

John then entered the tomb, saw what Peter had seen and believed. He turned and walked out of the tomb, the beginnings of hope dawning in his soul. Peter followed him out and they walked back to their house, leaving Mary to arrive at the tomb again alone.

Weeping, she looked into the tomb and saw two angels in brilliant raiment, one sitting at the head and one at the feet of where Jeshua had been. They said in gentle chorus, "Woman, why are you weeping?"

She sobbed, "Because they have taken away my Lord and I don't know where they have taken him." She turned away and through her tears saw a man standing a short distance away.

He too said, "Woman, why are you weeping?"

She thought him to be the gardener, "They have taken him away. If you know where they have taken him, tell me, and I will go and take care of him."

Jeshua said to her, "Mary," and her heart nearly exploded in joy.

Stunned, she took two steps and collapsed at his feet, "Master." She grasped his feet and began weeping again, although this time from sheer joy.

He knelt down and began to remove her hands from his feet. "You must release me for now, but go and tell my brothers, the disciples, and Peter, that I will meet them in Galilee." He helped her to her feet, and stepped back.

She looked at her Lord, standing there smiling at her as she wiped her eyes, and said bravely, "Yes, I will go!" She turned immediately and walked away, looked back to see Him still standing there, smiling at her. She sighed, smiled too, and turned again to fulfill His last command. And fulfill it she did. She ran back to the disciples and glowingly shared His resurrection with them. She shared it with the other women. She shared it with anyone who would listen. She shared and shared and shared for the rest of her life. For everything He had said was true and as the centurion had spoken, "Surely this was the Son of God," and He still is!

THE END

Glossary of Names

Abigail	Jeshua's youngest half sister
Adam	One of the paralytic's four friends
Ahlam	Janus' chief courtesan
Ahvram	Man born blind
Amulius	Jailor at Herod's Dungeon
Andrew	One of Jeshua's Disciples
Anna	One of Mary, Martha, and Lazarus' servants
Annah	Woman with the issue of blood
Annas	Faher of the high priest Caiaphas
Anthony	Herod's centurion
Archelaus	Herod the Great's son who became king after him
Balak	Singing sword given to Ishbe-benob, then to Nesher, won by Hannah and restored as Oz by Jeshua
Barabbas	Murderer and insurrectionist
Bartholomew	One of Jeshua's disciples
Batel	Herod's new sorceress
Chayeem	The Tree of Life in the garden Delight's center
Chemosh	Batel's & Mekah's god, another name for Halel
Chokmah (Chok)	Master of Religions
Claudius	Archelaus' former Master at Arms
Cleo	Mary, Martha, And Lazarus' servant
Clay	First man, caretaker of the garden, Delight
Crispus	One of Markus' soldiers

Cymon	The Egyptian officer's son, carries Jeshua's cross
Daath	The Tree of Knowing good and evil
Dawn	First woman, co-caretaker with man (Clay)
Deborah	A young blind woman
Delight	God's wonderful garden
Elizabeth	Mary and Joseph's daughter, Jeshua's half sister
Eliezar	One of the paralytic's four friends
Gamaliel	A young rabbi saved by Anthony
Halel	Conductor, choreographer of worship, covering angel of Delight who falls from his exalted position
Hane	Formerly Goliath's singing sword, Favor, now Mishimar's, then his son's, then...
Hannah	Seph's housekeeper, foster daughter, Mishimar's wife with the singing sword Oz
Hannah	Bent over 18 years with infirmity
Herod (the Great)	Current King of the Jews (Judea)
Herodias	Herod Antipas' wife (from Philip)
Isaac	Owner of the "Triumphal Entry" colt
Jairus	Ruler of the synagogue with a dying daughter
James	Jeshua's younger half brother
James	Mary, Martha, And Lazarus' servant
Janus	Master of the courtesans
Jerud	One of the paralytic's four friends
Jeshua	Son of Mary, also the Promised One
Joanna	One of the women that followed Jeshua
John	One of the disciple and Jeshua's inner three

John the Baptizer	(That pretty much defines him.)
Jonathan	Deaf and mute brother of Judah
Joseph	Jeshua's half-brother
Joseph	Jeshua's step-father
Joseph	(of Aramithea) The Pharisee who asked to bury Jeshua's body
Judah	His brother, Jonathan was deaf and mute
Judas	Jeshua's half-brother
Judas	The disciple who betrays Jeshua
Judith	Markus the Centurion's slave
Judith	Jairus' dying daughter's name also
Jude	A disciple of John the Baptizer
Julian	Anthony's wife
Julius	Herod Archelaus's personal guards
Justin	The paralyzed man with four friends; Adam, Jerud, Eliezar, and Shem
Kambroze	A Persian Prince, Halel in disguise?
Leah	A woman of the roads and her alabaster jar of ointment
Lazarus	Brother of Mary and Martha
Levi	A wealthy tax collector
Lydia	Isaac's wife (colt)
Malchus	High Priest's servant
Marduk	Nebo's god, another name for Halel
Markus	Herod the Great's centurion, Anthony's son
Marie	(from Magdala) Companion of Mekah, with seven demons later renamed by Jeshua, Mary
Martha	Mary And Lazarus' sister

Mary	Jeshua's mother
Mary	Martha And Lazarus' sister
Mathiah	Widow of Nain's (dead) son
Mekah	(Mehashephah) Meshel's companion (another sorceress)
Meshel	Batel the sorceress' daughter
Mishimar	Soldier, with a singing sword, who accompaniesHannah and the Masters to Jerusalem
Nathaniel	Jeshua's disciple
Nebo	Herod's wizard and master of the black arts
Nesher	Son of the wizard Nebo, possessor of the singing sword Balak
Nicodemis	One of the Pharisees, came to Jeshua at night
Philip	A disciple of Jeshua
Pilate	Roman governor
Pollux	Guard at Herod's Dungeon
Pricilla	Widow at Nain
Qadar	Mekah's familiar, a scrawny black cat
Rebecca	Bath slave that becomes Anthony's daughter, Marcus' wife
Raz	Master of the Mysteries
Rex	Markus the Centurion's slave who becomes paralyzed
Salome	Herodias daughter, the dancer
Sepheth (Seph)	Master of Languages
Shem	One of the paralytic's four friends
Simeon	Righteous old man who meets Jeshua in the temple at his dedication and then when he's twelve
Simon	Hannah and Mishimar's son, a zealot
Simon (Peter)	A disciple of Jeshua

Simon	Former Leper that Jeshua healed
Thaddeus	Wine merchant, former robber, met coming back to Nazareth
Thaddeus	Owner of the Passover Upper Room
Uriel	The angel that replaced Halel over Delight, who preceded the coming of the Promised One
Zacchaeus	Chief tax collector, short of stature
Zerah	The servant girl who introduced the King to Nebo, then served Nebo and his son
Zillah	Mishimar's black stallion Shadow

About the Author

Bill has always been a storyteller. His wife says he still tends to share the truth creatively and with a flair for the dramatic. He grew up in south Seattle and has lived in Tacoma, Washington since 1972.

He worked nine years in hospitals, completing half his RN education (if you had a heart attack, he could half save you), Bill joined the Boeing Airplane Company in 1979. The last 15 years of his 32 year career he taught Employee and Leadership Development. Bill often developed and taught his own material and has written numerous short stories and dramas, culminating in his first published novel "Amidst the Stones of Fire" in 2017, its sequel "Out of the Sanctuary" in 2018, followed by "The Magi and a Lady" (a Christmas Fantasy) and now "Hane and the Centurion" (a Gospel Fantasy).

Now retired, he spends his time teaching, mentoring, acting in community theater, writing, and enjoying his family. Bill and his wife of more than fifty years, Nancy, live near their three children and six grandchildren in Tacoma, WA.

If you can't find Bill in his home-office, with is next book all over the floor, then he is probably across the road playing with the neighbor's dog, Stacy.

Hane and the Centurion

Twenty-Seven Week Daily Devotional

By William Siems

First printing - November 2020

Scripture quotations from the SUV (Siems Unauthorized Version) of the Bible

Contact the author at chayeem10@gmail.com

Cover by Jacob Bridgman from artwork by Gil Henry

Interior design by Alane Pearce of Professional Writing Services
AlanePearceWrites.com

Preface

It is my suggestion that you read the fantasies, "The Magi and a Lady", and then "Hane and the Centurion", simply for the pleasure of their stories. Then, if you have found that they touched you in some way, that you would go back and reread the "Hane" using this guide and devotional to help you apply it to your daily life.

Table of Contents

Week One - Prologue & Chapter 1

Read the two chapters once first. Then review them daily using these questions.

Day 1.

Why would five special people make the long and arduous journey to find the Promised One?

____
____
____
____
____
____

Why is this important to you?

____
____
____
____
____
____

Day 2.

Why did Uriel (and later Hannah and Mishimar) "join" himself to the child and his family"?

____
____
____
____
____
____

How are you "joining" Him in your daily life?

Day 3.

Hannah retrieves the dark sword Balak (the Void) off the slain form of the wizard's son, Nebo. What is the significance of the young child, Jeshua, restoring it to its original glory as Oz?

What has He restored in your life?

Day 4.

Why is the story of Mishimar's sword, Hane, important to the children?

(2 Cor. 10:4-5 says "For the weapons of our warfare are not like the world's, but have divine power to destroy strongholds. We destroy arguments and every lofty opinion raised against the knowledge of God, and take every thought captive to obey Christ." What does that mean to you?

Day 5.

It has been said that we are "to respond in the opposite spirit" to the enemy. How would Mishimar's and Hannah's fighting with the sword Hane be an example of that?

How are you operating “in the opposite spirit” in your daily life?

Day 6.

Simon’s grandfather found Hane essentially by accident. Why is that important to the story?

What seeming unexpected provision has God supplied in your life?

Day 7.

As you review your answers to this week’s questions, what has the Lord been saying to you through this story so far?

Week Two - Chapters 2 & 3

Read the two chapters once first. Then review them daily using these questions.

Day 1.

Why would the rumor that the young girl Mekah was the offspring of the god Chemosh and a virgin make a difference in the power and the effectiveness of her sorcery and occult practices?

____

____

____

____

____

____

The enemy of our souls gains access and power over us through half-truths, lies, and rumors spread by others. Give an example in your own life and how you were (are) able to combat his schemes.

____

____

____

____

____

____

Day 2.

The penalty for witchcraft, sorcery, and divination in the Old Testament was death. Why was the penalty so severe?

____

____

What are the things in your life (counterfeits) drawing you away from God?

Day 3.

Why would the characteristics, "He has great instincts, reads wood well…works meticulously and patiently." make the six year old Jeshua an ideal woodworking apprentice?

What are the characteristics that make you well suited for what He has called you to?

Day 4.

Hannah was a fierce warrior, but also had a strong compassionate side of her nature that drew people and animals. Why are both these sides important?

____

____

____

____

____

____

Balance is important in the life of a Follower of Jesus. What helps you to maintain balance?

____

____

____

____

____

____

Day 5.

Jeshua seemed to especially enjoy the family's ceremony of "foot washing". What seems the significance of it, "wash, dry, kiss, bless, and welcoming 'home'"?

____

____

____

____

____

____

What ceremonies do you participate in with similar significance?

____

____

____

Day 6.

Uriel brings the children gifts, a smoky grey stone, a cloudy amber stone, and a seed from the Tree Chayeem. What might their significance be to each child?

Can you remember a significant gift you were given over the years? What did it mean to you?

Day 7.

As you review your answers to this week's questions, what has the Lord been saying to you through this story?

Week Three - Chapters 4 & 5

Read the two chapters once first. Then review them daily using these questions.

Day 1.

What was the response of the angel Uriel sharing with them, "Those who sought the life of Jeshua are dead…You can return to Israel…?"

Uriel: ____

____

____

____

____

Hannah and Mishimar: ______________________________

____

____

____

____

What would have been your response?

____

____

____

____

____

____

Day 2.

What is the small request, wish, that Uriel wants to fulfill before he leaves?

What wishes do you have that you deeply desire Him to fulfill?

Day 3.

How does Jeshua's smile and words fill the emptiness, the void, left by the two dances of the swords?

When and how has He filled the emptiness in your life?

Day 4.

Why was the Egyptian Officer of 100 Chariots so impressed with the table that Joseph and Mishimar delivered?

How are we to complete the work that He gives us to do?

Day 5.

Why do Mary and Hannah completely clean the house they are leaving?

What is the difference between being a "renter" and an "owner" of the house you live in with how it is usually maintained?

Day 6.

What had been said about this young boy, Jeshua, up to this point?

Knowing the "end of the story" what does it mean to you that this boy would grow up to fulfill all these prophecies?

Day 7.

As you review your answers to this week's questions, what has the Lord been saying to you through this story?

Week Four - Chapters 6 & 7

Read the two chapters once first. Then review them daily using these questions.

Day 1.

Why is Anthony bothered by nightmares?

____
____
____
____
____
____

What events have occurred in your life that affected you similarly?

____
____
____
____
____
____

Day 2.

How did Anthony's wife Julian try to help him?

____
____
____
____
____
____
____

How can you be most successful in your attempts to comfort someone else?

Day 3.

How did the bath slave Rebecca know what she did about Anthony and his current situation?

How might Rebecca's efforts to help Anthony aid you in your attempts to help others?

Day 4.

Why would God want to forgive Anthony for his part in the slaughter of the Bethlehem children?

How have you experienced His forgiveness and helped others do the same?

Day 5.

What did Julian think had happened when she noticed that Anthony had gone a week without any nightmares?

How do you notice the changes in the lives of those around you?

Day 6.

What convinced Julian of the truthfulness of Anthony's story of how Rebecca had helped him?

How do you measure "truth" in what you see and hear from others?

Day 7.

As you review your answers to this week's questions, what has the Lord been saying to you through this story?

Week Five - Chapters 8 & 9

Read the two chapters once first. Then review them daily using these questions.

Day 1.

Why did Jeshua read them stories from the Pentetuch until they had heard them often enough that they knew them by heart?

____

____

____

____

____

____

Why do you read, study, memorize scripture?

____

____

____

____

____

____

Day 2.

How did Joseph respond to Thaddeus' threat to kill Jeshua if they did not give him money?

____

____

____

____

____

____

How do you respond to the threats that you face?

Day 3.

Thaddeus' story remind you of what familiar story? Why does he become a robber himself?

How are you responding to the things God is allowing in your life?

Day 4.

How does Hannah help Thaddeus?

____

____

____

____

____

____

Explain how you have been used to lead someone to Jesus?

____

____

____

____

____

____

Day 5.

What is Jeshua's response when he and the other children are confronted by the three teenagers?

____

____

____

____

____

____

What do you think (feel) was the result of that encounter?

____

____

____

____

____

____

Day 6.

What was Uriel's response to Jeshua standing up to the three teenagers?

____
____
____
____
____
____

We do not do good in order to BE saved, why do we do good?

____
____
____
____
____
____

Day 7.

As you review your answers to this week's questions, what has the Lord been saying to you through this story?

____
____
____
____
____
____
____
____
____
____
____
____
____
____

Week Six - Chapters 10 & 11

Read the two chapters once first. Then review them daily using these questions.

Day 1.

What is Marie of Magdala's "back story"?

____

____

____

____

____

____

How can your past affect your present and your future?

____

____

____

____

____

____

Day 2.

Who (or what) is Chemosh? To whom did he introduce Marie?

____

____

____

____

____

____

How is demonic influence....oppression....possession possible today?

Day 3.

What was so special about Jeshua getting to celebrate Passover in Jerusalem?

What celebrations are special to you and how are they special?

Day 4.

Why did people sacrifice a lamb at Passover?

Why don't we still sacrifice lambs today?

Day 5.

What is the difference between killing/murdering a person (next door) and killing a person (the enemy) during war?

How are we supposed to treat our enemies as followers of Jeshua?

Day 6.

Why didn't the Rabbi answer Jeshua's question about marriage?

If you could ask the "Learned" a question today; what would it be?

Day 7.

As you review your answers to this week's questions, what has the Lord been saying to you through this story?

Week Seven - Chapters 12 & 13

Read the two chapters once first. Then review them daily using these questions.

Day 1.

How did Mekah respond to Marie's introduction to the Seven?

____
____
____
____
____
____

How do you (or should you) respond when confronted with evil in its purest and rawest form?

____
____
____
____
____
____

Day 2.

What were the noticeable changes in Marie as a consequence to her introduction to the Seven?

____
____
____
____
____
____

We often think we can get away with dabbling with the Darkness, but what always happens?

____
____
____
____
____
____

Day 3.

To further refine Marie's skills, she is given into the care of Ahlam. What impressed you about their first meeting?

____
____
____
____
____
____

Why are your first impressions so powerful?

____
____
____
____
____
____

Day 4.

Who is Simeon?

____
____
____
____
____

Why is the chance meeting of Jeshua and Simeon so important?

Day 5.

"So, you believe it is my destiny to bring salvation to all people? What does that even mean?" Why does Jeshua ask Simeon this question?

What are some of the questions that you have concerning your destiny?

Day 6.

Simeon responded, …but you must listen to Him." and he pointed upward. and Jeshua said, "He is also here," pointed to his heart, "closer than my next breath." What did Jeshua mean?

What do Jeshua's words mean to you and your relationship to God?

Day 7.

As you review your answers to this week's questions, what has the Lord been saying to you through this story?

Week Eight - Chapters 14 & 15

Read the two chapters once first. Then review them daily using these questions.

Day 1.

Anthony is ushered into the presence of the king, Herod Archelaus. What does the king want?

What is our attitude to be towards those who govern us?

Day 2.

Anthony is not worried about the "rule of law", but what does he worry about?

What should our response be when asked to do something illegal, immoral (or fattening)?

Day 3.

What comes along with Anthony's new position as "Master at Arms"?

How have you seen God provide for you beyond what you have expected?

Day 4.

Mary, Joseph, and Mishimar realize that Jeshua isn't with them, having left Jerusalem. What is their response?

How should we respond to the unexpected, even what seems like a breach of trust?

Day 5.

Anthony finds Mary, Joseph, and Mishimar at the inn. He has some good news and some bad news. What is each?

Share some similar kind of news you have received.

Day 6.

Mishimar gives Anthony a chance to wield Hane again and tells the sword's story. Afterwards, he thinks, "Anthony, Chayeem, and Hane, will wonders never cease?" What does he mean?

How has God surprised you?

Day 7.

As you review your answers to this week's questions, what has the Lord been saying to you through this story?

Week Nine - Chapters 16 & 17

Read the two chapters once first. Then review them daily using these questions.

Day 1.

How did Marie's instruction involve her entire being?

____

____

____

____

____

____

How are you growing and developing your entire being (body soul and spirit)?

Body ______________________________________

____

____

Soul ______________________________________

____

____

Spirit ______________________________________

____

____

Day 2.

Who was Marie's spirit guide? Who was she really?

How is it still possible for people to have "spirit guides" today?

Day 3.

How did Marie perform for Ahlam's master, Janus?

How does God test our spiritual development (maturity)?

Day 4.

What would Simeon miss about his time with Jeshua?

What would you hope people would miss about you (when you are gone)?

Day 5.

What was Jeshua's question for the learned men to answer?

What do you think of Jeshua's answer to his own question?

Day 6.

As Jeshua described his answers and questions among the teachers, what were Mary and Joseph's reaction?

Later (in Acts) the answers of the disciples would astonish the teachers of the Law, who would recognize that these ignorant men "had been with Jesus". How should that describe us as disciples following Him?

Day 7.

As you review your answers to this week's questions, what has the Lord been saying to you through this story?

Week Ten - Chapters 18 & 19

Read the two chapters once first. Then review them daily using these questions.

Day 1.

Anthony and Julian release Rebecca from her service on one condition. What was that and why?

____

____

____

____

____

____

Rebecca enhanced her swordsmanship from her secret place and did what with it?

____

____

____

____

____

____

Day 2.

How did Julian coax Rebecca out of her tomboyishness?

____

____

____

____

____

____

Raising kids is difficult. Share some of your joys and sorrows.

Day 3.

Anthony received a copy of the Hebrew Psalms as a thank you gift for saving a young rabbi. Why was it so precious to Rebecca?

What special things has God given to you over the years?

Day 4.

Rebecca nearly jumped out of his lap, "You've met the new king?" Why is she so excited?

Sometimes we have heard/read the story of Jeshua so many times that it has become commonplace. How do we regain our excitement?

Day 5.

Why did Jeshua "look up to" Mishimar?

What qualities and characteristics do you desire to have in your life for people to look up to?

Day 6.

In an ocean of anguish at the death of his father and friend, Jeshua utters, "Uriel, where were you?" What does Uriel respond?

What events have you experienced where it has been difficult to believe God was there?

Day 7.

As you review your answers to this week's questions, what has the Lord been saying to you through this story?

Week Eleven - Chapters 20 & 21

Read the two chapters once first. Then review them daily using these questions.

Day 1.

What was John the Baptizer's message?

____
____
____
____
____
____

What does Baptism mean to you?

____
____
____
____
____
____

Day 2.

Before John would baptize a person, what must they do?

____
____
____
____
____
____

I thought salvation was a gift, why must you do something first?

Day 3.

How did John respond when they asked him if he was the Messiah?

How do you respond when someone asks if you are Christian?

Day 4.

What had changed after Joseph and Mishimar's deaths?

How have you responded to similar difficult events in your own life?

Day 5.

Why did Jeshua want James to watch the shop?

How would change in our life be different if we expected and planned for it?

Day 6.

Why did Jeshua ask him, "James, how does God speak to you?"

How does God speak to you?

Day 7.

As you review your answers to this week's questions, what has the Lord been saying to you through this story?

Week Twelve - Chapters 22 & 23

Read the two chapters once first. Then review them daily using these questions.

Day 1.

Why did Jeshua get baptized by John the Baptizer?

When and why were you baptized?

Day 2.

What was John's response to Jeshua when he presented himself to be baptized?

What were the words spoken over you after you were baptized (if you recall)?

Day 3.

Why did the Father want Jeshua to go off into the wilderness?

How should we respond to times of trial snd testing?

Day 4.

What were some of teachings Marcus had learned from his father, Anthony?

What are some of the key learnings you have received during your life?

____

____

____

____

____

____

Day 5.

Marcus talked to Rebecca about everything, but what was the one thing difficult for him to discuss with her?

____

____

____

____

____

____

What things do you find are most difficult to discuss with those close to you?

____

____

____

____

____

____

Day 6.

Why did Marcus need to talk to his father about the way he felt for Rebecca by himself?

____

____

____

How can we help others talk about the difficult things of life?

Day 7.

As you review your answers to this week's questions, what has the Lord been saying to you through this story?

Week Thirteen - Chapters 24 & 25

Read the two chapters once first. Then review them daily using these questions.

Day 1.

Why did Jeshua fast in the wilderness for forty days?

____

____

____

____

____

____

Why do we fast now days?

____

____

____

____

____

____

Day 2.

How did Jeshua respond to the testings of the Tempter?

____

____

____

____

____

____

How should you respond to temptation when it comes?

Day 3.

After the testing was complete, what did Uriel bring to him and say to him?

What should you expect on the other side of successful testing, resisting temptation?

Day 4.

How did John the Baptizer respond to being asked if he were the Christ?

Who do we let tell us who we are? Who should we?

Day 5.

For two days in a row, who did John proclaim Jeshua to be?

What does it mean the he is "the Lamb of God" who is taking away the sin of the world?

Day 6.

Why did the first four disciples Andrew, Simon Peter, Philip, and Nathaniel all follow Jeshua?

Why do you follow Him?

Day 7.

As you review your answers to this week's questions, what has the Lord been saying to you through this story?

Week Fourteen - Chapters 26 & 27

Read the two chapters once first. Then review them daily using these questions.

Day 1.

How did Mary think Jeshua would handle the problem that they had run out of wine at the wedding at Cana?

____

____

____

____

____

____

When you have a problem what is usually your first response?

____

____

____

____

____

____

Day 2.

What was Mary's response to Jeshua's "What does that have to do with me, woman?"

____

____

____

____

____

____

What is your response to God's answer, when it is different than what you thought it should be?

Day 3.

What was the Master of the Feast's response to the water that had now turned into wine?

How have you responded to some of the miracles He has done in your life?

Day 4.

Why does Jeshua drive out the sheep, oxen, and money changers?

What have you experienced "righteous indignation" about?

Day 5.

Why did Simon the Zealot now join himself to Jeshua and the disciples?

What are some of the reasons you are following Him that may not be the right reasons?

Day 6.

How did Jeshua heal Deborah's blindness?

Why does it seem Jeshua heals each person differently?

____
____
____
____
____
____

Day 7.

As you review your answers to this week's questions, what has the Lord been saying to you through this story?

____
____
____
____
____
____
____
____
____
____
____
____
____
____
____
____
____
____

Week Fifteen - Chapters 28 & 29

Read the two chapters once first. Then review them daily using these questions.

Day 1.

Why did Nicodemus come to see Jeshua at night?

How willing is the Lord that you would come to Him with your questions and deepest desires?

Day 2.

Jeshua tells Nicodemus that he must be born again. What does he mean?

How does being "born again" relate to you and your relationship to God?

____

____

____

____

____

____

Day 3.

Jeshua calls after Nicodemus, "You must do much more than just think about these things. You must believe in the One who has said them." What does that mean to you?

____

____

____

____

____

____

How should you respond to what Jeshua said?

____

____

____

____

____

____

Day 4.

Ahlam is consorting with a priest and is drug out of the middle of……bound, and carried from her house. What is she expecting?

____

____

____

What should we expect as the penalty for our sin?

Day 5.

They drag Ahlam before Jeshua, and the spokesman says, "In the Law, Moses commands us to stone such a woman to death. " What does Jeshua do?

If you didn't know the end of the story, what might you have done?

Day 6.

Jeshua says to her, "Neither do I condemn you, go and sin no more." How could she possibly do that, sin no more?

What is your response to His forgiving you?

Day 7.

As you review your answers to this week's questions, what has the Lord been saying to you through this story?

Week Sixteen - Chapters 30 & 31

Read the two chapters once first. Then review them daily using these questions.

Day 1.

Jeshua never seemed restless or in a hurry. Why was that?

What causes you to get restless and be in a hurry?

Day 2.

What did Levi do when Jeshua asked him to "Follow me"?

Jeshua asks you to follow Him? What is your response?

Day 3.

A scribe asked, "Why does your master eat with tax collectors and sinners?" What was Jeshua' response?

Who are you reaching, your tax collectors and sinners?

Day 4.

What was Zacchaeus' response to Jeshua?

We do not "give" in order to earn salvation, why do we give?

Day 5.

Jeshua said, "Go, get your husband, and bring him back with you." Why was that so effective in reaching this woman?

How do you share your faith in Jeshua?

Day 6.

Jeshua stayed with them for two days, then what was their response?

How are people responding to what you say and do?

Day 7.

As you review your answers to this week's questions, what has the Lord been saying to you through this story?

Week Seventeen - Chapters 32 & 33

Read the two chapters once first. Then review them daily using these questions.

Day 1.

Why was Markus arresting John the Baptizer? How did John respond?

____
____
____
____
____
____

How are we to respond to those in authority (even when they are wrong)?

____
____
____
____
____
____

Day 2.

Who was John's jailor and how did he take care of him? Why?

____
____
____
____
____
____

What kind of treatment should we expect by the "enemy" as God's kids?

____

____

____

____

____

____

Day 3.

Describe the dialogue between John and the King.

____

____

____

____

____

____

How should we respond under persecution?

____

____

____

____

____

____

Day 4.

Jesus read from the scroll of Isaiah and then said, "Today, this scripture is fulfilled, right here." What was the response?

____

____

____

____

____

How will people respond to our testimony?

Day 5.

Jeshua heals a man with a withered hand in the synagogue, how do the people respond?

Will God ever ask us to do something that isn't right?

Day 6.

Jeshua heals a woman who had an infirmity for eighteen years. What was the people's response?

How are we to know the difference between the Law of God and the traditions of Man?

Day 7.

As you review your answers to this week's questions, what has the Lord been saying to you through this story?

Week Eighteen - Chapters 34 & 35

Read the two chapters once first. Then review them daily using these questions.

Day 1.

"Who sinned that this man was born blind?" How did Jeshua respond?

What are your views on the origin of sickness, deformity, etc.?

Day 2.

How did Jeshua heal the next blind man?

We tend to want formula's and magic words. What is the key to healing?

Day 3.

My favorite line in this particular story is, "You don't want to become his disciple too, do you? What is yours?

After Ahvram was cast out, Jeshua found him. Why did He take so much time with this man?

Day 4.

What impresses you about Justin's four friends.

How do you react to handicapped people?

Day 5.

Why did Jeshua first forgive Justin's sins?

How important to our whole well being is our spiritual purity?

Day 6.

Why did Jeshua spend the evening, alone, in the mountains with his Father?

How do you spend your extended times with Him?

Day 7.

As you review your answers to this week's questions, what has the Lord been saying to you through this story?

Week Ninteen - Chapters 36 & 37

Read the two chapters once first. Then review them daily using these questions.

Day 1.

How did Markus and Rebecca's slaves, Judith and Rex, become like family?

How should we treat our employer and fellow employees?

Day 2.

Jeshua offered to go with Markus and heal his slave. Why was this response unexpected?

We do not always get what we expect when we ask, but what do we get?

Day 3.

Why was Jeshua stunned?

How does it surprise you that you can stun and amaze God?

Day 4.

What is the difference between Leah and Ahlam? What is the same?

What is your alabaster jar of ointment?

Day 5.

Why did Leah weep on his feet, dry them with her hair, kiss them, anoint them with the perfume, and massage it into his feet?

What have you to offer Him?

Day 6.

What was the point of Jeshua's story?

What is the connection between love and forgiveness?

Day 7.

As you review your answers to this week's questions, what has the Lord been saying to you through this story?

Week Twenty - Chapters 38 & 39

Read the two chapters once first. Then review them daily using these questions.

Day 1.

Mekah thought she was summoning the god Chemosh, but what was really happening?

When have you been seeking one thing and found it was something totally different?

Day 2.

What happened when Chemosh breathed on Salome?

When have you thought yourself in control of the situation, only to find that you are not?

Day 3.

Chemosh exclaims, "How could this be hidden from me?" How could it be hidden from him?

Sometimes it appears the enemy knows the future, what does he really know?

Day 4.

Why did Herod ask John the Baptizer about Rabbi Jeshua?

Why did Herod keep coming back to talk with John (even though he had told him it was wrong for him to be living with his brother's wife)?

Day 5.

The entertainment included Janus' dancing girls, the sword dance of the Prince of Persia (who is he?), and Salome, to what end?

Herod is "tricked" into beheading John the Baptizer, how have you been tricked?

Day 6.

Why does John ask Markus to "dispatch me into the arms of Chayeem"?

Are you afraid to die? Why or why not?

Day 7.

As you review your answers to this week's questions, what has the Lord been saying to you through this story?

Week Twenty-One - Chapters 40 & 41

Read the two chapters once first. Then review them daily using these questions.

Day 1.

Why had the Syrophoenician woman come to Jeshua?

When have you come to Jesus, unworthy as you are? Why?

Day 2.

Why was Jeshua so mean to her?

When has He responded to you in ways you didn't understand?

Day 3.

Why did Judas think he could help the demon possessed boy?

What do you do when the evil seems beyond your control?

Day 4.

Who did the disciples think Jeshua was before the storm, after it?

Day 5.

Why did Jeshua permit the demons to enter the swine?

What has He done that you have not understood?

Day 6.

Why would Jeshua not let the (now in his right mind) man follow Him?

What have you learned it really means to follow Him?

Day 7.

As you review your answers to this week's questions, what has the Lord been saying to you through this story?

Week Twenty-Two - Chapters 42 & 43

Read the two chapters once first. Then review them daily using these questions.

Day 1.

What was Janus' response to Ahlam's request.

____
____
____
____
____
____

What difficult things have been asked of you by others?

____
____
____
____
____
____

Day 2.

What was Jeshua's response to their sneered, "Doesn't he know who she is?"

____
____
____
____
____
____

How have you misjudged others?

Day 3.

How did Jeshua exorcise Marie's demons (the Seven)?

We are often afraid of the demonic world. Why do we not need to be afraid?

Day 4.

How did Jairus see his daughter?

How are we supposed to see other people?

Day 5.

What made Annah think there was hope for her, even though she had spent all of her money trying to get well?

Where do you place your hope?

Day 6.

How did Jeshua raise Judith from the dead?

Why would Jeshua want to keep the healing of Jairus' daughter a secret, just among themselves?

Day 7.

As you review your answers to this week's questions, what has the Lord been saying to you through this story?

Week Twenty-Three - Chapters 44 & 45

Read the two chapters once first. Then review them daily using these questions.

Day 1.

What tragedies had befallen Pricilla?

____

____

____

____

____

____

How have you responded to tragedy in your life?

____

____

____

____

____

____

Day 2.

What did Jeshua do for Pricilla?

____

____

____

____

____

____

How has God responded to your tragedies?

Day 3.

Why did Jeshua think it important to still answer Mary of Magdela's question?

How does He answer your questions?

Day 4.

Jeshua asked Martha, "So, why have you asked us to supper?" How did she respond?

What kind of a relationship do you want Him to have with you?

Day 5.

Jeshua later says to Martha, "There will always be a lot of things, but only one thing that is really necessary..." What is that one thing?

How are you sure that you have found the "one thing"?

Day 6.

Why did Jeshua wait until Lazarus had died?

When have you felt that He has waited until it was too late to do something for you?

Day 7.

As you review your answers to this week's questions, what has the Lord been saying to you through this story?

Week Twenty-Four - Chapters 46 & 47

Read the two chapters once first. Then review them daily using these questions.

Day 1.

Why was Simon still called "the leper" even though Jeshua had healed him?

What labels and nicknames have followed you for years?

Day 2.

Why did Mary anoint Jeshua with the pure nard ointment?

When have you gone "above and beyond" to show your love for Jesus?

____

____

____

____

____

____

Day 3.

Why was Judas indignant at Mary's sacrifice?

____

____

____

____

____

____

How should we respond when others are praised for the good thing they have done?

____

____

____

____

____

____

Day 4.

Why did Uriel proceed the disciples and set up the borrowing of Isaac's donkey?

____

____

____

____

What have you done that you were later surprised at how much it was appreciated or how someone was touched/impressed by it?

Day 5.

How did the disciples respond when caught taking the colt?

It is said that "obedience is better than sacrifice", what does that mean to you?

Day 6.

After the Triumphal Entry, Jeshua cleanses the temple again, why?

Why do you suppose things had not changed in the temple?

Day 7.

As you review your answers to this week's questions, what has the Lord been saying to you through this story?

Week Twenty-Five - Chapters 48 & 49

Read the two chapters once first. Then review them daily using these questions.

Day 1.

Why did Judas think he was handing Jeshua over to the religious leaders?

____

____

____

____

____

____

What good have you done for the wrong reasons?

____

____

____

____

____

____

Day 2.

Thaddeus provided the upper room for the Last Supper, why?

____

____

____

____

____

____

When were you able to participate in something that was way beyond your gifts and talents?

____

____

____

____

____

____

Day 3.

At the end of the Last Supper, why did Jeshua sing a hymn?

____

____

____

____

____

____

How have you found praise and worship to help in difficult and troubled times?

____

____

____

____

____

____

Day 4.

What kind of men did Markus hand pick to go with him to arrest Jeshua, Why?

____

____

____

____

What is the basis or criteria for the friend you pick?

Day 5.

Jeshua prayed in agony while the disciples slept. Why did they sleep?

When have you not measured up for the task you were called to do?

Day 6.

Why did Jeshua allow himself to be arrested?

How is it easier to allow trials and trouble into our lives when we know God is working in and through them?

____

____

____

____

____

____

Day 7.

As you review your answers to this week's questions, what has the Lord been saying to you through this story?

____

____

____

____

____

____

____

____

____

____

____

____

Week Twenty-Six - Chapters 50 & 51

Read the two chapters once first. Then review them daily using these questions.

Day 1.

Why did Markus feel a shiver of acknowledgment from the sword, Hane?

How do you feel He is preparing you to fulfill your destiny?

Day 2.

Markus stepped out of the shelter...drew the blade and nearly came unhinged at the power and pleasure of wielding it. Why?

When was the last time you were overwhelmed at what God was doing in your life?

Day 3.

Caiaphas continued to pressure Jeshua, "Tell us. Are you the Messiah, the son of God?" Jeshua….said, "I AM!" Why is that significant?

How are you confessing to be a follower of Jesus?

Day 4.

Why is it significant that Markus accompanied Jeshua through the trial process?

What trials have you walked through with someone else?

____

____

____

____

____

____

Day 5.

Pilate laughed, "What is truth?" What is the deeper significance of his question?

____

____

____

____

____

____

____

How do you find "the truth" in the world today?

____

____

____

____

____

____

Day 6.

Jeshua said to Pilate, "You have no power over me." What did he mean?

____

____

____

____

How do we know that God is still in control?

Day 7.

As you review your answers to this week's questions, what has the Lord been saying to you through this story?

Week Twenty-Seven - Chapters 52 & 53

Read the two chapters once first. Then review them daily using these questions.

Day 1.

The soldier replied apathetically (to Markus' question about the crosses), "It makes no difference, there all the same?" Were they all the same?

____

____

____

____

____

____

Romans 14 says there are (at least) four kinds of Christians, those who eat only vegetables and those who can eat anything, those who celebrate special (holy) days and those to whom all days are the same (special/holy). Which are you?

____

____

____

____

____

____

Day 2.

What was significant about Jeshua knowing Markus' sword, Hane?

____

____

____

Sometimes things seem common, but are special. How can we see the special in the middle of the common?

____

____

____

____

____

____

Day 3.

Jeshua cries out, "Eloi, Eloi, lama sabachthani?" Had God forsaken him? Why?

____

____

____

____

____

____

How do we know that Jesus will never forsake us?

____

____

____

____

____

____

Day 4.

Jeshua whispered, "It is finished," and died. What did he mean? What happened next?

____

____

____

____

What do we mean by "the finished work of the cross"?

Day 5.

Why did Nicodemus and Joseph want Jeshua's body?

Why did the Pharisees and chief priests want the tomb sealed and guarded?

Day 6.

How did Mary finally know she was speaking to Jeshua and not the gardener? Why is that significant?

He may not have called your name as He did Mary's, but how has He spoken meaningfully to you?

Day 7.

As you review your answers to this week's questions, what has the Lord been saying to you through this story?